DANCE
— *of* —
DECEPTION

KIM SIMONS

PAGE PUBLISHING, INC.
New York, NY

First originally published by Page Publishing, Inc. 2018

ISBN 978-1-64424-173-8 (Paperback)
ISBN 978-1-64424-175-2 (Digital)

Printed in the United States of America

OMNI BANK

HIGH HEELS BEAT a tight staccato that echoes on the marble floors of the Omni Bank in Beverly Hills. All eyes are on the temptress as she makes her way into line. Kira makes eye contact with her spectators, obviously annoyed at all the attention she is getting. Their curiosity sated, the imposers return to waiting impatiently in the line.

All except one man—Lance McCann, a wealthy businessman, entrepreneur, and real estate mogul. He hungrily undresses her with his eyes, continuing along the lustful path he began when she entered the building. Kira's face flushes as her eyes meet his; he's gotten her attention. Lance smirks as he turns away; by the look in his eyes, he has already had her.

Kira is a beauty; more than that, she is sexy, which adds to her allure. She has a mystery about her; like the moon, part of her is always hidden. Behind her eyes, she wears a look of intelligence, which is uncharacteristic of most young bombshells. At the age of twenty-six, she has a demeanor reflecting that of a woman much older and with experience. She is a curvaceous blonde who is used to getting attention from all males in a room. This man is different, though—richer, stronger, more in control; she can tell that by the way he is dressed. There is something about a man in a starched white shirt with french cuffs. Maybe he is a bit too clean, too manicured, and yet irresistible. She can see the contours of his muscled frame through his custom Italian suit. Kira imagines what he would smell like—musk and spice, masculine and sensuous. Lance glances back. He smiles when he sees Kira looking at him. She quickly looks away, feeling the heat rise in her face as she realizes she's been caught. She feels as if he has penetrated her with his eyes.

The bank teller calls out, "Next in line." Lance glances back at Kira, smiling, fantasizing. The teller, a little louder, says, "Sir, you are next in line." Suddenly Lance wakes from his trance and steps up to the teller window.

"Sorry about that. I was a little distracted back there," he says as he glances again at Kira. Lance hands the teller his transaction.

The teller looks it over and then says, "This is over my limit. I need to get approval." The teller steps away, giving Lance one more chance to gaze at Kira. She is wearing a yellow silk dress; it is thin, and the light comes through—Lance can see the outline of her panties. His eyes work their way down her legs as he enjoys every inch of her well-defined calves.

Teller number two says, "Next in line," and Kira moves up to the window.

Kira speaks to the teller and Lance overhears her.

"I need some cash."

"How much do you need?"

"About four or five million, but I'll take a couple hundred today."

The bank teller laughs.

"I know the feeling. You know, the lottery is up to thirty million. Someone's gotta win. Sure gonna buy my ticket."

"What, and leave this fantastic job you have?"

"Only in about a split second."

The teller counts the twenties as he hands them over to Kira.

"There is twenty, forty, sixty, eighty, and one. Twenty, forty, sixty, eighty, two. Are you going somewhere special tonight?"

"Yes, I've been invited to the Grammys. I have to buy something exotic to wear."

Laughing, the teller replies, "I wouldn't worry about that. Most of those people just show up half-naked." Kira laughs at the teller's remark. Then the teller says, "The Grammys, how exciting. Have a nice time!"

Kira nods and smiles as she walks away. She glances back at Lance as she approaches the exit. Lance quickly stuffs his money in his wallet and rushes over to follow Kira.

Two men in camouflage with masks burst through the door, each pointing a semiautomatic.

"Get down! Everybody down!" yells one of the outlaws. The bank clerk shrieks; one of the gunman rapidly fires a round in her direction, shattering a chandelier over her head. Glass flies in every direction. All others drop to the floor as told, except for Lance, who is transfixed, staring at Kira's now partially bare ass that is now exposed, showing only the backside of her cream lace thong.

"Hey you, fuck face! Get down on it like I said! Or that'll be the last ass you'll ever look at!" Lance looks over and smirks at the man with the gun.

"What are you smiling about, asshole?" He comes closer to Lance, pointing the gun in his direction. "If you don't get down, I am going to splatter your guts clear to the wall!" The gunman charges at Lance, stepping over Kira as he goes. Kira uses the opportunity to put her leg up and trips the gunman to the floor. Lance grabs at the gun in his grip. They begin to struggle with the gun. The second gunman moves in, pointing his gun at Lance. He fires several deafening rounds, shooting out all the tellers' windows. The rounds barely miss Lance. Glass shatters everywhere; the people on the ground moan and scream. The gunman struggling with Lance gets cut by the glass. Drops of his blood drip at Kira's face. Kira winces and shimmies away from the blood. Lance seizes the gun from the man's hand and knocks him in the face with it. The man drops to the floor, knocked out cold, his face all bloody.

Lance swings the gun around, pointing it at the other gunman, who is now ready to shoot another round at Lance. Lance takes aim at him as well. They lock eyes; the thug is covered in sweat. He takes dead aim, and they both fire. The plate glass windows at the bank all shatter with the shots from Lance's semi. The force of the bullets pushes the robber straight through the shattering glass as he falls into a pool of his own blood, shot in the head and the face. The first gunman rises and runs out of the bank, leaving his gun and his accomplice behind. Lance tosses the gun to the ground. The bank's alarm system goes off with an ear-piercing volume. Lance takes this as a cue for his exit. Ten cop cars fly up to the curb in front of the bank. Two cop cars jump the curb and stop just short of the front door of the bank. The police all bound from their cars with guns drawn; some kneel behind their car doors using them as shields. The people in the bank start to shuffle to their feet. Kira slowly gets up, spreading her legs as she does, and Lance gets a full view of that cream lace thong. He helps her to her feet, and they quickly move to the exit of the bank, bypassing the commotion and avoiding the police. He holds the door open as Kira walks through.

Kira's eyes meet Lance's as she passes through the door.

"So not only can you stare, apprehend criminals, and save the day, but you can open doors as well. You are a very talented man. Do you have a name?"

"My name is Eric. Ryan. Lancelot. McCann. But you can call me Lance."

"Well, that's a relief—it would take me all day just to say it, and I don't have much time." Kira glances at her watch, trying to avoid Lance's hypnotic eyes. "So did you like what you saw?"

"Actually, I was a little disappointed."

"Excuse me?"

"That you wear panties at all. A woman with an ass like yours should never wear panties. It is a bore when you don't expect one."

Kira's face turns red; she can feel it burn, placing her hands on her hips, clearly irritated.

"Well, I can see this is going to be a short conversation."

"Why do you have to be in such a rush? How about I buy you lunch?" Lance's eyes work their way up and down Kira's body as he speaks. He looks as though he may want *her* for lunch. Kira can clearly see Lance is determined to get his way. She sees him as a man who does not take no for an answer, ever.

"No, I can't—I'm being picked up in an hour, and I have to find a dress before then."

His advances do not waver after her brush-off. "So you still have to eat, don't you? Call and say you're running late."

"A limo is picking me up—it's probably already on the way. Arrangements have been made, and it would be so rude to make that call. You seem determined—why don't you give me your card, and I'll call you sometime."

"Beautiful girls learn to lie easily; I know you would never call." Kira laughs, which breaks the intensity of the awkward moment. "All right, I will shop with you, then. I have great taste when it comes to dresses—and the women who wear them."

"You must be kidding. With the way you handled those bank robbers? You are most likely an ax murderer."

"I'm sorry. Here's my card. My office is the penthouse of the bank building. Everyone at the bank knows me. I'm a businessman, more likely to kill you with kindness."

Kira's spine tingles with Lance's words, her keen intuition kicking in. She feels somewhat uneasy and starts to step away. Lance quickly steps toward her and blocks her way.

"All I am asking is if I can walk with you, share some air. Come on, we are in a public place. What do you think I'm going to do?"

"All right. It's a free country. I suppose I can't tell you where you can walk."

Lance smiles, seeing that he has gotten his way—he is used to it and expects it. Kira is still not sure about him. There is an unsettling intensity about him—she can see it in his eyes. It's in the way he breathes so deeply while all the while trying to seem so casual. He is anything but casual: every molecule in his body is contrived, every move planned, every word carefully chosen. Kira is well aware of this type of man; she seems to attract them like bees to the hive.

Lance and Kira walk down the steps of the bank and pass a fountain. Tourists are flocking like pigeons in Beverly Hills. The sidewalk is crowded as they walk along Rodeo Drive and pass several stores. Kira did not plan to shop here and is feeling very distracted—even manipulated. Suddenly Lance stops and opens a door to a clothing store in the center of Rodeo Drive.

"I've bought a few things here before. I think you will like what they have."

"You just got through telling me how normal you are. Now you are telling me you wear women's clothes?"

"No, silly, I buy clothes for the women I like. If I like you, I might do the same for you."

"Lucky me," Kira says sarcastically, smirking.

Entering the store, Kira realizes she is in over her head; Lance has successfully manipulated her.

Inside the store, a crystal chandelier hangs over a marbled entry, beautiful cases accented by the glitter of the perfumes, and jewelry just in front of them. Kira eyes the case as she walks by and can't take her eyes off some emerald and diamond dangling earrings—she freezes briefly, imagining herself with them on.

A salesclerk approaches them.

"How are you today? Are you looking for something special?"

"I think she would be interested in an evening dress," Lance answers for Kira.

Kira blushes, although she really wants to bolt. She is running out of time.

The salesclerk walks over to several dresses on a rack. Turning to Kira, she says, "Something formal?"

"I was thinking cocktail, meaning less formal."

The salesclerk picks out a lovely dress off the rack. It is a dusty-rose-pink silk with a rolled collar and deep V-neck slit up the side. Kira gasps; she loves it. She would have chosen it herself. Her heart beats harder. Lance can see it in her eyes—she wants it.

The salesclerk says, "This is one of my newest arrivals. I happen to love this one." She holds the dress out to Kira. "This is a Valentino. It would be stunning on you."

Lance says, "That is a beautiful dress. You must try it on."

"Well, yes, I really like it, but I was not planning to purchase a designer dress for this occasion." Kira turns to the salesclerk. "Would you have something like a festive top?"

Lance, not taking no for an answer, says, "Don't be ridiculous. You have to try the dress on."

Kira feels pressured.

"It's just more than I wanted to spend."

Lance is lusting to see Kira in the dress.

"Forget about the money. Just put the dress on."

Kira takes a deep breath and takes the dress from the salesclerk, who says, "I'll show you to a dressing room."

Lance watches Kira intently as she enters the dressing room, and the salesclerk returns to answer a ringing phone. Lance tries to busy himself by looking at his cell phone. His expression changes from complacency to sheer enchantment when Kira reenters the room, wearing the seductive silk dress.

"You are stunning in that dress."

"Thank you. It is a beautiful dress. I would love to have it, but—"

Lance quickly pulls the tags off the dress.

"If you want it, it's yours."

Kira protests.

"I can't let you do this."

"It's done; the dress is yours. The money means nothing to me. No worries, no strings attached."

Kira stares at Lance for a beat. Lance, smiling back, hands the price tags to the salesclerk. Kira walks back to the dressing room. Kira is thinking, *No strings attached?* This really means he is planning to lasso her with a rope and tie her to him. She is feeling very uncomfortable with Lance's attempt to impress her; she reluctantly goes back to the dressing room. She comes back with the dress and places it on the counter as the sales-clerk rings up the sale. "That will be 877 dollars, would you like to pay cash or charge?"

"Cash." Lance reaches into his pocket and pulls out a huge roll of hundred-dollar bills held together in a silver money clip engraved with the initials LM. As he pulls the bills out, a shiny object drops from his hand and falls to the floor. Both Lance and Kira reach for it, and their eyes meet. Lance, amused, stands back up to allow Kira to grab the object. He peels out hundreds to the salesclerk, who turns back to the register to complete the sale. Lance returns his attention to Kira, who is examining the silver object in her hand. Kira runs a finger over it and presses a button—a switchblade flashes open. She is frozen—the blade is at least six inches long. Her eyes blaze at Lance.

"You should have told me it was a knife before I picked it up."

"That would have ruined the surprise," Lance snaps back with a grin.

"You said you're not an ax murderer."

"*That* is true—I do it with a knife."

"So you *are* dangerous."

"Just enough to be interesting."

Handing Kira the bag with the dress, the salesclerk says, "Thank you so much. I hope to see you again." Her eyes linger a bit too long on Lance.

Kira takes the bag.

"Thank you," she says as she starts walking out with Lance following. Standing outside the store, Kira hands the knife back to Lance with a disturbed look. "I think you'll need this," she says and then turns away and begins to walk.

"At least you can let me take you to dinner. I want the pleasure of seeing you in that dress."

"All right. Maybe we'll go out sometime."

"Not sometime, tomorrow night."

"Tomorrow?" She hesitates and then says, "Call me—I'll write down my number."

"No need; just tell it to me."

"Seven, six, six, eleven, eighty-four." Kira looks at him suspiciously, thinking, *Can he really remember this, or is he just playing me?*

"I will call you tomorrow at five. Just plan on me picking you up at eight. You know what to wear."

"Fine, tomorrow it is." Kira continues to walk away. Lance watches as she goes. Kira turns back to see if he is watching; he is. Kira gives a wave and a smile. Lance does not wave back, nor does he smile; his look is very intense. Kira anticipates what his plans must be. Her mind is aflame. Lance—devil or an angel? She expects both. Kira is confident she can handle either one. Lance continues watching Kira until she is out of sight.

FBI HEADQUARTERS, LOS ANGELES

T WO FBI MEN are reviewing the tape of the bank robbery. They get a close-up on Lance's face.

"Who the hell is this guy? He wasn't questioned as a witness."

"Better yet, who is this girl?"

They zoom in on Kira, getting a close-up on her bare butt. One of the guys breaks into a smile.

"Wait, I know someone who would like to see this." They message to another agent to come into the room. Jimmy is sitting at his desk, eating a sandwich left over from yesterday, when he gets the message. He quickly moves into the office across the hall where the tapes are being surveilled.

The screen has a close-up on Kira.

"You know this girl?"

Jimmy's eyes light up. They zoom in on a close-up on her exposed bottom. There are wide smiles all around; one agent breaks into a laugh.

"Thought you might like that," one of the agents says.

Jimmy responds, "Certainly has put a spark in my day," with his face flushing.

Then on a more serious note, he says, "It's nice to see she is at least keeping busy."

The other agent responds, "She is busy, all right. She has got her hands full this time."

Jimmy thinks on this for a beat and then heads to the door.

"Yeah, well, no surprise here. Keep me posted."

KIRA'S APARTMENT

K IRA'S APARTMENT IS small but well furnished, light and airy with a deco feel. Everything is in black and white—she has black-and-white prints of famous movie stars as artwork, and her bed is all-white satin. Her apartment is luxurious for a woman of her means.

The living room of her one-bedroom apartment has a fireplace with an antique clock on the mantelpiece that includes a loudly ticking pendulum. The clock chimes at five o'clock, and the phone rings at precisely the same moment. Kira picks up.

"My plans have changed. Can you be ready by six?"

"Six? Fine—I can do that."

Before Kira can say anything else, Lance hangs up. Kira is startled for a moment but then realizes she has only an hour to primp. She walks into the bedroom to pull her new silk dress out of the closet. She slips out of her robe and slithers into the dress. She looks into the mirror to check her backside. All good—she works out hard and it shows. She chooses some hot stilettos and a bag. Looking back into the mirror, she brushes her hair and does some touch-up on her lips. She is going for sexy and thinks she has achieved it. She smiles at her reflection as she takes one last look in the mirror.

The doorbell rings. Opening the door, Kira is taken aback by the sight of a uniformed driver instead of Lance.

"Ms. Kira Michaels?"

"Yes."

"I am Mr. McCann's driver. I am here to pick you up for your dinner engagement."

"So where is Lance?"

"He is waiting in the car; may I help you carry anything?"

"All I have is a purse, just one minute." She leaves the driver at the door and rushes into the bedroom, grabs her bag, and tosses in a lipstick before returning. She steps out, she and the driver walk to a black limousine. The driver opens a back door—Lance is sitting inside. He is strikingly handsome in a black suit, white shirt, and french cuffs embroidered with his initials. Both his suit and shirt appear to be custom-made.

Lance smiles.

"Aren't you a vision of loveliness this evening?"

"Aren't you full of surprises?"

"I am just getting started," Lance cracks back.

Kira gets into the limo next to Lance. The driver closes the door and then walks around to get in.

"What do you have planned for us this evening?"

"An enchanted evening with a beautiful lady."

"Because the limo driver seemed to think I would have luggage."

"Why don't you leave this evening's plans up to me? Can I offer you some champagne? I trust you like champagne."

"I love champagne."

"Is Dom Pérignon all right?"

"It's okay. Cristal is really my favorite."

"But you will *settle* for Dom?"

"I'll settle." Kira smiles as Lance removes an already-open bottle from an ice bucket; the bottle is carefully and perfectly wrapped in a white cloth napkin. He pours champagne into a glass. The champagne is exquisite, and so is Lance—in fact, everything about him is perfect. His hair looks as if he has just stepped off a Paris runway. His smile is pristine and white; he looks polished and planned. Kira sips the champagne as Lance pours a glass for himself. Kira is focused on Lance's panache; she is thinking he may have a shot at getting her.

"You are certainly difficult to impress." Lance smirks casting a sharp look at Kira.

"But if there *is* a way to impress me, I know you'll find it."

"Or possibly be destroyed trying." After saying this Lance's mood turns more serious, looking at Kira straight in the eyes.

"So now it's *me* who's become the dangerous one? I assure you I am as meek as a lamb." After saying this a small fire rose in her brain knowing she had lied. She blushes crimson red, almost giving herself away. Lance is staring so deeply in her eyes she is afraid he will see her poorly concealed deception.

"I assure you—I don't believe most of what you say. But you have certainly caught my interest."

Kira can see by the look in Lance's eyes that his mind is traveling a lot faster than that limo. What is he planning to do with her? He wears a mischievous grin as he glances out of the window. The butterflies in her stomach fly into her head and are floating around. Her thoughts twirling, the monster she is seeking to destroy might be the man she is destined to love. Why did she just think that? Before she can have another thought, the limo comes to a stop.

Kira looks out and sees that they are at a private airport, and a jet is waiting.

"You have a jet?" Kira asks, her eyes wide open.

"It is mine. Does that impress you?"

"I would say you've scored some points."

"You are easier than I thought."

The limo door opens, and they step out. The evening sky has taken on a pink glow as the California sun sets. It is a balmy, breezy night. Kira is in awe as she examines the outside of the jet—white, streamlined, and elegant. The limo driver holds the boarding ramp secure as Kira climbs the stairs and steps into the jet.

Inside, Kira takes notice of the jet's cold, powerful interior, reflecting Lance's taste and demeanor. The entire interior is black-and-white, with black leather seats and touches of chrome. There are passenger seats with belts just like any other jet but also a lounge area with a table and sofa as one would find in the interior of an expensive yacht—except that this one flies.

Lance enters the jet.

"Go ahead, take a seat." Lance motions to one of the passenger seats. Kira takes the seat that Lance has pointed to, visibly impressed.

"This is quite the setup you've got here."

Her back is toward the cockpit, Lance's seat directly opposite hers. Within reach of the seats is a silver butler table centered to the left and a full bar to the right. Lance sits across from Kira, with nothing between them but air dense with anticipation—and power. Lance takes in Kira with his eyes, and she gazes back, holding his stare, sexual tension rising.

Kira is suddenly distracted by noise from the cockpit as the pilot and copilot flip switches and speak to the control tower as they prepare for takeoff. The pilot gives notice over the PA.

"We are ready for takeoff. Is everyone buckled in?"

Lance gets up and feels around Kira's hips, reaching for her seat belt. Kira starts to gasp at his touch and then realizes what he is doing. Still, why does he feel the need to buckle her in? It is not as if she were a child and unable to help herself. She hears the seat belt clasp snap as Lance finds the belt. He leans into her even further, his chest coming up from her thighs and sliding along her breasts while his face moves from her cleavage to her neck. He lets his face linger there, and his nose touches her ear as she feels hot, moist air hit her earlobe and neck, making the tiny blond hairs on her neck tingle. Finally, Lance sits back in his seat, snaps his seat belt closed, and answers the pilot, "We are ready."

Kira is anxious about the takeoff.

The copilot slams the cockpit door, and the engine roars. The jet accelerates and speeds down the runway. Soon the jet is airborne—the pressure glues Kira to her seat. Kira peers out the passenger window at the sunset, the last light coming through the pink clouds signaling the start of their journey.

But to where? She was so enthralled that she forgot to ask. *What the hell am I thinking? Immediate answer—I am not thinking.* With the liftoff, she realizes that she is now completely in Lance's territory and at his mercy. Not thinking is absolutely correct.

Kira looks away from the window and glances at Lance. She looks like a deer caught in the headlights.

Lance senses her tension.

"Can I get you a cocktail?"

"How disappointing. You mean you don't have servants?" Kira says with a smirk.

"Actually, I do. I just wanted to be completely alone with you."

Kira musters a smile.

"Vodka tonic."

Lance leans toward the bar and pulls open the small refrigerator door, checking the stock.

"Sorry, we seem to be all out of tonic. How about vodka straight?"

"Straight is how I usually drink it. I was merely trying to be polite."

Lance takes two glasses, plops ice cubes into both, and pours the vodka. He hands one to Kira. He takes his drink to his lips and slowly sips it down while taking in Kira with his eyes. Kira lifts her glass as if to toast, takes a sip, and looks Lance in the eyes.

"Are you going to tell me where we're going?"

"You will know when we get there."

Kira becomes even more anxious but tries to hide her concern by looking out the window again. Lance, meanwhile, never stops watching her.

"You wore panties." Stunned, Kira shoots a hard look at Lance. "A woman with an ass like yours should never wear panties—I told you, it's a bore."

"So now I'm a bore?"

Kira feels the heat rising in her head.

"Not you—your panties. I hate them. Take them off."

Kira feels as if Lance has set a match to her as anger burns like flames down her back.

With a disbelieving look, Kira asks, "What do you mean?"

"You heard me. I hate them. Take them off."

Kira is shocked by Lance's words.

Lance grabs the drink from Kira's hand, spilling vodka all over her. He slams the glass down on the table.

"Do what you are told!" Lance shouts as if speaking to one of his employees. Kira's eyes open wide in disbelief. Her heart is racing; she feels her cheeks searing with the heat from her anger.

"Take. Them. Off!"

Kira's eyes blaze at Lance.

"You are crazy. No one speaks to me like that! Who do you think you are?"

Lance speaks more calmly.

"I am asking you as nicely as I know how to. Now do as I say."

"You're insane. Land the plane—I want out!" Kira gets up and pounds on the cockpit door to get the pilot's attention.

Lance laughs.

"Just where do you think you will go? We are fifteen thousand feet above the ground with no airport in sight. Do as you are told, you stupid woman." Kira turns back and flashes her eyes at Lance in disbelief for a stunned second then turns back to the cockpit door.

Kira pounds harder and more desperately, hot with anger and numb with fear.

"I need help. Open the door!"

"You are ridiculous. They can't hear you."

Kira pounds harder in more desperation.

"Is anyone in there? I need help! Open the fucking door!"

"Do you realize how foolish you are being? Number one, who do you think they are going to listen to—you or me? No one does anything in this plane unless I give the order. Secondly, why are you so hysterical about being asked to take off your panties? Is that such an unusual request? Don't you think you are overreacting?" Lance's eyes grow wide, and he shakes as he restrains himself. He seems just seconds away from striking Kira. Her fear is stinging like arrows going through her stomach.

Kira turns from the cockpit door and faces Lance, breathing heavily and trying to compose herself, her heart pounding like a race-horse's. Lance walks to where Kira is standing. He puts his face so close to hers that she feels the heat radiating from his flushed cheeks.

Speaking pointedly and calmly, he says, "I have gone to a great deal of time and expense to entertain you. I swear I will not ask another thing from you this evening. You can make me very happy by appeasing me and slipping off those panties."

Kira's mind races. No matter what she thinks, she is not getting out of this one—at least not until the plane lands. Accepting her fate, she slowly sits down. Looking at Lance, Kira gradually slips her panties down underneath her dress. Lance stares at her with lust in his eyes as he sips his drink, clearly entertained and pleased at getting what he wants. She slips off her shoes, pulls her panties from her ankles, and hands them to Lance.

He leisurely holds the cream lace thong up and pushes his face into it, taking a deep breath. His eyes roll—he appears intoxicated. Then he tosses the thong aside and smiles wide.

"That wasn't so bad, was it? All that fuss over nothing."

Kira peers out the window, raging inside. She catches a glimpse of the Las Vegas skyline, lights coming up from the shining jewel in the middle of nowhere. The runway lights flash on. The landing gear roars and grates, and then the wheels of the jet touch down, hitting a few bumps on the runway before slowing to a stop.

Lance turns to Kira and says, "I hope you are hungry. I have a fabulous dinner planned for you." With that, Lance stands, takes Kira by the hand, and guides her from her seat. She rises with uneasiness, still feeling captive and under siege.

The cockpit door opens, and the pilot emerges. He steps over to the passenger door and opens it. Lance and Kira walk down the stairs of the jet to a waiting limo. Lance holds the door open—Kira gets in and he follows. As the door closes, the limo immediately begins to move. They sit in silence long enough for it to become awkward.

Lance folds his hands in his lap, looks up at the ceiling, and laughs.

Kira says, "Really, is it that amusing?"

Mocking Kira, Lance says, "Open this fucking door."

"So pleased with yourself, aren't you?"

Lance is quiet for a minute as he takes in Kira's displeasure then says, "You are so hot right now, naked under that dress. I do not care if you are mad at me. It was 100 percent worth the effort to get your ass naked. And yes, I am very pleased with myself." Kira's eyes grow wide as she blushes. Lance tries to kiss her, but she pulls away and looks out the window.

The limo comes to a stop, and the door opens. Kira steps out of the limo into a perfectly hot Las Vegas night, at the entrance to the Bellagio Hotel. She can see the picturesque fountains of the Bellagio dancing in the moonlight. The wind whips at her dress, lifting it. It feels good against her naked flesh. She feels as hot as the desert wind.

Lance opens a door, and Kira walks in, still shunning him as she walks confidently through the hotel. He takes her hand and leads her to Le Cirque restaurant, where they are immediately greeted by the maître d'.

"Mr. McCann, how very nice to see you this evening. Your table is ready."

Lance and Kira are escorted to a very private booth. The restaurant is romantic and dark except for the twinkling of candlelight on the tables.

Quickly a waiter appears.

"Can I start you with a cocktail?"

Lance says, "Yes, we will have two Belvedere vodkas straight up."

Kira adds, "Make mine on the rocks, please."

"Right away. I'll leave these menus and the wine list for you, Mr. McCann. I'll be right back with your drinks."

Lance takes both menus. The waiter leaves to get the drinks.

Lance says, "I hope you don't mind if I do the ordering. I think it's rude to offer a lady a menu. I'm sure you will be pleasantly surprised."

Kira jeers back, "You think it's rude to offer a lady a menu but not to order her to take off her underwear? The only thing that would surprise me now is if I actually *was* pleasantly surprised."

"Oh, now, now. Such sarcasm coming from such a beautiful vessel. That just should not be. You are going to have get over that." He pauses for a second. "Actually, I do understand some of your reservations about me. I can't say that I blame you entirely. I don't think

I know how to behave in front of such a flawless creature as yourself as I have never been in the presence of one. So excuse me while I adjust to this."

The waiter reappears with the cocktails and places them on the table in front of Kira and Lance.

"Shall I take your order now, or would you like more time?"

"I think we would need a little more time. I am not sure if we will be staying," Lance tells the waiter.

"Very well. I will come back in a bit."

Lance shoots a cold look to Kira.

"Can you get over this trifling incident? Or shall we end this evening?"

"I am really uncomfortable. I think it would be better if you took me home." Kira is cold and distant. She looks away from Lance and out at the fountains. They are changing colors, putting on a private show just for her" She knows she is being a bitch, but he deserves it.

"I am sorry for offending you. I am offering to make up for my clumsiness. I think if you spend enough time with me to get to know me, you may find that I have some redeeming qualities."

There is a long pause as Lance gathers his thoughts.

"I feel like every woman I have ever known just ends up running from me. My own mother put me in boarding school when I was just six years old. I only got to visit her on holidays."

Kira looks at Lance, who seems to be pouring his heart out. The ice starts to melt, and she listens on. Her heart slightly warms to room temperature now.

"My father died before I was born, or at least that is what I was told. Maybe I do act unsociable. Maybe I am cold, but it is all I know. Why don't you teach me how to be better?'

Kira finally softens a bit.

"I'm sorry to hear about your father. Did your mother ever marry again?"

"Sure, she did. About four times. Who knows? By now maybe five."

"So you don't stay in touch with her?"

"Not at all, and why should I? We are truly strangers."

"I am a stranger, and you are out to dinner with me."

"You have not hurt me like she has."

"Have you ever been to therapy?"

"Yes, for a short time. What good can it really do? You can do many things in life, but one thing you can never do is change the past. So what good does it do to talk about it?"

Lance is clearly hurt and haunted by his painful childhood. Kira can relate, but that will remain her secret. At a certain point, everyone has skeletons in their closet. But not everyone lets them out to play.

The waiter returns.

"Have you made any decisions on dinner?"

Lance looks at Kira.

"Are you hungry?"

"I'm sorry—I've lost my appetite."

"How about if we skip straight to dessert?" Lance smiles widely at Kira, and she smiles back.

"Okay, dessert then."

"We'll have one of every dessert on the menu." Kira laughs. The waiter nods, leaves for a moment, and returns with seven desserts. Lance and Kira share bites of every one of them, and their conversation loosens up.

Not finishing most of their desserts, Kira and Lance leave the restaurant and are whisked back to the airport. As they board the jet again, the mood is brighter and calmer. Kira, although still intimidated and uneasy, is dealing better with it now. After they have buckled in, Lance laughs, pops a bottle of champagne, and pours two glasses for them to enjoy on the flight home.

Sitting across from Lance again, Kira is more at ease but ever aware of her naked crotch, feeling the steam coming through her dress. She thinks Lance can feel it too.

Lance looks at her as if the steam just hit him in the face.

"I've been talking about myself so much, I have not learned a thing about you. What do you do? Are you a model?"

"Yes, I model from time to time when I can get the work. I do some acting as well—small parts mostly, on soaps and things. I work a lot as a body double. Sometimes I even do stunt work, believe it or not."

"Stunt work? That is hard to believe."

"Yeah. Well, I know some martial arts, though I am not very good at it, just good enough to spoof a movie camera. Anyway, it pays the rent." Kira seems intimidated talking about herself. She nervously shifts in her seat and quickly changes the subject. "When you said, 'Let's skip straight to dessert in the restaurant,' I thought you meant something else."

"I was trying to get you to stay, trying to come up with something you might like. Now I think I know something you will like even better."

Lance leans toward Kira and kisses her on the lips. At first hesitant, Kira returns the kiss. Lance moves on, kissing and biting Kira's earlobes before putting his tongue in her ear. He makes his way down her neck, slightly biting as he makes his way down. Out of his seat and kneeling at Kira's waist, he slowly lifts her dress and kisses and licks her well-toned thighs. Resisting, Kira pushes Lance's head back. Lance doesn't stop, but instead his hands stroke her thighs on their way to softly massaging her hot wetness. Kira loses all remaining resistance, lunging into Lance's fingers and pushing them deep inside her. She is in a trancelike state and can hardly breathe.

Lance stops and looks up at her for a moment.

"This is why I wanted you to take off the panties." He pulls the dress all the way up and licks her swollen clitoris. Kira moans and gyrates on Lance's face as he moves his expert tongue between her legs. She grabs his head, pushing it into her as she spreads her legs wider. Better than dessert—true ecstasy.

Kira rolls her head back as her face flushes with her climax. She looks out the window at the sky as the plane touches down in Los Angeles and sees the pink sunrise. Red sky at morning, sailors take warning. Red sky at night, sailors' delight. Now she has had both.

ON LOCATION

I T IS 7:00 a.m. the same morning. Kira is on the set after a night of no sleep and several glasses of champagne, among other things. She is working with a small film crew doing some pickup shots. Kira is doubling today, wearing a dark wig and dressed like a hooker.

The director yells, "Three, two, one, and action!" Kira walks down an alleyway. The cameraman is getting a close shot of her legs. A muscle car comes barreling down the alleyway toward Kira. As the car passes, it drives into a huge puddle of water, splashing Kira from head to toe.

"Cut!" After a pause, the director adds, "Okay, that was good."

Kira walks back to one of the trailers, mud and water dripping from her limbs, shivering in the cold morning air. A costumer walks up and kindly hands Kira a towel. She dries herself off as she passes the film crew.

The director walks up and places his hand on her shoulder.

"Thank you, Kira." He looks into her eyes, almost apologetic.

"Yeah, that was fun," Kira gibes back then smiles to let him know it's really all right.

Kira steps into the trailer she is sharing with another bit player named Tanya. Dripping wet, Kira pulls off the wig, shakes her blond hair all around, and continues to dry herself off completely with the towel.

Tanya is around Kira's age, is small and stylish, and has lots of red curls. She has a sarcastic sense of humor that Kira really likes. They work and play together and tell each other all their secrets—she is Kira's best friend. Actually, she is her only friend. Tanya points to a dozen gorgeous red roses in a vase on Kira's dressing table.

"Hey, check out what came for you while you were on the set."

Kira walks over and sniffs the bouquet, touching one long-stemmed rose, then continues to take off her wet clothes.

Tanya continues, "Me, I'm lucky if they ever call again, and this one's getting roses. Oh, and yes, I read the card." She picks up the card and reads it out loud. "If I could write the beauty of your eyes and in fresh time, number all your graces, the ages to come would say, 'This poet lies.'" She holds the card out to Kira, who doesn't take it. "It sounds like Shakespeare, although I'm not sure what it means. Hope you don't mind. I couldn't resist. What are you, a witch or something? You must have put a spell on this guy."

Kira finally takes the card from Tanya and looks at it.

"I can't believe it. How did he find me? I never said where I would be. It's kind of weird, actually."

"Yeah, the kind of weird I would like to happen. So if you don't like him, hand him over to me because I could totally handle this."

"He's got a private jet. He took me to Vegas in it."

"Private jet? Oh man, I am dying!"

"Gives great head too."

"Get the hell out!"

Kira bursts out laughing, now in her panties and bra.

"He's kind of cute too."

"Cute? A guy doesn't have to be cute if he has a private jet. Just at least invite me along next time if he has a friend."

Kira pulls on some sweats and slips on some flip-flops.

"Sure, I'll check and see if he has a friend." Kira heads toward the door to leave. "Bye."

"Some girls have all the luck. Wait, what about the roses?"

Kira smiles back.

"That's okay—you keep them."

Kira walks from the trailer and to the spot nearby where she's parked her car. It's a little MG Midget, not fancy, but it gets her where she has to go. She drives off the lot at Warner Brothers and heads to her apartment in Studio City. She has the top down, and her blond curls fly all around as she drives. There is a great pink sunset, and it is a hot Valley night. Life is good when you are Kira.

KIRA'S APARTMENT

WHEN KIRA ARRIVES at her apartment, she finds a note on the door—a UPS delivery notice. She looks down and sees a box. She picks it up and carries it inside.

She puts her purse and the box down on the kitchen table then grabs a knife from a kitchen drawer and cuts into the mystery box. She pulls out still another box, this one wrapped in gold paper with a beautiful shocking-pink bow. She peels off the paper and opens the gift. She finds, wrapped in layers of tissue, a small statue of Galatea from Greek mythology. She is perplexed by the gift, though it is very beautiful. She takes it into her bedroom and places it on her dresser, where she can see it from her bed. As she takes a moment to admire the gift, her cell phone starts to ring. She runs to the kitchen and grabs her phone from her purse.

"Hello?"

"I've been waiting all day to hear how much you love the roses and the precious statue of Galatea."

Kira immediately recognizes Lance's voice.

"I hope you have a good explanation as to why you did not call me immediately to express your delight."

"Lance, I just walked in the door. Who is Galatea?"

"Oh, the story of Pygmalion and Galatea. Pygmalion was a gifted sculptor who hated women so much that he chose not to marry. He decided to sculpt the perfect woman to show other men how inferior their wives were. As he sculpted his beauty, he began to fall in love with her.

"He brought her gifts, and he kissed and caressed her as if she were alive. He was so passionate about Galatea, he even slept with her. He longed for more than anything else in the world that she would come alive and return his passion.

"So he began to pray to the goddess of love, Venus. The goddess of love heard the prayer and brought Galatea to life. Replace Pygmalion with me in the story. You are my Galatea, brought to life, only for me."

"That's a very nice story. But I am not your Galatea."

"You are. You just don't know it yet. You will, though. I want to own you—body, mind, and soul."

There's an uncomfortable silence as Kira considers what to say—she really does not know how to respond to this. Is it flattering? Or is it strange obsession? Should she be frightened and back away? Or should she run into his arms, letting him lavish her with gifts and affection, letting him think, at least, that he "owns" her while living in the lap of luxury?

"When will you be here for dinner? I have had my chef prepare saltimbocca. I don't want it to get cold. I like to eat things while they are still hot and fresh. But then I guess you already know that."

"I'm sorry, but I'm dead to the world right now. Maybe I'll call you tomorrow, depending on how my day goes."

"No—that is not going to work for me. I have planned for tonight. You have to come; I have something that can make you feel less tired."

"Well, that sounds interesting."

"So I am learning more about you all the time. I live at 1542 Stonehenge Road. Don't wait much longer."

"Yeah, okay."

Kira tosses the cell phone down on her bed. She goes to her desk and opens her computer. She logs in then googles Lance McCann. There are several mentions of him in newspaper articles—"Making a Killing in the Real Estate Market" is one headline. *Forbes* lists him as one of the richest men in California. His list of properties is extensive and impressive. Numerous articles in trade magazines name him as the youngest multimillionaire several years ago.

So he really is all that he says he is. Or is there more? How does a man with such a sordid past and childhood make his way to such success? Is there more to him? Kira digs in deeper:

Another news article, an arrest, domestic violence. Lance's girlfriend gets a restraining order. The next piece, Lance McCann, wealthy real estate investor, is being investigated for selling properties to Mexican drug lords using shell corporations to conceal their identities. The article details how the drug lords used the properties as fronts to launder their money. Lance is accused of money laundering and abetting the drug lords. Through a high-priced attorney, Lance is acquitted of all charges, proving that money can buy anything, including freedom and innocence.

She knew he was a criminal. She is like a shark; she can taste it when blood is in the water.

Kira quickly shuts down her search then pulls up directions to Lance's house and prints them out. She goes to her dresser and picks up a bottle of Obsession perfume, perfect for the occasion, and sprays herself in all the right places. She pulls out a shade of hot-pink lipstick and paints her lips. Steam rises from her as she walks out the door.

CRISP CANYON

K IRA SLOWLY DRIVES up the steep driveway to Lance's residence, where it sits alone, high on a hill—a majestic metaphor for Lance's plot in life. Kira gets out of her car and creeps toward the front door while taking in the surroundings. There is a 180-degree view of the city, and twinkling lights rise from the metropolis below. Built in a modern style, the house looks as if it were set on a pedestal. There are plate glass windows all around, allowing one to peer into the house. Shadows mill about the fenced yard to the side where the infinity pool is. It appears to spill out over the city, with a lit waterfall just above, water cascading down onto lava rocks. Steam rises from an adjacent hot tub. Kira reaches the door and rings the bell. The door opens, and Kira gasps as she finds herself face-to-face with a huge Great Dane that looks more like a tiger. Startled, she jumps back, almost falling off the steps as she does.

"Go lie down, Zeus! Pardon Zeus—he tries to steal every girl who visits." Zeus saunters away. "Not this one, Zeus—she belongs to me. Come in."

Kira is still hyperventilating and trying to calm herself as she steps inside.

"Oh my god, I can't even breathe! Is he gone?"

"Don't worry about the dog—he is not the one who can hurt you. He does what he is told."

Kira is still apprehensive as she steps farther inside.

The house is completely dark except for hundreds of lit white candles all around. Cold and austere, the house is decorated almost entirely in black. Black marble floors reflect the candlelight, and the furniture is all black leather with some shining bits of chrome sparking here and there. One wall is covered completely by a moonscape. Pillows covered with exotic animal skins are strewn about. Light comes from only one other source, a huge saltwater aquarium that takes up another wall. Kira approaches the aquarium and sees a small shark swimming about. The shark swims up to a beautiful angelfish and bites into it. There is blood in the water. Kira winces and looks away.

"Too bad you didn't get here earlier. I just finished the dinner." Lance walks over to a leather sofa. Kira looks in the dining room and sees the maid clearing dishes from the table. She glances at Kira briefly as she picks up a platter then turns her back as she goes into the kitchen.

Walking into the living room, Lance pulls a small white folded envelope from his pocket and, using his silver switchblade, tosses it onto the large glass coffee table.

"This is for you; you won't be hungry after you have some."

Kira picks up the envelope and slowly opens it. She lays it out on the table, revealing the white powder inside. Lance takes the switchblade off the table and opens it very near Kira's face. Kira looks at him, hesitating for a moment to see what he intends to do. Lance smiles wickedly as he hands the knife to Kira. He then reaches into his pocket and tosses a hundred-dollar bill on the table. Kira kneels at the table and cuts lines of cocaine. She rolls the bill into a straw, and putting her head down to the table, she snorts the powder through the "straw."

"If you like that, I can get you as much as you want. In fact, I can give you anything you want. But you are going to have to prove to me that you are worthy."

"So just what do I have to do to make myself worthy?"

"Do as you are told."

"You want me to be just like Zeus over there? You can't train me like a dog. That is not going to happen."

"That's too bad, because you could use some training."

"Fuck you. Just who do you think you are, God or something? That you can take people and control them like playthings just there for your entertainment? Nothing more than pieces that you move around on a chess board? You are a spoiled brat, like a little child who always has to have his way. You can no more control me than you can control yourself and your selfish ways."

"It's too bad you feel that way, because I am prepared to take care of you in the highest fashion."

"Yes, it is too bad, because I am not prepared to be your amusement."

Kira stands up and starts walking toward the door.

"Thanks for the treat. Here comes the trick."

She is almost at the door when Lance puts his hand on her back and grabs on to her sweater.

"You can't leave unless you give me your sweater. That way I know you have to come back." He tries to pull her sweater off her arm.

Kira swings around and faces Lance.

"Get your hands off me! You can't have my sweater! And I am never coming back!"

Lance quickly blocks the door.

"Then I won't let you leave."

"You can't keep me here if I don't want to stay. This is not like in your jet."

Zeus jumps up and bounds toward Kira. Kira turns to face Zeus, stunned. Zeus growls and barks. Kira starts to back away then steps sideways toward the knife on the table. Lance lunges for the knife and gets to it first. He points it at Kira.

"Are you insane?"

"Give me the sweater." He looks at Zeus. "Go lie down." Zeus looks at Kira and slowly goes back to his corner.

Kira looks at Lance disgustedly; she takes off the sweater and hands it to him.

"This is all you are going to get from me."

"I doubt that."

Kira walks toward the door, and Lance follows her. She is glad to open the door—as the cool air hits her face, she feels freedom and it is good. She continues to walk toward her car.

"So I have misbehaved. Give me a chance to make it up to you."

"You are really pathetic." She gets to her outdated MG convertible; she opens the door. She is starting to get in when Lance grabs the door handle, stopping her.

"That car doesn't even look safe. I cannot let you drive that around. Here, take my Mercedes." Lance reaches into his pocket and pulls out his keys. He dangles them in the air in front of Kira's face. Kira stares at the keys and then at her old car, then at the brand-new Mercedes 500SL. In the driveway, next to the Mercedes are Lance's Maserati and Bentley.

"You can take it. I have others."

Kira hesitates.

"Has anyone ever offered you a two-hundred-thousand-dollar car before?"

Kira grabs the keys from his hand, and with a click of the key, the car lights up and sounds off. She jumps in the car and starts it up then rolls down the window.

"I will call you," shouts Lance.

She blasts music as she backs out of the driveway and then peels rubber as she drives away, leaving Lance standing in the driveway. Her hair flies out the window as she blasts off.

Lance is mesmerized; he wants her in the worst way. He hates himself for it. He slowly walks back into the house.

SUNSET BOULEVARD

TANYA IS SEATED at a sidewalk café when she sees Kira pull up and park the sleek Mercedes. Her eyes pop open wide when she sees Kira get out of the car and walk toward her. Kira takes a seat at the table with Tanya.

"So what, did you rob a bank or something?"

"Actually, I think I earned it if you ask me. No one else would even go out with that lunatic."

"This is the same lunatic that sent you roses and took you on a date in his private jet?"

"Lance McCann, lunatic, yes, that's the one."

"Ah yes, a rich lunatic, those are my favorite kind. Did he buy you that car? Or is this one of his many?"

"It's one of his. I'm going to give it back though."

"Now who's the lunatic? Are you *crazy*? You shouldn't give it back. If a guy gave me a car like that, he would have to chase me to hell and back before I would give it to him. Then I still wouldn't give it to him."

"No, you don't get it. A guy doesn't give you a car like that and not expect something in return. I expect a lot of something in return."

"Wait, back up. Are you telling me that you haven't even slept with him and he has given you all this stuff? Isn't that, like, against the law?"

"Not only have I not slept with him, I also never want to. It's not even my ass I am worried about giving away. It's more like my life. I think I am better off just staying away from him. He's the kind of guy that if I went out with him once more, you might not ever see me again. He's that scary. He's got a dark, dangerous side. I think there is a lot in his past that he is hiding. He is someone I would have to keep my eye on, you know. He is dirty."

Kira's cell phone starts ringing in her purse; she takes it out and answers it.

"Hello, Lance." She pauses and rolls her eyes at Tanya. "I am having lunch with my friend, Tanya. Sure, of course I like the car. Next I want a Rolls Royce though," she says jokingly, but, she means it. "A party? At your house? Can I bring my friend?"

Tanya sits up and sends out a silent "Yippee!" She is jumping around in her chair.

Kira continues the conversation with Lance: "What kind of party is this? I guess we should bring our swimsuits, then. Of course, I have one. Well, okay, seven o'clock, fine. We will be there"

Kira puts the phone down, looking over at Tanya and smiling.

"I thought you said you didn't want to see him again."

"I am doing this mainly for you. He probably has at least one hot friend. Plus, this is safe enough. It's a party with lots of people. You will be there, so what can he do? He's not going to eat me, right?"

"Well, I don't know about that."

"You will have my back."

"True that."

"Come on. Let's get out of here. We need to go shopping. I need a new suit."

"What? We haven't even eaten yet. On the other hand, I would rather ride in that car than eat."

"And I would rather shop than eat. So let's get going."

Kira and Tanya get into the Mercedes and drive off.

The Beverly Center is close by. The girls head on over and park at the valet. They ride the elevator up to Bloomingdales. Getting off, they head straight into the store's bathing suit department.

There are racks of bathing suits and several on display. Kira is attracted to a fuchsia print micro bikini, perfect for her. She goes right to it; it's a 4, her size. She takes it off display and holds it in her hand. Tanya is going through racks. Frustrated at not being able to find one she likes, she looks over at Kira.

"Aren't you even going to look?"

Kira answers, "No, this is the one I want."

"Really, it's that easy for you? It's the first one you saw."

"I always know exactly what I want."

"Go to the dressing room and try it on."

"I don't have to. It's my size, and I know it will fit."

"Oh, that easy? Has everything always been so easy for you?"

"Not really, but I learned to overcome it."

"Someday we are going to have to talk about that. I need to get clued in on some of your wisdom. You certainly seem to always get what you want."

"First you have to know what you want. I always do."

Tanya looks over at Kira whimsically, you really do know, don't you?"

Tanya pulls a yellow knitted bikini off the rack.

"This one."

She starts to walk over to the register with the suit in hand.

"Aren't you going to try it on?"

"No, this is my first lesson, doing it your way. I like it. It's mine." They continue to the register where they pay for their items, getting their bags and walking toward the exit.

There is a handsome man walking by, taking close notice of Kira. His eyes go up and down her legs. Tanya is watching him ogling her. Kira looks over at him and smiles; the girls keep walking.

The man chases after them. Catching up to them, he says, looking at Kira, "You are stunning. I just want to give you my card. I am Darren Phillips. If you ever find yourself alone, call me." He hands her the card while staring into her eyes. He flashes a big white grin, then he walks away. Tanya is breathless; she stares in amazement as he walks away. Kira smirks as she places the card in her purse.

"What is it with you? This is getting freaky."

Kira laughs out loud; she loves it. Every drop of attention, she drinks it in; she thrives on it.

They go to the valet desk, and the car is brought up.

They get in and speed away.

The Party

KIRA AND TANYA walk up to Lance's door. Kira looks sexy in her yellow crop top and tight white jeans and heels. Tanya is in a denim miniskirt and platforms. The ladies look as if they just stepped off a page in a Victoria's Secret catalogue. Another party guest opens the door and waves the girls in. They walk through the house and outside to the patio. The sun is setting, and the music is loud. There are about twenty people gathered around, some drenched in the pool and others basking in the sun. There is a bar set up close to the pool with a bartender there. A waiter is circulating with a tray of appetizers.

"California roll, ladies?"

Kira says "Thanks" as she takes a roll and eats it. Tanya takes one too as she is looking around. Kira grabs Tanya's arm and leads her over to the bar. The bartender is a hunky guy with a dark tan and sky blue eyes. In Los Angeles bartenders are always actors waiting for their big break; this guy should be the next sexiest man in the world.

"What can I get for you ladies?" Tanya, disabled by his eyes, dazes off. Kira speaks up, "I'll have a shot of Patrón."

The bartender quickly picks up a shot glass and fills it with Patrón tequila and hands over the glass to Kira with a wedge of lime. Kira shoots it down and bites the lime.

He turns to Tanya, who is still dizzy, and she finally gets the clarity to speak up, "I'll have a margarita; make it a Cadillac, on the rocks, no salt."

The bartender mixes up the drink and pours it into a glass, handing it over to Tanya. Smiling at her and with a little wink, he knows she wants him. Tanya takes a big sip and smiles back.

Kira looks over to find Lance is standing right next to her. He is dripping wet from the pool; he obviously works out. He has a six-pack to show for it and some enormous biceps. Tanya is clearly impressed.

Lance is intense on Kira.

"I was worried about you last night. You seemed upset."

Kira is so focused; she does not blink an eye.

"Lance, I would like you to meet my friend Tanya."

Tanya is jolted back to reality.

"Hi, Lance, this is a great party. Thank you for inviting me."

Lance looks at her deadpan.

"I didn't invite you. Kira invited you. I allowed her to do that."

Tanya blushes with embarrassment, getting her first taste of what Lance is all about. Lance continues.

"Come with me. I have a gift for you Kira. Tanya can come too." He grabs up a towel and dries himself off, leaving the towel hanging around his neck.

The girls look at each other for a beat and then follow Lance. He leads the girls though the house, into his bedroom. The room is stark and cold with a lot of black leather and chrome, Lance's iconic branding. There is a set of shiny chrome barbells and a weight lifting bench in one corner. The bed has a big headboard in tufted black leather. A black satin bedspread and animal print pillows are thrown about.

Lance walks over to one of the walk-in closets and opens it up, revealing a full closet of women's clothes and shoes.

Tanya is astonished; Kira, not so much. She knows he will go to any extent to impress her.

Lance, looking at Kira, says, "They are all for you. I guessed you are a size 6 and wear a 7 1/2 shoe."

Kira thinks to herself, *Size 4, you must be kidding me.*

Kira gazes briefly into the closet but does not enter. She does not want Lance to think she is excited or impressed. She keeps her gaze low and will not look Lance in the eye. She dazes off and acts detached, if not bored. She knows that her indifference will spike Lance's attention that much more. Tanya walks right in and looks around. Tanya starts to check out the price tags still hanging from the clothes.

"Gucci, nice."

Lance and Tanya are now looking at Kira for a response. She remains detached.

Lance speaks up.

"She is difficult to impress, isn't she? Maybe if she decides to spend the night, she can have all of this. She will have to leave them here though, she can't take them with her." Lance speaks firmly, looking directly into Kira's eyes.

Still no response from Kira, she is deadpan.

Lance, "Well then, come; let's see what the rest of the guests are doing. Kira looks like she could use another drink."

Lance walks them back through the house and onto the patio.

Lance walks up to the bar.

"Get Kira another shot of Patrón, I'll have a vodka, and get Tanya whatever she wants." He looks over at Tanya.

Tanya says, "Another margarita, please."

The bartender gets Lance his drink first, handing it to Lance, who is being called away by one of his colleges. Lance turns to Kira and Tanya and says, "Excuse me, please."

The bartender hands a shot over to Kira, who quickly shoots it down. Then he hands a Margarita to Tanya. The two stand there for a snap, just taking things in.

The party is in full swing. There are more people now. The sun is setting, and there is a fire in the outdoor fireplace. Candlelight flickers on the outdoor tables. All the lights from the city are sparkling across the skyline. The view is spectacular as you can see the city on all sides of the yard. There is an orange and pink sunset— Kira's favorite. She is breathing it in.

Finally, Tanya turns to Kira.

"What are you going to do?"

"No way am I going to take the bait. Don't you see? It's not me. It's a control thing. He wants to own me. And I won't, under any circumstances, allow myself to be controlled."

"Unbelievable, Gucci and Marc Jacobs? Just spend the night, what the fuck?"

"That's not me. It's the principle. He thinks everything can be bought, except I have no price tag."

Kira sits in a lounge chair and kicks off her shoes. She peels down her jeans and flips off the little crop top. Underneath is the shocking-pink bikini she bought earlier. Tanya follows suit and takes off her clothes, revealing her bikini, and they both descend into the frothing Jacuzzi.

Tanya faces the edge of the Jacuzzi, still pondering what Kira should do. What would she do? Kira is sinking into the hot swirling water, letting her cares drift away momentarily. Tanya finally has a thought bubble in her brain that must come out.

"Seriously, haven't you done a lot more for a whole lot less?'

Kira shoots a look over to her. Tanya is taken aback by her darting eyes.

"I have, with one excuse. I was in love. Women who place their value in what a man buys them are selling out. I may be a slut, but I am not a whore. I sleep with the men I want to sleep with because I want the sex. If I am not feeling it, there is nothing they can do say or buy that will change my mind."

Tanya rolls her eyes sarcastically.

"Those are rock-solid standards, good for you."

There is a shadow hanging over them; they look up to see it is Lance. The first thing Tanya notices is the bulge in his bathing suit; she thinks it's quite nice. She smiles up at Lance.

"Mind if I join you, ladies?" Lance steps down into the water, sitting between Kira and Tanya. "Hope you two are enjoying yourselves. You are invited to spend the night, too, if you wish, Tanya."

"So you are inviting me now? What an honor."

"I hope I didn't seem rude to you before. Sometimes you have to overlook some of the things I say. Apparently, I lack social graces. I never mean to put off a pretty girl."

Tanya smiles back at Lance. He called her pretty; maybe, he might not be so bad. That and the bulge can get him far with Tanya.

Lance looks over at Kira, who is still elusive. He puts his arm around her and pulls her closer to him; Kira shrugs him away. Lance continues to stroke Kira on the shoulder. He turns and kisses her on the cheek; Kira's gaze remains straight ahead. Lance starts to nibble on Kira's ear.

Lance uses his other hand to slip her bathing suit strap down. Kira quickly puts it back on, remaining otherwise unresponsive. Lance is undeterred, kissing Kira down her neck and nibbling her shoulder. Kira starts to wiggle about, trying to push Lance away. Lance pulls Kira's other bathing suit strap down and forcefully rips off her bathing suit top, leaving her breast naked and exposed. Kira gasps and tries to get away, thrashing in the water. Tanya moves away in alarm.

Lance starts to fondle and kiss Kira's breast, his breathing getting harder, his passion growing. He seems to thrive on Kira's displeasure and with the attention he is drawing. All party guests begin to notice, but no one says a word.

Tanya's eyes grow wide, her panic growing deeper. Lance's fervor is raised; he seems to have lost control as he takes one of Kira's nipples into his mouth. Kira tries to push him away.

"Don't, please, Lance." Lance's intensity is blazing as he is grinding into her; he is getting increasingly harder, rougher.

Tanya lifts herself out of the water and sits on the edge of the deck, aghast at what she is seeing.

Lance kisses Kira with such craving, such greed for her body, both of his arms now pinning Kira to the side of the Jacuzzi, grinding against her.

Kira pushes harder.

"Don't, please." She forces him with all the power she has and then shouts "Don't!" with a harder shove.

Kira starts to struggle hard to get away. She is splashing and kicking in the water. She has the attention of all the guests now. All eyes are on the altercation in the Jacuzzi.

Lance puts his mouth on her shoulder and bites it.

Kira screams out loud. Lance is forcing himself so hard onto Kira, she is being forced underwater.

Kira is fighting fiercely now, digging her nails into Lance's back. Tanya watches in horror as Kira's nails go into Lance's back, ripping his flesh.

Tanya feels helpless and afraid.

Lance yells out in wrenching pain as the blood flows down his back; he releases Kira. She jumps up, trying to cover her breasts with her hands. She reaches for her bathing suit top and starts to run. Tanya follows behind her.

"YOU FUCKING BITCH! You scratched the shit out of me. You fucking bitch! Get the hell out of here!"

Kira and Tanya continue running out of the house as all the shocked guest look on.

Kira is throwing her top and grabbing up her keys on her way as they make their escape.

Kira and Tanya jump into the Mercedes. Kira peels rubber as she tears out of the driveway. She drives wildly down the winding canyon road. When she is far enough away from Lance's house that she is sure she can't be found, she pulls to the side, bursting into tears and crying hysterically.

Tanya feels ashamed that she did not do anything to help Kira.

"Oh, Kira, I am so sorry. I wanted to do something, but I was just so scared."

"I hate him. I HATE HIM SO MUCH! What an asshole! I swear I feel like taking this car and running it off the cliff."

"You can't possibly be thinking of that."

"Get out of the car."

"No, please don't. You are freaking me out! He will no doubt kill you!"

"Get out of the fucking car!"

"I am not going to get out of this car! Calm the fuck down! You are losing it! Yes, the guy is an asshole, but you are risking too much. Listen to me."

Kira takes some deep breaths, trying to compose herself; she wipes her tears away. Her breathing slows as she starts to gain more control.

"You are so right about him. He is a lunatic. He is everything you said and so much more. However, don't let that make you do anything crazy. You could file charges, you know."

"I should file charges against him!" Kira screams back. "I have the witnesses. Everyone was watching!"

Kira looks over at Tanya; her eyes seem to glaze over. She focuses straight ahead and gets lost in her thoughts. Tanya tries to bring her back to the here and now.

"We left all our stuff. Not that I care all that much, I mean I care more about you. But it's our driver's licenses and all the money I have until next week, I'm just saying. Well, I am sure you are not planning to go back."

"Oh yes, I will. He's not going to keep anything of mine! I am going to take his car back to him too and shove it right up his ass."

"I don't think you should ever go back there."

"I am not afraid of him. He's a complete wimp. I want to tell him what a loser he is to his face. After that I never want to see him again."

Kira takes another deep breath, and with that she starts the car. She pulls out onto the canyon road and continues to drive. Tanya breathes a soft sigh of relief; she is dazed and confused after what they have been through. She just wants to get home to a hot bath, wishing that they had not gone to that party.

KIRA'S APARTMENT

KIRA HAS DROPPED Tanya off at her apartment. She lets herself into her security building and goes into the elevator. Kira's apartment is on the third floor so that it feels extremely secure. There is no access to her windows or doors from the outside. Kira loves security; she checks doors and locks often. She is very aware of her surroundings, acutely aware. Kira puts her keys in the door and unlocks it; she has a sigh of relief as she steps inside her apartment.

She turns and double locks the door and puts on the latch. Turning on the lights, she sees everything is just how she left it; that is a good sign. In her bedroom, she goes to the nightstand and takes out a gun. She checks it to see if it is loaded; it is. She takes it off the safety lock and places it on top of the nightstand. She notices the card there given to her by the man at the mall.

Darren Phillips, commercial real estate. Another real estate guy? Where are all the doctors and attorneys in LA?

Kira goes to her desk and turns on the computer. She googles up Darren P. There are interesting news items about him; he seems to do well. There are newspaper articles about his last record sell. He was appointed to a prestigious board of directors. In addition, he does charity work—must be a nice guy. He coaches baseball—maybe too nice—and he must have kids. She goes to toss the card in the trash but then thinks twice. She puts it in her desk drawer, where she has a stack of men's cards, just like Darren's. She keeps it for a rainy day, when she may find herself alone—if there ever is such a day.

She goes into the bathroom and runs a warm bath; she can hardly wait to get in. The bathwater is steaming up the bathroom. Slipping off her wet bikini, she stands naked in front of her bathroom mirror. Kira inspects her face carefully in the mirror as she puts her hair up in a bun. She stops as she notices small scratches on her neck left by Lance. She looks over to see the teeth print in her shoulder. She touches it softly and thinks of how she is going to make him pay—not if but how. She sinks her head down and takes some deep breaths. She will think about it again in the morning but not a second more tonight. Kira steps into the hot bath and sinks in; her pain drowns under the fragrant water.

Her thoughts drift to her boyfriend in high school. How very sweet and simple it all was. How has her life become a roller-coaster ride? But then actually, she loves the thrill of a roller-coaster ride. She loves the feeling of falling hard down a dark hole and then rising again to soar like an eagle. Life is not much of anything without the ride. She smiles at the thought of that insight.

LANCE'S HOUSE

I T IS AN overview of the once-pristine house now in shambles. There has definitely been a party here. Stacks of beer and wine bottles lie everywhere, with cigarette butts in dishes and plates of dried-up food. Zeus takes advantage of a plate on the floor, eating a rib from it; he likes party food.

Morning light has just started creeping in, and Lance is sprawled out asleep in the bed. His cell phone starts to ring; Lance continues to sleep. The cell's voice mail picks up, and the caller hangs up without out leaving a message.

The house phone starts to ring; Lance flips over in bed and lets it ring. It finally stops after about eight rings. Lance has ten minutes more of uninterrupted sleep, and the phone starts ringing again. Lance opens an eye and glances at the clock. Ten a.m. He reaches over to answer the phone.

Half-asleep, he says, "What?"

Kira's voice comes though the phone.

"We need to talk."

"About what? So we had a disagreement. I'll allow for that."

"No, it's more than that. I want to talk."

"Fine, come on over. We'll talk."

Lance hangs up the phone, lying back down and rubbing his face. Seriously hung over and still half-asleep, he lies there, trying to remember what went on last night. Suddenly the memory pops into his mind, Kira in the hot tub. He rises in the bed and looks at his swollen face in the mirror then turns to look at his back, now scabbed over with Kira's nail marks all down the sides. Lance goes into the bathroom and brushes his teeth. He jumps into the shower. Steam rises out of the shower. Zeus is busy chewing the rib bone in the living room that looks like a bomb had been detonated in it.

Lance gets out of the shower, drying off. He slips on some jeans and combs his hair. Looking at his ripped body in the mirror, he is most likely thinking, *Kira wants this.* Lance's face is ruggedly handsome and masculine. He epitomizes what a man should look like.

The doorbell rings.

This is it. Kira is here. Lance goes to the door, opening it to see Kira in tight jeans and a low-cut blouse. She looks like she wants it, and he can give it to her.

Kira steps inside, looking at Lance.

"You look like shit."

"I don't know how to respond to that." Kira passes up Lance and has a look around the living room.

"What happened? Did your maid quit?"

Lance walks over to the sitting area; there are two chairs facing out to the front of his house. As he looks out the window, there is a view of the entire San Fernando Valley. There is a table between the two chairs; cigarettes and bourbon in a large crystal decanter are on the table. Lance sits in one of the chairs. He lights up a cigarette; although he doesn't usually smoke, this seems like a good time to start. He pours himself a bourbon; although he normally does not drink in the day, it also seems like a good-time to start.

Looking over at Kira now, he says, "I thought you wanted to talk. Did you want to talk about my maid, my looks, or what? Get to the point."

"You have problems, Lance. You need to face them head-on."

"Why is that such a big revelation to you, little girl? Everyone has problems. If you are looking for the perfect man without any problems, I assure you that you will be looking for quite a long time."

"No, I mean you are sick."

Lance burst out in uproarious laughter.

"So I am sick, am I? Oh, thank you. Thank you so much, wise doctor Kira."

He laughs even more then takes a huge drag from the cigarette, blowing the smoke out of his nose. Suddenly serious now, he says, "So why don't you heal me?"

Kira comes over to take a seat in the chair beside him. Lance reaches over and pours Kira a glass of bourbon. He pushes it over to her. Kira looks at him for a beat and takes a sip.

"You are beyond my help, Lance. You need a doctor. You hate all women because your mother abandoned you. You want to possess me but only to hate me. You see yourself as the center of the universe, as if you were the sun and everything else evolves around you for your use and your pleasure. Well, you can't have me. I won't be possessed. I just came to get my things back, and that is all I wanted to say."

Kira looks defiantly into Lances eyes.

"Oh yes, and here's your keys." She reaches into her pocket and tosses the Mercedes keys onto the table. "You can have your car back too." She stands up and swigs down the rest of the bourbon. She cracks her glass down on the table and turns to pick up her belongings.

Sitting on a stool in the corner, Lance puts out the cigarette and stands up.

"You think it's that easy? Like *you* can just toss *me* away? Think again, little, little girl."

Kira turns back to see the look in Lance's eyes. They are glazed over; he looks possessed. Jolts of fear rise in Kira's stomach and shoot though her back, spreading all though her body.

Lance places both hands on her neck, squeezing until Kira gasps and jumps back.

Kira slaps his hands away.

"You don't scare me, Lance. You would like to scare me, wouldn't you? But you don't."

Kira picks up her and Tanya's bags. She continues to walk toward the door.

Lance grabs her arm from behind. Kira quickly wrings herself away, turns around, and in an automatic reflex motion, slaps Lace squarely in the face.

In an equally automatic movement, Lance slaps Kira right back. The sting of the slap sends jolts of fire through Kira's face.

"Fuck you!"

She turns to leave again. Lance comes at her, grabbing her arm. This time Kira kicks him as hard as she can. Lance is ready and blocks the kick. He grabs her foot and takes her down.

She hits the floor with a thud; the hit to her head on the floor makes her sick and dizzy. She has to fight' there is no other way out.

Lance jumps down on top of her, straddling her body; he pins her arms down to the floor. Kira starts to flail around, attempting to throw him off her.

She spits in Lance's face; he releases her hands to wipe the spit off his face. Kira takes the pause to roll over and get to her feet. She jumps up and kicks Lance in the stomach. She runs to the alarm system next to the door, pushing the panic button. The button alarms directly to the police. The alarm starts to sound; it is deafening.

Just as quickly as Kira sets off the alarm, Lance uses the code to diffuse the alarm. He throws Kira violently up against the wall, pinning her arms above her head.

"Now are you afraid?"

Lance has his face pressed up against Kira's. Kira can see he is excited by the fight, even aroused; he is a monster.

Kira screams and brings her knee up, kicking him in the groin; Lance falls to the floor, moaning.

Kira runs to the door, and with her hands shaking, she starts to undo three locks.

As she fumbles at the locks, it has only been seconds, but it feels like an eternity. Suddenly she feels something hard and cold pressing to her temple. She looks to the side to see a gun at her head. Lance's other hand grabs her by the neck while he continues to press the gun into her temple.

Kira stops, stunned and frozen. The fight is over, and Lance has just won.

Panic takes over her body; she starts to shake from head to toe.

"You should learn to do what you are told. Get into the bedroom."

Kira starts to walk toward the bedroom as Lance holds the gun to her head, forcing her to the bedroom. They walk down the hallway and into Lance's room.

"Lie down on the bed."

Kira lays down on the bed. Still holding the gun, Lance reaches with the other hand into a drawer by the side of the bed. He pulls out some handcuffs and cuffs Kira's wrist to a post on the bed, locking the cuff tight.

Lance is out of breath from the fight. Hot sweat runs down the sides of his face. He sits down in a chair across from the bed. There is a table next to the chair that is more like a minibar from a five-star hotel. He pours himself a stiff drink and throws it back, his hands shaking all the while.

Kira stares at Lance in terror.

Lance is still breathing hard and keeps running his hands through his hair as in deep thought. He stares back for a moment at Kira. The silence is deadly and awkward. Kira has never felt so completely helpless. She is used to having the upper hand. Being a victim is just not her comfort level; it's not who she is.

Lance starts to calm down, now taking some deep breaths.

"Why did you do that? You made me get rough with you. I didn't want to do that, but you made me."

He stands now and starts pacing at the foot of the bed.

"All I want is to take care of you. Your life could be so rich, so comfortable if you would only let me take care of you. You have to stop fighting me this way." Lance takes the glass in his hand and hurls it at the wall just above Kira's head. The glass bursts into shattered pieces, falling all over Kira. She quickly throws her face aside to avoid the shattered glass.

"You bitch! Fighting stupid Bitch."

"I'm sorry."

"What did you say?'

"I said I'm sorry."

Lance looks at Kira as if he is in wonder, astounded by her apologies. He goes to the side of the bed and sits down beside her; his tension seems to subside. Facing her, he touches her face and brushes the hair from her eyes.

Kira is shaking in terror.

Lance leans down and softly kisses her on the mouth then slowly down her neck. He climbs on top of her and straddles her over her waist. He slowly starts to unbutton her blouse.

He opens it, and her breasts are bare. He slowly goes down and takes her entire breast in his mouth, savoring the taste of her flesh.

Kira's eyes are still filled with terror. Lance moves down her body, licking her stomach as he goes down. He peels down her tight jeans.

Slowly he pulls down her panties. Kira knows what is coming; her heart sinks in pangs of anguish.

The panties are slowly making it down her hips to her thighs and past her ankles and finally on the floor. She watches as Lance flings them across the room, stopping only for a second. His head goes down as he spreads Kira's legs wide apart. He dives his head into Kira's crotch.

Kira feels his wet tongue on her clitoris, moving in circles around it, sending shock waves through Kira's body. She arches her back and tries not to lunge deeper into Lance's advance, but her body moves into Lances face involuntarily. She feels Lance's fingers twisting in her vagina.

Kira is momentarily lost in the sensation. She cries out in a whimper.

"Please don't do it."

But her body is bearing down to his deep thrust into her vagina, and the heat seems to have melted all reason from her.

Kira clenches the pillow beneath her with a free hand; it is wet in whiskey and her sweat.

Kira's body starts to tingle, all her nerve endings standing at attention. Then her body convulses in a wild sensation as her orgasm consumes her.

Lance rises, his face wet with her juices; he unbuttons his jeans and takes them off.

Kira is still convulsing in remission to her orgasm.

She manages to look at Lance one more time.

"Please no."

Her words are worthless; he has her now just the way he wanted her.

Lance's pants are off, exposing his huge hardness. Kira breaths in deep and turns her head away.

Lance positions himself between Kira's spread legs.

She feels him enter her; it is so intense, the feeling of the fullness inside her. Lance is grinding into Kira, harder, deeper. She screams out, arching and moving into Lance's assault.

Kira can see the reflection in the mirror of her scratch marks in his back from the night before. She is proud of her work; it should have been worse.

Lance continues to thrust inside her, slamming really deep.

Through clenched teeth, he says, "You like this don't you? Say it." Grinding in deeper, he yells, "SAY IT!"

Kira is starting to collapse; she feels a huge growing orgasm about to collapse in her like a wave. She screams out, "Yes!"

Through hard breaths, he says, "Good girl."

Lance grabs on to her hips and thrusts into her as far as he can go, moving very roughly now.

"Say my name."

Kira is moaning and whimpering, trying to say his name, and the words won't come.

"SAY MY NAME!"

"Lance, Lance!" she yells out.

That sends him over the edge, and clenching his teeth and groaning, Lance releases with a huge orgasm into Kira, moaning and breathing hard. He collapses on top of her, his body drenched in sweat.

His head is resting on her stomach. He grabs her sides, kisses her all over her belly, and lays his head back down on it. His breathing slowing down now.

Kira is lost and confused. She feels a release but with such great regret. This is not what she wanted. It was not what she planned.

Lance is resting so comfortably on her.

"I can be gentle, but you wouldn't like gentle, would you?"

Kira looks down at Lance, who glances up at Kira. Lance smiles and rests his head back down. Holding Kira tightly now, he drifts off into sleep.

Kira tries to wiggle her wrist, still in a cuff attached to the bed. Her arm is getting cold. Silently, she starts to cry. The bitter tears go streaming down her face, biting her tongue so as not to make a sound.

Kira looks out the window to see the sun slowly going down. She closes her eyes as well. Maybe she will wake up to find this has all been a dream, a very bad dream.

Next Morning

T HE MORNING LIGHT peaks through the curtains. Lance's room is still in shambles. The glass is scattered over the floor from the night before. The stench from the whiskey seems worse. Lance starts to move, still holding Kira around the waist. He rises to look at the clock. He looks over at Kira and seems confused, sitting up. He rubs his hands through his hair. He looks back at Kira, and the light streams over her face; he remembers it all now. He picks up his jeans from the floor and puts them on. Stepping gingerly across the floor to avoid the glass, he walks into the bathroom.

Kira hears the toilet flush and the water go on. She takes the pillow from underneath her and places it on top of her naked body. She is cold, in shock, and still afraid. She looks over at the gun by the bed, out of reach and still a threat.

Lance comes out of the bathroom, rubbing his face with a towel.

"Lance, can you uncuff me?"

"No."

"Please, my hand has fallen asleep, and it's getting numb."

Lance looks over at Kira and turns back around, thinking; he walks to the window and opens it up. He breathes in deeply and turns back around.

"I can't let you go. I know you will leave me."

"Lance, please. I promise not to leave. I need to go to the bathroom. You have got to at least let me do that. Where could I go? I have no clothes on."

Lance hesitates.

"Please, I swear. I am going to pee all over your bed."

Lance removes a key from the drawer and unlocks the cuff. It clicks open. Kira rubs her wrist, trying to get the circulation back.

Kira sits up and puts her feet on the floor, feeling weak. She is trying to get her strength back.

"I need my purse."

"No."

"Come on, Lance. I think I am getting my period."

Lance goes into the living room, bringing back Kira's purse and handing it to her. Kira goes into the bathroom and closes the door.

"Don't lock it," Lance yells from the bedroom.

Kira turns on the faucet in the bathroom to make the sound of running water so that Lance cannot hear what she is doing. She slowly opens the bathroom window, looking down at the ground to see what the drop is like. She thinks she can make it; she must make it.

She runs to the toilet and flushes it to be sure all the sound is drowned out. Grabbing a towel off the rack, she wraps it around her. She grabs her purse to take it with her. Pulling a trash can over and standing on the inverted trash can to lift her up, she opens the window further and heists herself through it.

She drops to the ground, falling on her knees; the towel drops away, the fall hurts, but she is free.

Wrapping the towel back around herself, she runs down the driveway to her old car. Grabbing the car door and flinging it open, she jumps behind the wheel, slamming the door shut. She puts the keys in the ignition and tries to start it.

Lance hears her car door slam in the driveway from the bedroom. He throws open the bathroom door and sees the bathroom vacant, the towel gone and the window open. He picks up the gun next to the bed and runs to the front door.

Kira sees Lance run out the door and is standing in front of her car. She is trying to start the car and get away, but it is stalling.

Lance lifts up the gun in his hand and points it directly at Kira. Her car is failing her; she pushes the gas and tries starting it again as Lance cocks the gun.

Finally, the car turns over. She quickly throws it into reverse and peels rubber down the driveway.

Lance fires three shots, hitting Kira's car. One shot penetrates the front of the car, and one hits the side; she does not know where the third one goes. She swerves onto the street and puts the pedal to the metal.

In the rearview mirror, she sees Lance in the street, pointing the gun. She hits the gas harder until he is out of sight.

KIRA'S APARTMENT

KIRA IS ON the phone to the police. She is in a fog, still suffering and traumatized from her injuries from Lance. Yet she has the state of mind to make the phone call.

"How soon can you be here? No, I haven't showered. I need help. I am in fear for my safety. He has a gun. He knows where I live. I may only have minutes or even seconds. Fine, then I will wait."

Kira puts on a large white terry cloth robe and curls up in a fetal position on the sofa.

Time is running slowly now, as if the world had shifted into slow motion; everything is in soft focus and gray. It's more soothing this way, almost bearable.

The doorbell rings. Kira slowly rises from the sofa and stumbles to the door. Opening the door, she sees two police officers.

"Hello, Kira, I am Officer Kelly." Kira looks to see a young cop, no doubt new on the force.

"Ms. Daniels, I am officer Ruiz." Kira looks to see a veteran officer.

The younger officer speaks up, "You called to file a report on an attempted murder and rape."

"Yes, come in."

The young rookie officer and the senior officer step inside and look around. Kira is disheveled and not entirely coherent. She shows the officers in and takes a seat on the sofa. The officers sit in chairs across from the sofa, and so it begins.

"I was raped and held at gunpoint."

The younger officer questions, "You were raped? Can you identify this person?"

"Yes, his name is Lance McCann. I was dating him."

Ruiz is now asking, "You were dating? Did you have sex with this man before, or was this the first time?"

"I said I was raped. I never had intercourse with him before, and nor did I want to. I told you, he had a gun to my head."

Ruiz continues, "You specifically said you never had intercourse with this man. Does that mean you engaged in other sexual acts but just not intercourse?"

"Yes, I had oral sex, or I mean, he did with me. Does that mean it is okay to hold me at gunpoint and rape me?"

The two officers look at one another for a beat, at a loss for words. Kelly starts writing the report and briefly glances up at Kira.

"He used a gun?"

"Yes."

"Any other force?"

"He hit me, and I fought with him. He also used handcuffs to restrain me."

"Handcuffs?" The younger officer looks confused, which turned to concern after seeing the bruises on Kira's wrists. "We will have to take a picture of the bruises."

He stands up and takes a camera from a bag, taking shots of Kira's injuries. There are bruises on her wrist, a small cut over her eye, and various lacerations on her arms and thighs.

Ruiz speaks up, "Were you on a date with him when this altercation took place?"

"No, I had actually gone over to break up with him and get my things."

"He has things of yours?"

"Well, I have my purse now, but he has a sweater of mine and my friend's purse."

Kelly is writing all this down as Kira speaks.

"You said he used a gun. Was this just to threaten you? Or at any time, did he fire the weapon?"

"Yes, he fired at me as I was trying to escape. He shot my car, but he was trying for me."

The two officers look at each other at that.

"He shot your car? We will need to see the car."

"My car is down in the garage."

"We can follow you out there."

Kira goes into the bedroom and slips on some shoes. She walks back out and the two officers follow her to the elevator. They get in and take it down to a subterranean garage.

The car is riddled with gunshots. Kelly's eyes grow wide as he photographs the evidence, taking shots of the front side and the rear of the car, writing more on his report.

He looks at the other officer, and they nod in agreement that the report is finished.

Kelly sticks the report under his arm then speaks to Kira: "We are going to need you to go to the hospital for an examination. We will need DNA evidence. We need you to go without delay."

The older officer speaks up.

"These things are very hard to prove. It is basically your word against his. It can be very messy. If you want to think about it, we can hold this report on our desk, and you can let us know later if you change your mind about filing."

"No, I want to file this. He tried to kill me. He is a dangerous person. He has to be stopped."

"I advise you not to shower, then, and go straight to Valley Hospital. We will call ahead and say you are coming. If you do not feel well enough to drive, we can take you or get an ambulance.

"I think I can drive."

Kelly writes on a pad and then rips the paper off the pad, handing it to Kira.

"Give them this for the examination."

He also rips off a copy of her report.

"Here is a copy of the police report." He hands her a card. "This is my card. Call me tomorrow, and I will get a police escort for you to get your things from his house. In the meantime, go to the hospital and get the examination. We need all the evidence intact."

Kira takes the card and turns to go back in her apartment. The officers leave out the garage's security door.

Kira walks back into her apartment, and the house phone is ringing. She picks up the phone.

"Hello?"

The voice on the other end is a man.

"Kira, I am Stanley Mays, Mr. McCann's attorney. I know about what took place over the weekend. I am calling to make you an offer."

"Go to hell and take your client with you."

"Don't be so quick, Kira. My client is prepared to pay you a nice sum."

"The next contact I will have with Lance will be when I meet him in criminal court. I am sure you will be there with him."

"Think about it, Kira. If you let this go to trial, I am going to make you look like last week's garbage. I will make you look so bad, your own mother won't take your side. Be a smart girl, take the money, go shopping, and get on with your life."

"The only person who is going to look like last week's garbage is going to be Lance and you for defending him."

"Suit yourself, but you are making a very foolish mistake."

Kira hangs up the phone then rips it out of the wall and throws it on the floor. Screaming and crying in anguish, she throws herself down on the bed and cries into her pillow.

The cry is good for her; it is cleansing. She will need a lot of that.

Her crying subsides, and she raises her head up, gathering her thoughts. She must make it to the hospital and get the examination. She throws on a black knitted dress and some flip-flops and heads out the door.

She arrives at the hospital and is greeted by a receptionist. She says who she is and hands the woman the slip of paper the police gave her. She walks to an examination room, where a nurse greets her.

"Kira Michaels? Detective Kelly has ordered a rape kit. Do you know what is involved?"

"Not really."

"We are going to have you undress. I will give you a gown, and we will be taking DNA evidence from underneath your nails, and we will be doing a pelvic exam with a pap smear."

"All right then."

"We will also be taking pictures of any wounds or lacerations. If you want someone in for support, we have counselors that can speak to you. Would you like for me to call someone?"

"No, I am okay. I think I can get through this."

"Here is a gown for you to put on. You can hang your clothes behind the door."

The nurse leaves the room, and Kira undresses, slipping into the hospital gown. It is cold in the examination room, and she starts to shiver. The nurse returns and has an assistant.

"We need you to lie down on the table." Kira lies down but continues to shiver. "Can I get you a blanket?"

"Yes, please."

The assistant gets a blanket out of the cabinet and covers Kira. It really doesn't help; she is shivering from the inside, from the shock, from lying on this hospital bed, and from the journey before her. She is cold through to her core.

First they take swabs and start scraping underneath her nails, placing the matter into small test tubes. Next they ask to remove the blanket and open her gown, observing many bruises and lacerations and taking Polaroids of each as well as using a digital camera. Then Kira is asked to put her feet into the stirrups and slide down. Seated at the bottom of the table, the nurse is facing Kira's vagina; she shines a bright light on it and flashes a picture. There must be some cuts there; she has felt them. They insert a cold hard instrument and open Kira up. The pain is intense from the roughness from the night before. It sears like a knife. The nurse starts scraping the sides of Kira's vagina with a swab, placing it in a test tube. Kira winces in pain, digging her nails in the bed.

"Don't worry, Kira. Try to relax. We are almost done. You are doing great."

That's strange because I don't feel great. Strange thing to say, Kira thinks to herself. *The scraping is done, thank God.* They take the instrument out.

Kira can go now. She has never been so glad to get something over with in her life.

She walks out into the warm Valley air and gets into her car.

KIRA'S APARTMENT

KIRA HAS HAD a shower and is walking around in her bathrobe with a towel on her head. There is a knock at the door.

Kira goes to the door and opens it to see Tanya.

"I came as fast as I could."

"I am a wreck. I haven't slept in two days."

"I can't even believe you went back there. I told you not to go."

"JUST SHUT UP!" Do you really think I want to hear this?"

"Well, aren't you more afraid now? Don't you think Lance is going to come after you?"

"Of course I am afraid. Don't you see I got my gun out?"

Tanya looks over to see the gun out on the table. She is a little surprised that Kira has a gun but also relieved.

"I told you that guy was an evil lunatic. He should be shot—or no, tortured."

"Don't worry. I will get revenge. The tables are about to turn."

"Have you thought of an attorney? You should file a civil suit. You need that famous one, Dana Spears. She handles only women, mostly abuse cases."

"I have already thought of that. She is the one I will call. She has a very good reputation for winning cases like this."

"You should call her before the criminal trial starts. You need some good advice." There is a quiet pause, Kira contemplating what is to come.

Kira takes a deep breath and sinks into the sofa next to Tanya. Tanya continues.

"You should also get a counselor, a psychologist."

"I am my own best psychologist. What are they going to do for me? Talk about it until I can't stand it anymore? There is no real resolution. It's a facade. You think you have been fixed, but the past lives on inside you. It can't get undone."

"You need some professional help. You are saying this now because you are angry. You may be able to get some resolution and healing."

"I am going to handle this on my own terms, Tanya."

"You always do."

Kira feels so weak and tired that she is finding it hard to stay awake.

Tanya sees Kira nodding off.

"Have you had anything to eat?"

"I am not a child, Tanya! I would eat if I was hungry!"

Tanya knows it is just a lack of sleep. She is not upset with Kira's outburst.

"All right, I think I should go, and you should get some sleep."

"I am sorry if I upset you."

"You will get better. It's going to take some time."

"Tomorrow the police are coming to take me to Lance's house to get my things. I will get your purse."

Tanya gasps at this.

"Do not go there, of all things! This guy just tried to murder you. I will get another fucking purse, and you will get another fucking sweater! Have you actually really lost your mind?"

"I am not backing down, Tanya. Lance will have to face me, and he will pay for this."

"That is right, but it is something you do in court."

"It's already been arranged. I mentioned I will have a police escort right? What's he going to do to me? Anyway, I want to get into his face."

"I am really going to have to leave you with this. Get some sleep."

Tanya goes out the door. Kira locks all three locks and puts the chain guard on. She looks out her third-story window. The night is quiet and still; all the stars are shining. There is no wind, just an eerie, still night. It is the quiet before the storm. And what a storm it will be.

Morning, Kira's Apartment

K IRA IS AWAKE, having her coffee in the kitchen with her laptop close by. She reads the news and checks her social networks. She pours another cup of coffee and then googles up Dana Spears, the attorney she and Tanya had discussed. Dana's website states that she is an avid advocate for women's rights and fights successfully to represent victims of sexual assault and rape. She has handled many high-profile cases, has been a news commentator on many cases, and has won high awards for her achievements. Kira thinks her ego is huge; she will win at any cost, perfect. She closes her laptop and makes her way into the bedroom, throwing on some jeans and a top. The doorbell rings; Kira goes to the door. It is the police officers, Kelly and Ruiz. Kira grabs up some empty bags and goes out the door with them to the police car; she is seated in the back. They all proceed to Lance's house. Kira's heart beats faster and faster as they drive up the street. When they drive up the driveway, her heart is in her throat.

It is as if she is on automatic, just like a machine that can't be stopped. This attitude will work in her favor; she has mountains to climb.

Kelly turns to Kira.

"You all right to do this?"

"I'm good." Kira fakes a smile.

They all get out of the car, and Kelly leads the way up the walkway, ringing the doorbell. You can hear Zeus barking inside, then Lance flings open the door, looking very casual in jeans and a T-shirt.

Kelly speaks up, "Lance McCann, we are here to assist Kira Michaels in retrieving her belongings from your house."

Lance smiles and seems amused.

"Ms. Michaels, well, of course. Come in."

Kelly says, "Mr. McCann, I am going to have to ask you to step outside, sir."

"Fine, no problem." Then he steps out with Kelly in the front while Kira and Ruiz enter the house. Ruiz follows Kira into the bedroom, where you can overhear Lance speaking to Kelly.

"Sorry you guys have to waste your day doing this. It is just an overblown lovers' quarrel. You know how dramatic women can be. This is really senseless."

Kira continues on to Lance's bedroom, oddly left in the same disarray as when she left. She expected it to be all tidy and clean as if nothing had happened. He knew the police were coming, so why not clean up? She had no time to consider the puzzle; she went quick to her work. Opening the bags she brought, she goes about filling them with the designer items in the closet. She grabs up her sweater and Tanya's purse as well.

Ruiz looks around as Kira is in the closet. They can still hear Lance speaking to Kelly on the front porch.

"I guess I really know how to pick them. It seems like the pretty ones are always the crazy ones. Maybe someday I will learn. I'll bet you have had experiences like this with women, haven't you?'

"Actually, no, nothing like this. I am married," answers Kelly.

"Lucky guy. Well, you have seen your share of crazy women, I am sure."

"We have your story on file, Mr. McCann."

Kira walks out of the closet to find Ruiz inspecting the room. He walks to the head of the bed and sees the mark on the wall where Lance had thrown the glass. He bends in to look very closely at it. Then looking down behind the head of the bed, he sees the shattered glass. He bends down to pick up a piece. He looks up at Kira, who is stoic.

Kira turns to walk out, and Ruiz follows her.

They walk out of the door past Lance and Kelly. Kira turns back to look at Lance.

Lance wears a fake goofy smile, pretending to be casually laughing this off.

"Well, as I say, sorry you guys had to waste your day with Kira. I am sure you have better things to do."

"No problem, it's all in a day's work," says Kelly.

"That's it, then? Are you finished with the investigation?"

"That's it for now. You know not to leave town, don't you?" Ruiz asks Lance.

"Sure, I know."

"That's it, then," Kelly adds.

As they walk to the car, Ruiz sees something shiny on the ground. He reaches down to pick it up; it's a bullet.

Kelly says, "What is that?"

"Nothing, man. Just can't pass up a lucky penny."

He slips the bullet in his pocket and continues to the car.

They all get into the car and drive off. Lance stands on the front porch and watches them drive away. His arms are crossed; his body language screams defensive, Kira thinks to herself. Although he acted self-assured, it won't be for long; her mind is churning.

Kira will be glad to get home behind her locked door. She has a sense that she had a small victory just now. Still, a locked door and a glass of wine will do her a world of good.

KIRA'S APARTMENT

K IRA CLOSES THE door to her apartment. She goes through the ritual with the locks. Next it is into her bedroom to recover the handgun out of her drawer that she had put away before the police arrived. She unlocks the safety lock and places it on the nightstand next to the bed. She looks out the window, inspecting the street for any strange cars or one of Lance's. Finding it to be safe enough, she closes the blinds. She sits at her desk in the bedroom and turns on the computer. She googles up Dana Spears and picks up the phone.

"Law office of Dana Spears," a receptionist answers.

"I am Kira Michaels, calling for Dana Spears."

"Do you have a case with Ms. Spears?"

"No, I would like to file one."

"What is the nature of your case?"

"Rape, attempted murder, and false imprisonment."

Kira speaks very calmly, enough to be disconcerting to the receptionist. There is a pause on the part of the receptionist.

"I will need you to speak to our paralegal. Please hold."

Kira is put on hold. She grabs a tablet of paper and a pen to get ready for anything she may have to write down. She draws targets while waiting. The paralegal comes to the line.

"Hello, I am Lucy Diaz, Ms. Spears's assistant. To whom am I speaking?"

"I am Kira Michaels."

"I was told you have a complaint of a rape and attempted murder?'

"That's right, and false imprisonment."

"Kira, I will be recording this conversation. Is that all right with you?"

"Yes."

"I need you to be truthful in giving me your details of this case. I am starting the recording. Ms. Michaels, you have told me that you have been a victim of a rape and attempted murder and were held against your will. Is that correct?"

"Yes."

"Do you know who your assailant is?"

"Yes, his name is Lance McCann."

"What is your relationship to Lance McCann?"

"I dated him."

"Were you on a date with him when this altercation took place?"

"I was at his house. I had gone there to break up with him."

"You drove yourself to his house?"

"Yes, I wanted to get my things I had left there."

"So briefly describe the attack."

"I wanted to end our relationship. When I got up to leave, he tried to stop me from leaving. He grabbed me and pushed me to the floor. A fight broke out. I was struggling to get away. Then he somehow got a gun and put it to my head. He took me to the bedroom and handcuffed me to the bed, and he raped me." Kira's voice starts to quiver; she is feeling weak at recalling the incident.

"Did you clearly say no?"

"Yes, I fought him hard and I screamed no, but he had a gun. What could I do?"

"How did you get away?"

"I convinced him to let me go to the bathroom. It was the following morning. I was able to escape out of the bathroom window."

"Have you filed a police report?"

"Yes, with LAPD officers Kelly and Ruiz. They took a report, and I got an escort to his house to get my things. I can give you the case number and their phone to call."

"Yes, I will need that. What I will do is email you a form to fill out. On that you will need to give the details and your case number. Hold on. I will see when Ms. Spears is available to see you."

While Kira is on hold, she draws targets then punches the pencil through the paper, creating bullet holes. She rips the paper to pieces and tosses it in the trash. The receptionist is back on the line.

"Can you come in tomorrow at 2:00 p.m.?"

"Yes, I will be there."

"Just so you know, this is only an interview to see if Ms. Spears wants to take your case. This does not mean she will take your case. Do you understand?"

"Yes, thank you."

"See you tomorrow at 2:00 p.m."

"See you tomorrow, then, thanks."

Kira hangs up the phone and prints out the directions to the office. She thinks Dana will take the case; it is rock-solid.

She spends more time before bed, googling Lance. She finds he has an impressive portfolio of real estate. She finds he has holdings in other counties as well, most likely in overseas bank accounts. There have been some inquiries from the government over some deals he did in Mexico. There are some possible connections to drug kings in Mexico. He was investigated and let go. He apparently represented them in buying properties in the United States under a false corporation.

Not exactly Mr. Clean, are you, Lance? The government couldn't take you down, but I will. Kira feels sure of it.

DANA SPEARS'S OFFICE

K IRA STANDS OUTSIDE the twin towers in Century City, where the office of Dana Spears is. She looks up at the towering building, wondering how the meeting will go. Will Dana agree to accept her case? She is nervous, her hands sweating as she opens the door to the huge high-rise. She is greeted by a security officer at a desk that leads to the elevator.

"Who are you here to see?"

"Dana Spears."

"And you are?"

"Kira Michaels."

He checks his roster, finding her name on the list. Looking up, he says, "You can take the elevator on the left to the penthouse." He presses a button that opens the elevator doors to the penthouse. Her stomach sinks as she is lifted up to the forty-fourth floor. Kira looks out of the glass elevator at the sprawling city below and thinks of what it would be like to be able to fly like a bird. The freedom that would bring, she would fly right out of here now with the wings of an eagle. The elevator door opens, and she is in Dana Spears's office. It is light, airy, and feminine. With white walls and light aqua sofas with accents of soft pink pillows, huge picture on the wall of white cranes in a creek in blues and pinks. It was serene and peaceful, it put her immediately at ease. Sitting at the front desk is the receptionist, who smiles at Kira as she walks in.

"Kira Michaels?" Kira shakes her head. "We were expecting you. Ms. Spears can see you now." She motions to an office where the doors are open. Kira walks down the hall to the office. She sees Dana Spears on the phone. She is surprised at how pretty she is—with long brown hair and green eyes, dressed perfectly in a St. John suit. Dana peers up at Kira only for a second while she is on the phone and motions for Kira to sit in the chair across from her desk. Kira sits and looks out over the expansive view. Kira can only think how powerful someone like Dana must be to have an office like this. Above Dana's head hang the many diplomas and accolades that are a testament to her accomplishments. Finishing up her phone call, Dana is speaking in an authoritative tone that is very intimidating.

"No, I will not file that petition. This action is totally unacceptable. I will go to the Supreme Court if I have to. Don't fuck with me, Jerry. I will have your ass disbarred, I swear." She hangs up the phone.

Kira thinks Dana is badass. She's a pit bull in sheep's clothing, just exactly what she needs to win this case.

"Kira Michaels. I got your police report. I read Lance's deposition. I had a look at your hospital examination. I will tell you straight. The outcome of the police report is not good. There is not enough legally admissible evidence to take this to criminal court. The district attorney has decided not to take further action."

Kira's head is burning; her heart pops into her throat. Without thinking, Kira gets up and slams her fist on the desk.

"No! No way! You can't let him get away with this!" Kira stands up and starts to pace the room. "He must have paid them off. There is so much evidence! The DNA, the bullet holes in my car, bullets found in the driveway."

Dana walks in front of her desk, standing and leaning back on it, legal papers in her hands.

"Hold on, calm down, and listen. We have some pictures the police took of your bruised wrists the day after the incident. There are also pictures of marks on your car that could be bullet holes or not. In Lance's deposition, it says, and I will read it to you, "I handcuffed her because she asked to be handcuffed. Kira loves rough sex, the rougher, the better. She's a nymphomaniac. She can't get enough. She can go on for hours. I was tired, I wanted to stop, but she just kept begging for more."

"That sick fuck. You don't believe that, do you?"

"It doesn't matter what I think. It matters what the jury thinks. It matters that we can prove otherwise. The police report says that there could be bullet holes in your car, or that it could be damage from just being towed, perhaps. They also remark that it is not in the best repair anyway, so it is hard to tell."

"I can't believe this is happening. I WAS RAPED. DOES ANYONE CARE? He shot at me in my car as I was trying to get away! I could have been killed! He was trying to kill me! This is outrageous! I even saw the policeman Ruiz pick up one of the bullets there. He saw the broken glass in the room. There was obvious evidence of a struggle."

Anger churns away inside Kira; she sits back into the chair at Dana's office. Tears start to flow out of her eyes. Hot tears of outrage burn as they flow down her cheeks. Her head is pounding but not nearly as hard as her heart.

Dana goes to the door and shouts out, "Lucy, will you please bring Kira some water?"

Lucy appears at the door with a glass of water for Kira. Kira briefly looks up through her tears to see an attractive small Hispanic lady with a kind face. Lucy hands the water to Kira. Kira's hands are shaking as she takes the water, almost spilling it.

"I know what is going on here. Lance is no doubt paying someone off to slant the evidence."

"The examination and the rape kit shows evidence that a rape took place. The pictures are clear. But Lance's written statement is very credible as well."

Dana kneels down close to Kira in the chair, looking into her eyes. Lucy stands beside Kira and puts a compassionate hand on her back.

"I want you to understand, I care. I am going to do everything possible to help you win this case. That is number one. We will file a civil suit asking for twenty million dollars. I am going to need your complete honesty and your focused attention to do your part. It is going to be a very rough road."

"So do you think we have any chance to win? Or is this a long shot?"

"If I thought you couldn't win, I would not take the case. I will carefully choose the jury so that we have more women. I think empathy will be on your side. I'm not going to lie. It won't be easy. You are going to have to hang in tough with me. I have to be sure you are credible and can stand up in court."

"I will show you, I can take it. I am as tough as they come. I want to get Lance bad."

"All right then. We are a team."

Dana reaches over and squeezes Kira's hand. Lucy smiles warmly.

Kira feels as if the clouds opening and a glimmer of hope is trickling in. She is feeling somewhat less vulnerable, more on solid ground, and she knows an alliance has been formed.

KIRA'S APARTMENT

K IRA DRIVES UP to her apartment. As she pulls into the driveway to the underground security garage, she sees Lance's Mercedes parked in front. She drives frantically into the secured garage. She parks her car and carefully looks around to see if Lance could be hiding in the garage before she gets out of her car. Her heart pounding and terrified, she anxiously gets out of the car. She dashes to the elevator and pounds on the button several times. The elevator is taking forever, and as if she can rush it, she starts to bang on the door.

Lance suddenly appears at the garage gate. He starts to jiggle the gate, trying to open it. Kira bangs harder and harder on the elevator door. She is all alone in the garage and starts to panic. Lance pulls a gun from his pocket and quickly fires at Kira. Kira drops to the ground and dodges the bullet; she screams out.

"Help me please! Someone dial 911!"

Lance is undeterred and fires another shot, hitting close to the ground where Kira lies. A scrap of concrete splinters off and flies in her face; Kira screams out in pain.

The elevator door opens, and Kira crawls inside. She pulls herself up to push the button, her legs trembling beneath her. She is panting and her heart is racing as the elevator climbs.

Finally, the elevator reaches her floor. She gets out of the elevator and starts to walk. The hallway goes black with darkness; the electricity has gone out. She hits a wall and slides along until she can find her door, struggling nervously with her keys to try and unlock the door. There is a loud noise, a door opens, Kira screams and looks toward a bright light now shining on her face. It is her neighbor with a flashlight.

"I'm sorry, honey. I didn't mean to scare you. I guess we lost our electricity. I'll put some light on your door so that you can get the key in."

Still trembling and panting, Kira mutters a "Thank you."

He puts a beam of light on the doorknob. Kira's hands are shaking so much, she cannot get the key in the door.

"Are you all right?"

"I am just really scared."

"Here let me."

He takes Kira's key and opens the door for her. It is pitch-black inside. Kira walks in.

"Are you going to be all right?"

"Yes, I'll be fine. It's okay, thank you."

The neighbor looks puzzled as he walks away.

Kira steps in and bolts the door behind her. She quickly goes over and lights a candle, her hand still shaking as she lights the match. She strikes two matches in the dark before the candle finally ignites. She picks the candle up and carries it into the bedroom with her. She picks up her gun next to the bed. She sees a shadow in the moonlight, moving on the balcony. She throws open the drapes and points the gun. It is a black cat that hisses at her then jumps off the balcony.

Kira picks up the phone and dials.

"Tanya, oh my god, he is here. I can't call the police. They are against me, I know it. You have to come. Please, I am so afraid!"

Kira hangs up the phone and sits in the darkness except for the tiny light from the flickering candle.

She sits and waits for what seems like eternity. The lights come back on. The microwave starts to beep. She goes to reset it, and the doorbell rings. Kira opens the door to see Tanya.

"Thank God, you are here. He was out front when I came home. He shot at me."

"You need to call the police. If you don't do it, I am going to do it for you."

Tanya goes to the house phone and picks it up, ready to dial.

Kira runs over and wrenches the receiver out of her hand and slams it down.

"No, you don't! I am tired of fucking with the police. I am going to get Lance now. You are going with me."

"If you are planning to do what I think you might, I want no part of this."

"YOU ARE COMING WITH ME, GODDAMN IT, TANYA! You don't have to do anything. No one will even know you were there. I swear it." Tanya relents and decides to go along.

Kira picks up her gun and sticks it in her purse, and they both exit the apartment. Kira feels like she is getting her power back.

Kira and Tanya pull up in front of Lance's house. It is completely dark inside. Kira gets out of the car and walks up the walk. Standing silently, she stares at the house for a moment. You can hear the dog start to bark a warning.

Kira takes the gun from her purse. She points the gun at one of the huge plate glass windows and fires a shot. The widow shatters with a spectacular crash. The alarm system is set off; the noise is deafening. The dog is barking and frothing at the mouth. Kira can see his huge white teeth bared at her as she takes aim. Then Kira points the gun at another plate glass window. She fires the shot, and the next glass explodes with a tremendous blast. Aiming now at a third window, she fires the shot. The glass explodes into smithereens and crashes down in an enormous explosion. Lights go on in the house. There are police sirens in the background. Kira hurries to the car where Tanya is waiting. She gets in and very calmly and slowly drives away. The police sirens get louder and louder. They can now see the red lights flashing as they come toward Kira and Tanya. Tanya is transfixed in time and glued to the seat while Kira calmly keeps driving. The police are now right in front of them. Tanya gasps and covers her mouth, afraid they may be coming after her and Kira.

"Don't you dare blink an eye, don't say a word, and do not even look over at them!" Kira is blasting orders at Tanya.

Kira pulls to the side, giving full access of the street to law enforcement. Tanya's heart is palpitating up into her throat. Kira keeps her eyes fixed in front of her, but her breathing gets shallow.

The police drive right past the girls on their way to Lance's house. After they pass, there is a sigh of relief from Tanya. Kira starts to catch her breath in a short reprieve.

Kira slowly pulls back onto the road and continues home.

"You have totally fucking freaked me out! What if you killed Lance or the dog?"

"The dog is fine. He was barking as I walked away. None of the glass or the bullets came even close to hitting him. I know what I am doing with a gun, Tanya. I have had lots of practice. The light came on in the house. I know it was Lance. He was back in the bedroom the whole time, so the fucker is alive."

"Still, that was nuts. What if the neighbors saw us? What if they got your license plate?"

"The bushes are too high for them to have seen us. I needed to do that. You have no idea how good that felt. I want to make it rain fire down on that man."

"You will have your day in court, you need to lay low. You are freaking me out taking too many risks."

"Right, I am a risk taker." Kira continues the drive home.

NEXT DAY, SIDEWALK CAFÉ

S EATED AT A sidewalk cafe on Sunset Plaza, Kira is alone. She is nervous due to the events of last night. Dana called first thing in the morning to ask to meet for lunch. Although Dana's call may not be about last night at all, or could it be? Kira fidgets anxiously with her ice tea and rips a sugar package to shreds. It is a typical beautiful sunny day that becomes just what you expect when you live in Los Angeles. Kira has her sunglasses and her designer jeans on with her favorite pink pumps. Kira wore pink, thinking it will make her look more innocent—just the impression she needs to give in meeting with Dana today. She sits sipping a hibiscus iced tea. She checks her watch. Dana is late, which makes Kira even more anxious.

Kira spots Dana coming across the street. She is dressed in a slick white suit with a black-and-white top; she looks chic and professional. Dana gets to the table and sits across from Kira.

"So I understand you had quite the eventful night last night."

"I don't know what you mean," Kira answers defensively.

"You can bullshit all you want, Kira, but don't even think of lying to me. I can see right through you. Lance had all his windows shot out of his house last night. Fortunately, no one was hurt."

"It could have been anyone. You have to get in line to hate that guy."

"Except the police think it was you."

"They have no proof. Besides, I have an alibi. I was out with Tanya. So what are they going to do, arrest me?"

"No, it is like you said—they have no proof. But let me warn you. If you ever get caught going anywhere near that man again, you stand the chance of ruining this case, and I will drop you like a hot potato."

"So who is going to keep him away from me?"

"Has he been bothering you?"

"He showed up at my apartment last night."

"Showed up at your apartment? Are you sure it was him?"

"I saw him very clearly. He shot at me through the gate in my garage."

"He shot at you? I will file a restraining order today. In the meantime, you stay inside as much as possible. Keep away from Lance. I am going to need you alive if you want to win this suit."

"So you already filed the suit?"

"Last week, I filed a civil suit asking twenty million dollars' damages. I need you to see a shrink to prove emotional distress. Here is the card of a doctor I have used in other cases."

Dana reaches into her purse and pulls out a card, sliding it across the table to Kira. Kira takes the card and reads it, placing it in her bag quickly.

"I am sorry. I am out of time. I have to be in a deposition. I won't have time for lunch. I will call you tomorrow and check on you. In the meantime, call and make an appointment with that doctor. I am going to need her expert testimony."

Dana gets up and leaves. Kira checks the bill on the table, throws down some money, and leaves. She gets up and walks across the street to do some window-shopping.

Kira notices a man keeping about ten steps behind her who seems to have his eye on her. Every time Kira stops, he stops and looks away. When she starts walking again, he follows along.

Kira is becoming anxious.

As she passes several shops and looks back to see if he is following, each time Kira glances at him, he looks at his cell phone and pretends not to notice.

Kira is panicky now, rushes to the cross walk, and starts frantically pushing the walk button. Seeing this, the man runs to his car parked at the curve, jumps in, and starts it up.

The light turns green. Kira starts to walk across the street. The man in the car revs his engine and drives like a maniac straight for Kira in the cross walk. Seeing this, Kira drops and rolls into the gutter. He narrowly missed her.

The man continues driving recklessly on Sunset, weaving in and out of traffic.

A man who saw what happened comes running over to help Kira up. He lifts her from the street and helps her to her feet.

"That was brutal. Are you all right?"

"I think so." Kira starts bushing herself off, very shaken. "I am more dirty than hurt."

"Are you sure? I can call an ambulance. You should at least be checked out."

"Thanks, but no, really, I am okay."

"I have never seen anything like that happen before. I am shaken up just by watching. It looked intentional. I was so shocked that I didn't even get the license plate. The guy must be crazy."

"I am alive. That is all that matters."

Do you need me to drive you anywhere? I am not in a rush or anything. You seem hurt."

"That is very nice, but I have my car."

"Are you sure? Maybe I could buy you a drink. Maybe you could use one."

"That is very nice, but not today. I am not feeling very sociable right now."

"I am Jeffrey. Here's my card anyway, maybe when you are feeling better, then."

"Thanks, Jeffrey."

"And you are?'

"Oh, sorry, Kira, nice to meet you. Thank you for lifting me up today."

Kira walks away toward her car. The man watches her as she walks away.

Kira turns around briefly and smiles. She thinks he is very attractive, but she is not in the mood for any man, attractive or otherwise. She will be happy to be safely tucked into bed alone.

KIRA'S APARTMENT

KIRA SITS IN the dark at her computer table. Just the soft haze from the computer lights the room. The card of the man whom she met today is on the table next to the screen. Next to it is a martini, which Kira sips as she is on the computer. She looks over at the card and enters his name on Google, Jeffrey Miller. He is on the usual social sites, Facebook, LinkedIn, and Twitter. She checks for his picture and profile on each. He is a good-looking guy and seemed very nice. Apparently, he works in the financial world. For Kira, there has to be a thrill involved in meeting a man. Something about a man with a touch of danger attracts her like a lightning bug. He just doesn't strike her. She takes a sip of the martini and turns off the computer.

LANCE'S OFFICE, THE NEXT DAY

T HE PLUSH PENTHOUSE office of Lance McCann is exactly like the interior of his house—cold and severe yet elegant. There is a spectacular view of the Century City skyline. On a clear day, you can see to the ocean. His office walls are lined with pictures of buildings he has sold and huge office complexes he has developed. There are various news articles with pictures of him in magazines, on the covers of *Time*, *Forbes*, and *Business Week*, very impressive. He sits at his desk and studies his computer screen. His secretary calls on the intercom.

"Mr. McCann, Stan Mays is on the line."

"Good, put him though." Lance pushes a button on his desk, and the call is on speakerphone.

"Talk to me, Stanley."

"I've got some good news and some bad news."

"I need some good news."

"The district attorney is an ex–fraternity brother. So the case with Kira Michaels will not be going to criminal court. I got him to drop the case and not prosecute. However, bad news now, her attorney has filed a civil case against you. Now, are you ready for some very bad news?"

"All right, I can manage some bad news. My MicroComp stocks just made a killing in the stock market today."

"Good, sell."

Laughing at this, Lance says, "That bad, huh? Don't worry, Stan. I'm not that surprised. So what does she want?"

"Twenty million."

"Twenty million! That bitch, I should have killed her while I had the chance!"

"I certainly hope no one heard that. She has also filed a restraining order against you."

"Smart."

"Kira has alleged that you shot at her in her garage the other night."

"She is delusional."

"That may be, but when we get to court, it will go against you. So as your attorney, I have to advise you to comply with the restraining order."

"This won't make it to court. She just wants money. Warn her that we plan to rip her apart in court. Offer her eight million to settle out of court."

"I'll do that, but we have to brace ourselves for the possibility that she turns the offer down."

"All right, all right."

"This may be some comfort to you. We are doing some investigating on your little friend. It looks like she may have some questionable background flaws."

"Background flaws, now *that* is good news, almost as good as my MicroComp. Good work, Stan."

"You know I always have your back. Don't forget about that restraining order."

"You've got it. Keep me updated on those background flaws."

Lance cancels the speaker call. He goes to the sprawling plate glass window and pounds his fists so hard on them, they start to vibrate. Sounds of the vibrations are echoing through the halls of the office.

"Bitch!" he yells out in his office.

The intercom comes on, his secretary.
"Is everything all right in there?"
"It's okay."
Lance paces the floor, brushing his hands through his hair, fuming over Kira's lawsuit.

KIRA'S APARTMENT

K IRA IS DRESSED in oversized pajamas and looking disheveled, the loss of sleep showing in her face; she is feeling drained and distressed. Her intercom at the door is buzzed; it is Tanya, who always lifts up Kira. She will be a welcomed respite. Tanya comes in carrying a large tote.

"What is in the bag?"

"I knew from the tone of your voice you were down. So I brought you something I think you are going to love."

Tanya reaches in her bag and pulls out an adorable kitten.

"Oh my god, she is precious!" Kira takes the kitten into her arms, and the kitten starts to purr, Kira cradling the kitten close to her as if it is a baby.

"She can be your friend and your watchdog, or I mean, watch kitty."

"This is the sweetest thing anyone has ever done for me."

"Sometimes there is nothing more comforting than a pet. I know you need a little TLC right now."

"You are my best friend. You always have my back."

Kira gives Tanya a hug. She thinks of all that they have been through together in such a short time. Tanya's support is critical to Kira; she has no one else in her life. She hides very well the loneliness behind her beautiful face. Kira is keenly aware that no one knows her soul. They only take her at face value, never looking deeper. There is an unprotected child inside her looking for refuge, hidden beneath a hard crust of a bombshell.

Tanya answers, "I will always be there for you."

"Can I get you a glass of wine?"

"Sure."

Kira goes to the refrigerator, gets out the wine, and pours it into two stemmed glasses.

Looking at the bottle, Tanya remarks, "Oh, fancy, French wine, ooh la la."

"Only the best." She hands the glass over to Tanya. The kitten is on the floor now, rubbing itself on Kira's legs. She seems to be bonding well.

"Let's have a toast to my new kitty. What shall I name her?"

The girls toast with the glasses. Tanya is thinking hard while looking at the kitten. She reaches down to pet her.

"Well, she is supposed to be your watch kitty, so I am going to say some warrior name."

"No, an angel name, she is my guardian angel."

"Sorry, I am fresh out of angel names."

"Her name will be Uriel, the angel of light and guidance.

"Then to Uriel, may your light shine down on us."

They toast again.

The phone rings. Kira goes to answer it.

"Hello, yes, this is Kira. I know who you are, Lance's attorney. What do you want? You know you should be speaking though my attorney, now, don't you? Hopefully, you understand how these things work. Make me an offer?"

Tanya frowns at this. She shakes her head as though to say "No way."

"No! Not a chance! Let Lance know I am so not afraid. I will see you both in court, Mr. Mays."

Kira slams down the phone; she wants to take it and throw it at the wall, but she stops short.

Kira stifles her anger. This started out to be a special night of celebration, her one bright spot. Now they have stolen that from her as well, fucking bastards.

Kira slumps down on the sofa, the torment showing in her face. She thought she was strong. Maybe she overestimated herself; these guys are out for the kill. Does she really have the fortitude to get through this struggle? She is about to find out.

Tanya sits beside her and places an arm around her. Uriel jumps into her lap.

COURTHOUSE

KIRA AND TANYA are waiting on a bench outside the court-room; dressed in conservative suits, they look like they could lead a church choir. Kira gets up and paces the marble floor; her hands are wringing wet. Her mind is racing a million miles a minute. It is never about justice; it is just about who has the best attorney. Dana has a good reputation, but can she really be as tough as she seems to be? Will she crumble if everything does not go in her favor? If she does, Kira knows she is tough enough to pick her up. Kira is only focused on winning; it is in her DNA. She sees Dana approaching; she stops pacing. Dana has the eye-of-the-tiger look, this may give her the edge in winning. She could use the tiger's aggression to her advantage.

"Are you ready? It is going to be a bumpy night." Dana says to Kira.

Dana looks down at her watch, very focused. "It's time. Let's go."

Kira's heart sinks deep into her chest as they walk into the court-room. Lance is already seated across the courtroom with Stan Mays as they take their seats. Lance barely glances in Kira's direction. He looks at her very briefly and then quickly away, whispering to Stan sitting next to him. The air is thick, like you can't breathe it, heavy with the smells of despair and justice all at the same time. The walls echo the cries of the victims as well as the corrupt. Does anyone really win? Or do they all lose?

Kira sits down next to Dana in front of the courtroom. Tanya is directed to sit directly behind them both. Kira is nervous and uncomfortable. Her skirt hikes way up as she sits down, and Kira tugs at it to pull it back down, modestly. She looks over and Lance is staring right at her, and he smiles broadly, watching her tugging at the skirt. Kira looks at him and blushes, her face burning as she looks away.

Kira only gets a quick glimpse of the jury. Looks like mostly women, which is good. She notices all races are represented. There are three men. She is careful not to make eye contact with the jury, which feels uncomfortable.

The bailiff stands up in the front of the courthouse.

"All rise." Everyone stands. Kira's ankles feel a little weak; they are shaking. She steadies herself on the table next to her. The bailiff continues, "The superior court of Los Angeles, Honorable Judge Prescott residing. Hearing *Michaels versus McCann*, the court is now in session. You may be seated."

The judge comes in and takes his seat. He is a heavyset middle-aged man with light eyes that are hard to see behind the thick black-rimmed glasses he wears. He has a military haircut and a stern look. Kira observes immediately he is military trained by his posture and attitude. He is a tough dude, but maybe there is a big heart underneath that exterior. He glances briefly at Kira and clears his throat.

And so it begins.

"Will the plaintiff call the first witness."

Dana stands at her seat.

"Your Honor, the plaintiff calls Kira Michaels to the stand."

Kira stands up and walks apprehensively to the witness stand, her legs shaking; she takes a seat.

"Kira, can you tell the court in your own words what happened at Lance McCann's house on April 15?"

Kira's mouth is so dry from nerves, it is hard for her to speak.

"I went to Lance McCann's house to get my friend's purse and some items I had left the night before at a party there."

"Explain what your relationship was with Lance. How were you invited to a party at his house?"

"I had dated him a few times."

"You were romantically involved then?"

"No, not in my opinion. I had a couple of dates with him, but I wanted to end the relationship because he was too much."

"What exactly do you mean by too much?"

"He was constantly calling me, texting me, and being so demanding and controlling."

"Would you say he was obsessed with you?"

"Yes, exactly, he was obsessed."

Stan Mays stands and says, "Objection, Your Honor. Council is leading the witness."

The judge barks an order, "Ms. Spears, please let the witness give her own testimony. Please do not put words into her mouth. Court, strike the word *obsessed*. Go ahead, Ms. Spears."

"Rephrasing, Your Honor. Please describe this behavior that you found to be too much."

"I felt like he was stalking me, the constant calling, texting, and sending gifts, keeping up on my every move. On one date, he had taken me on a private jet and ordered me to take my panties off. I was so humiliated and afraid, I actually did it. I found his behavior to be bizarre.

"Why, then, did you agree to see him again and go to the party at his house?"

"I thought I would be safe with so many people there. I thought my friend would enjoy the party and possibly meet someone. I also wanted her to meet Lance and see what she thought of him."

"How did that go?"

"It was terrible. He got me in the Jacuzzi and tried to force himself on me. He got very violent, and I had to fight to get away. That caused me and my friend to have to run out of there, leaving our things behind."

"So you went back to Lance's house the next day to get your things. Tell us what happened then."

"I went back there and let him know that I didn't want to see him anymore. That is when he started to become violent with me. He tried to force me to stay."

"He became violent with you? Please tell us exactly what happened then? Describe this violent behavior."

"I was trying to make it to the door, and he grabbed my neck and started to strangle me. I kicked and pushed my way free. Then he held me by my arms. I slapped him, and then he slapped me back. He pushed me to the ground and jumped on top of me. I was fighting hard to get free. Finally, I broke free and went to push the panic button on his alarm system to summon the police. But he silenced the alarm. I kicked him in the groin and tried to run, but before I could get the door unlocked, he got a gun and put it to my head. He forced me into the bedroom, where he handcuffed me to the bed. That is when it happened."

Kira breaks down crying on the witness stand. She goes for a Kleenex in her bag, fully sobbing. There is a huge lump in her throat. She tries to speak more but cannot.

"What happened, Kira? Tell the court what Lance did next."

Through sobs Kira tries to answer the question, her misery-worn face looking over at Lance, who she can barely see through the tears.

"He hurled a glass at my head."

"Did the glass hit you?"

"No, but there was glass all over me. Then he got on top of me a started taking my clothes off."

Kira breaks down sobbing again.

"Please finish, Kira. The court needs to hear the complete story."

"He took his shirt off and then his pants down."

Kira is sniffling and grabbing for another tissue.

"I knew what he was going to do. But I was totally helpless. I closed my eyes so I wouldn't see."

"Can't you tell us what Lance did next? Please try."

"Raped me, he raped me! I couldn't get away until the next day. I convinced him to let me go to the bathroom, and then I escaped out of the window. He chased me and shot at me."

"He shot at you, with a gun?"

"Yes, he did. The bullets hit my car as I was trying to make my escape down the driveway."

"Do you believe Lance was trying to kill you?"

Stan Mays stands.

"Objection, Your Honor, the witness cannot speculate as to the intention of my client."

Prescott presides, "Objection sustained. Ms. Spears, stick to your client's testimony. Do not speculate on Mr. McCann's intentions."

"Let me rephrase that, then. You knew that Lance was pointing a gun and firing in your direction?"

"Yes, there is no doubt that he was."

"Did you fear for your life?"

"Yes, I felt like I was going to die."

"Can you tell us now what your life has been like since the rape and attempt of murder?"

"I am afraid all the time. I can't even leave my apartment. I feel like there is no one that I can trust. My self-confidence has been stripped away. I feel ruined, damaged beyond repair."

"Thank you, Kira. That is all, Your Honor."

There is silence in the courtroom. Lance looks at the floor as Dana walks by him to her seat, jury members shifting in their seats. Kira feels she has hit a nerve. She feels the sympathy streaming over her like a soft, warm flood. She feels confident again, secure she has presented her story in the best light.

Judge Prescott shuffles papers, again clearing his throat.

"Defense, are you ready to cross-examine?"

"Yes, I am, Your Honor." Stan rises from his chair and approaches Kira on the stand. He looks as if he is amused. It is unsettling to Kira, and her newly won confidence melts to the ground before Mays even utters a word.

"Ms. Michaels, in your testimony, you state that Lance McCann was stalking you, is that correct?"

"Yes, he was."

"Yet at least five times, you met with Mr. McCann socially and quite voluntarily, isn't that correct?"

"Yes, that would be correct."

"At least one of those times you met with Mr. McCann, you had consensual sex with him, isn't that correct?"

"Well, no, I did not have intercourse, if that is what you mean."

"Not intercourse? Then what kind of sex did you have?"

"Oral sex."

"Oh, so I guess you came from the Monica Lewinsky school of sex, where oral sex is not really sex."

There are giggles from the jury. Kira uncomfortably shifts in her seat, looking toward Dana like a lost little puppy.

Dana bounds from her seat.

"Objection, Your Honor. Is the council entertaining us or questioning my client?"

"Objection sustained. Mr. Mays, please stick to questioning the plaintiff."

"I understand that on at least one occasion, you took cocaine at Mr. McCann's house. Do you use drugs as a habit?"

"No, I do not. That was just one night."

"That is not how some of your friends describe you. They say you take drugs and drink quite a lot. In fact, they say you are a regular party girl."

Furious now, Dana jumps from her seat.

"Objection, Your Honor, this is hearsay. It cannot be permitted."

"Objection sustained. That should be stricken from the record."

Stan is getting his point across. They can strike it from the record but not out of the minds of the jury. Kira is getting pelted by Stan, and he is enjoying it.

"In your testimony, you state that you fought with Mr. McCann. Basically, you make it seem as if you were at his mercy the night of the alleged rape, isn't that true?"

"Yes, I was at his mercy. After all, he had a gun."

Kira feels she has made some points with that remark. Who could argue with a gun?

"Ms. Michaels, I have evidence that shows you were once an FBI agent, a person that is highly trained at disarming an opponent, that you have a black belt in karate and are actually very capable in overpowering any man, is that not true?"

There are gasps all around the courtroom. Tanya looks astonished. Dana leaps up again.

"Objection, Your Honor. I was not made aware of this information. It is therefore inadmissible."

"Your Honor, please, a simple background check reveals all this
information. This is, like, law school 101."

"Council, will you both approach the bench, please."

Kira looks straight at the floor as Dana approaches the bench.

Dana is fuming now as she tries to catch Kira's gaze.

"Your Honor, I could easily call a mistrial. I was not made aware
of any of this evidence prior to the trial."

"Your Honor, I intend to show that Ms. Michaels is grossly
misrepresenting herself as a hapless victim."

"Ms. Spears, I must say that this is highly negligent on your part
for not properly investigating your client's background."

"With all due respect, Your Honor, it is not my duty to inspect
my client's background. It is my duty to present her case."

"I am going to allow this."

Both attorneys walk away from the bench. Dana is livid as she
walks back to her seat. She stiffly pulls out her chair, sitting down,
and shoots a burning look at Kira.

How could this be admissible? Kira thinks to herself. She thought
all her FBI files had been sealed. Pangs are shooting though her
stomach.

"Continue, Mr. Mays."

"You were an FBI agent, weren't you, Ms. Michaels?"

"Yes."

There is chatter among the courtroom.

Prescott pounds his gavel.

"Order in the courtroom."

Stan continues, "Are you a black belt in karate?"

"Yes, I am."

Dana suddenly jumps up.

"Your Honor, I ask for a recess so that I can meet with my
client."

Prescott looks at Dana and then over to Kira. "The court is adjourned until one thirty." He bangs his gavel.

The courtroom stands up. Dana grabs up her papers as Kira steps down from the stand. Lance and Stan whisper to each other, both smiling as if they have already heard the verdict and it is in Lance's favor.

Dana storms out of the courthouse, and Kira tries to keep up with her. Tanya looks at Kira and throws up her arms as if to say, "What the hell?" Kira ignores Tanya's expression, passing her by in her haste to catch up with Dana. She has been left aghast from what just happened in the courtroom. Kira does not know how to explain this to her friend. She has not thought this far in advance; she knows that she should have.

Kira catches up to Dana as they head into a private conference room. Although Kira has not thought this out thoroughly, she blurts out, "Dana, I can explain."

Dana walks all the way into the conference room and stares down Kira. She slams the door closed as Kira walks though.

"WHO THE HELL ARE YOU?"

"All right, I was in the FBI. I was working on some intelligence matters. I realized it wasn't for me, and I quit. What is the big deal?"

"WHAT IS THE BIG DEAL? You totally misrepresented yourself to me. You make yourself seem like a weak victim when in fact, you are a highly trained professional! You made me look like a fool in there, and worse, you made yourself out to be a liar."

"Maybe your life has been perfect. Maybe you always knew who you were and where you were going. My life has not been so black-and-white. I've made a few mistakes, had some rough landings. But that doesn't make what happened at Lance's house that night any less of a crime. So I worked for the FBI. It's just a law enforcement agency. That doesn't make me a superhero with the strength to take down any man. That is so overplayed."

Dana is staring Kira down. There is a stark silence in the room; the air doesn't even move. Dana is not buying any of this; she is visibly shaken. Dana is usually always the one in control; she knows she should have looked further into her background. Kira is determined

99

to retain Dana as her attorney. She has to win this case. In fact, Kira always has to win; loosing is just not in her blood.

Kira continues, "If you are the attorney you apparently think you are, this is not going to stand in your way of winning my suit. So why don't you go out there and do your job?"

That was an order, not a question, and more of a challenge. Coming from Kira, Dana knows she has been duped all along. Now seeing Kira's true colors for the first time, she wonders, *Is there more?* dumbfounded by the way Kira just spoke to her. The two just stare at each other in silence.

Her hands shaking, Dana reaches into her bag and pulls out a cigarette, lights it, and inhales deeply, knowing full well smoking is not allowed in the building. But at this point, she really doesn't give a shit. She has seen her whole career life flash before her eyes, and she knows she really needs a cigarette, although something stronger would be better.

Dana offers a cigarette to Kira, who declines. Dana leans back on the wall to think a moment.

Dana can't help but think Kira is a con. To admit that in a court would be unthinkable; with her reputation at stake, she has to move forward.

"Any more surprises?"

"None that would be pertinent to this suit."

Dana takes one last drag off the cigarette and stamps it out on the floor. Leaving Kira and the cigarette behind, she walks out of the room.

Kira is left alone in the room. She pounds her fist into the wall, so angry with herself for being in this position. How could she have been revealed like this? Her cover completely blown.

She picks up the cigarette butt and puts it in the trash as if she were picking up toys from a naughty child.

She walks out of the room to see Tanya waiting in the hallway. She has a perplexed look on her face. She feels betrayed. She needs an explanation now. There is not enough time for Kira to explain. Any words she could muster right now would just be "I am sorry," which is not enough.

The courtroom door is opened by the bailiff. Kira looks up to the clock to see it is one thirty.

The court is back in session. Kira is first through the doors as everyone files in. Dana is already in her seat. Lance and Stan enter the court, looking smug. They take their seats; Kira has to file past them to get to her seat. Lance will not even look her way; this has become a war.

The bailiff stands up in front of the court and says, "The court is now in session. Superior court of Los Angeles, Judge Prescott residing."

Prescott takes his seat.

"Ms. Spears, do you have any other witnesses to call?"

"Yes, Your Honor, the plaintiff calls Tanya Torrey."

Tanya is clearly afraid but makes her way to the stand. On her mind is what was brought up in court about Kira, thinking all this time they were best friends. Why was there so much that she never knew about Kira? Does she really know her at all? Her questions all unanswered, she takes the stand.

Dana starts with her questioning.

"Tanya, you accompanied Kira to Lance's house for a party, is that correct?"

"Yes, that is true."

"Can you please tell the court what you saw take place that night?"

"Yes, well, Kira and I were in the Jacuzzi. Lance got in the Jacuzzi with us. The next thing I know, he is, like, kissing Kira all over. Then it was like he went nuts or something. He ripped her top off and just started crawling on top of her. It was obvious that Kira didn't want that because she was pushing him away. But he would not stop. It turned into a scary fight. So when Kira finally got away, we both ran. We had to leave all our things and just get out of there as fast as we could."

"Did you feel Lance was out of control?"

"Yes, totally. I was really scared. He acted like an animal, I swear."

"Thank you, Tanya. That is all, Your Honor."

Prescott looks over to Stan.

"Mr. Mays, your witness."

Stan walks over to the stand.

"Tanya, that night at the party, you had some cocktails, is that correct?"

"Yes, I did."

"How many would you say?"

"Three or four margaritas."

"Did you witness Kira have any drinks at the party?"

"Yes, I did, she was doing shots."

"Shots? Of tequila, is that correct?"

"Well, yeah."

"So you girls were pretty drunk by the time this alleged attack took place, were you not?"

"We were sort of high, yes."

"Would you say your judgement was impaired at the time?"

"Maybe, a little."

"I would say by a lot. I would say you were drunk and you had no clue as to what was going on at that party."

Dana leaps from her seat.

"Objection, Your Honor, the counsel is leading the witness."

Prescott is gruff.

"Objection sustained. Mr. Mays, please stick to questioning the witness."

"No further questions, Your Honor."

Prescott calls out, "The witness is excused."

Tanya steps down from the witness seat. She glances toward Kira, seeking her approval. Kira nods back, feeling that Tanya made a favorable impression on the jury for her. Kira feels the eyes of the jury on the back of her head, like someone is pressing with force. She does not know which is worse, the judgment of the jury or having to face down Lance. Or maybe it is the obvious seething of Dana sitting right next to her. Kira looks up at the clock; the court must be at least halfway through, and this torture will be ended, she hopes.

Prescott asks, "Any more witnesses?"

Stan stands up.

"Yes, Your Honor, the defense calls Officer Ruiz of the Los Angeles Police Department."

Officer Ruiz is escorted into the courtroom. He makes eye contact with Stan as he is sworn in. Kira notices right away there is familiarity between the two. He nods to Stan as he is about to start the questioning. Kira feels fire starting in her stomach and rising to her head as Stan approaches the witness stand to start the questioning.

"Officer Ruiz, you are the investigating officer in the case of *Michaels versus McCann?*"

"Yes, sir, I am."

"Tell me what your findings were in this case."

"My partner, Officer Kelly, and I took the report from Ms. Michaels. We later went to Mr. McCann's house to question him. Mr. McCann was very cooperative. We searched the house and found no signs of a struggle. In reviewing the reports from both parties involved, we excused the incident as nothing but a lover's quarrel."

"Nothing more than a lover's quarrel, thank you. No more questions, Your Honor."

"Ms. Spears, do you have any questions?"

"Yes, Your Honor."

Dana gets up and crisply approaches the witness stand. She has papers in her hand, which she holds like a weapon.

"Officer Ruiz, you took the report from Kira after the alleged rape. You took some pictures, did you not?"

Dana hands the pictures to Ruiz on the stand. Ruiz looks, and his expression changes immediately, looking sheepish now.

"Are these the pictures you took?"

"Yes, my partner, Kelly, actually took the pictures."

"Can you tell the courtroom what the pictures show?"

"Yes, these are bruises on Ms. Michael's wrists."

Dana then takes some enlarged pictures off the table and places them on a board for the court to see. Her wrists are very badly bruised and magnified in the pictures.

"In your expert opinion, doesn't that show that force was used?"

"Yes, well, normally, it would."

"What do you mean, *normally?*"

"Later, when we questioned Mr. McCann, he told us that she likes to be handcuffed and that she loves rough sex."

"Do you always take the word of an accused rapist over a victim? Is that what they teach you in the Police Academy?"

"No, I don't. I just gather the evidence, ma'am."

"Really, then in gathering the evidence, you must have left out a few things in your testimony on the stand. For instance, your report reads that there was broken glass in the bedroom. Does it not say that?"

"I must have forgotten that."

"Really? Then perhaps we need to review it."

Dana hands the report over to Ruiz. The part that tells about the broken glass is highlighted in yellow.

Ruiz looks it over.

"Your report clearly reads; broken glass is observed on the floor around the bed and under the head of the bed."

"Yes."

"Furthermore, there were bullet casings found in the driveway, were there not?"

"Yes, there were."

"So still no signs of a struggle?"

"Some things slipped my mind."

"It is a good thing you wrote a report."

"I didn't make the decision not to try this case in criminal court. The district attorney did."

"Thank you, that is all."

Prescott presides, "The witness is excused."

Officer Ruiz steps down. He looks over at Stan Mays, who nods approvingly. Ruiz is escorted out of the room.

Prescott continues, "Plaintiff, do you have some closing remarks?"

"Yes, Your Honor."

"Let's hear them."

Dana stands up and walks over to the jury, facing them and looking them in the eye.

"You heard my client's testimony. She is a victim of a cruel and violent act. She was beaten and held hostage at gunpoint. She was even shot at in her attempt to escape from Mr. McCann, to save her life. Regardless of my client's background, although you may think she used poor judgment in going to Lance's house that fateful night, this is no less of a crime. It should hold no less of a punishment. The district attorney chose not to try this case in a criminal court. But you and I know rape is a crime, and it is wrong. You and I know that Lance McCann should be made to pay for his crime. Therefore, I ask you to reach the only reasonable verdict and find him guilty. Make him pay."

Dana walks back to her chair and takes a seat.

The courtroom goes stone-cold silent.

Prescott speaks up, "Defense, your remarks."

Stan stands up and walks to the Jury. Standing in front of them, he clears his voice. There is a lot of tension in the air as he begins to speak.

"You have heard the testimony. Yes, the accusations are disturbing. But the fact is that they are only accusations. In fact, the evidence is so weak that the district attorney chose not to try the case. Ms. Michaels dated my client, admittedly had sex with him. Ms. Michaels is a drug user, and she has a reputation as a party girl. She has chosen to take advantage of a very prosperous and successful man. That is the truth of it. You must choose to acquit Lance McCann and drop this case. It is the only way justice can be served."

Stan turns around and looks at Kira with a very stern look as if he had just passed judgment on her that will stick, like he just tarred and feathered her in front of the courtroom. He is very proud of his performance today, and he wears it like a badge. He steps arrogantly back to his seat next to Lance. They both sit and gloat. Kira is thinking, *That was a good rebuttal, but how good would it be? Enough to sway the jury?* Her stomach aches with apprehension.

Prescott bangs the gavel.

"The court will adjourn until Monday. We will readjourn when the jury reaches a verdict, following the weekend."

There is rumbling in the court room as all get out of their seats. Lance and Stan are quick to exit. Dana gathers her papers angrily; she is still seething at Kira. She looks in Kira's direction just once.

"I will call you Monday," she says bitterly as she quickly exits out the courtroom door. Slowly everyone clears the courtroom. Left there is just Kira and Tanya. Tanya slowly approaches Kira, not knowing what to say after hearing about Kira's past in the trial. She had believed they were best friends and had no secrets between them. She now knows Kira has a very secret life that no one else shares. She feels like she has been on the outside looking in, when all the while she thought she was in. She really doesn't quite know what to say; she has been stymied by her new knowledge of Kira.

Sensing Tanya's discomfort, Kira speaks up as they walk out of the courtroom together.

"I know I never told you all my past, work history, and so many things. I know you are hurt because there are things I kept from you. I don't blame you if you think I'm a monster. I have spent the last three years trying to become someone new, repairing my life, creating a new identity, and getting away from the past."

The women are out of the courtroom now and walking to the parking lot. Tanya is clearly distressed by the conversation, her shoulders tight with tension. Kira takes her hand and tries to get her to sit on a nearby bench.

Tanya pulls away.

"I really need time with this. I thought we were friends. I thought I knew you, that we shared all our confidence in one another. I feel like I just got punched in the stomach, and you did the punching."

"Please try and understand. I was forced to create a new identity. I am under confidence of witness protection. That is something I can never share with anyone. I just shared it with you."

"I am sorry, Kira. I don't know now if what you say is true. I am really confused. I just need to go."

"I am sorry. I really am.," Kira says this as Tanya walks away to her car.

Kira goes to her car and hangs her head on the steering wheel. Is this worth it? All the pain and struggle? Even if she wins in court, will it ease the pain? Can money cover the wounds? You can't put Band-Aids on bullet holes. They don't stop the bleeding. Huge gashes are already in her heart. Now her one and only friend—has she lost her too?

Pull it together, her inner voice is telling her. She has been through hell and back. This is just one more hell.

Kira starts the car and drives out of the parking lot, getting on the 101 freeway and heading north to Santa Barbara. She can't spend another night in that dingy little apartment. She knows she needs to be buried under her layers of comfort.

DANA'S OFFICE

D ANA STORMS INTO her office, walking past Lucy briskly. Lucy picks up the scent of something wrong. Dana walks into her office and stiffly sits in her chair, turning on the computer. Lucy walks in.

"I take it, by the look on your face, things didn't go well."

Dana looks up at Lucy with a long pause, looking very serious.

"Go do a background check on Kira Michaels. Check for schools she has attended—past employment, residences, anything you can find. Crawl right up her butt. I want to know just who I am dealing with."

Looking very puzzled, Lucy says, "Sure."

Lucy leaves to get the information. Dana goes to work at her own computer. Not being able to concentrate, Dana gets up from her desk and paces in her luxurious office, looking out at the view of the city. Pacing not being enough, she goes for a cigarette. She hasn't smoked in a year, and here she is, nail biting, cigarette smoking, mad. Dana is always used to winning and being on top of her game. Who is this little bimbo to take her down? Is she a bimbo or really just good at what she does? The questions are burning in her head. In this day and age when all you have to do is google someone, is she that easily fooled? Questions burn away at her brain.

Lucy walks back in.

"Are you ready? Kira has been a very busy girl. First of all, she attended Dartmouth. She got her degree in psychology. She graduated Phi Beta Kappa. She lands a job with the FBI. Special intelligence. Investigating domestic companies with major holdings. She is an FBI profiler with a keen sense for picking out the people who will have criminal behavior. She leaves the FBI or is fired, and we can't find that out because it has been classified. She comes to Los Angeles and opens a big, fat bank account using the alias of Kim Michaels. Checking legal files, I was able to find out she has won three similar suits to the one you filed for her on Lance McCann. Accusing very wealthy men of assault, this little girl has tied up a tidy fortune."

Dana puts out her cigarette; she is spinning and thinking.

"Out of curiosity, go check for any real estate holdings."

Lucy rushes to it. Dana flops down on the sofa in her office, staring at the ceiling. Has she been duped? Yes, she has.

Lucy returns momentarily.

"Bingo. She has a small retreat in Santa Barbara, 3.5 million dollars small."

"Got an address?'

"Got it."

Lucy hands a paper over to Dana. Grabbing the paper, Dana quickly goes to her desk, typing in the address on her computer.

"Beach property in Santa Barbara. Just to think, I actually felt sorry for her."

Dana prints out the directions and rips it out of the printer, heading for the door. She says to Lucy, "Don't expect me back."

Dana jumps into her Mercedes and heads out the 101 to Santa Barbara. It is about an hour-and-a-half-long drive, but she needs the time just to chill. She turns the radio up full blast and settles back for a long drive up the coast.

Passing miles and miles of beautiful California coastline, Dana soaks in the scene. The sun starts to set on the ocean, tinting the sky beautiful shades of pink to purple.

She thinks, in terms of her career and her past achievements, why does this seem so significant to her? It's just that she did not see it coming; being taken by surprise is not her place in life. She thinks of herself as bulletproof; clearly she is not.

Dana finally reaches the city of Santa Barbara. She drives the graceful neighborhoods with their perfectly manicured lawns, looking for the address. When she finally finds Kira's residence, it is dark now, and the house lights are on. Dana parks her car on the street in front of the enormous white estate with exquisite lush gardens. Through the front window, Dana can see Kira walking inside in a flowing white silk robe. She is holding a glass of wine and has a fire glowing in the fireplace. For just this once, she wishes she were Kira—an elusive, puzzling woman with a sordid past, a vessel set to sail on a tumultuous ocean with nothing to anchor her and nothing to hold her back, able to sail away at her own free will. What would that feel like?

Kira walks to the window and looks out, as if she senses that someone is watching her. Dana starts the car and turns around, driving away.

Moments later we see Lance drive up and park in front of Kira's house. His breathing is heavy; a close look at his face shows him dripping in sweat. His eyes are wild as he sees Kira lounging in her white silk robe. It slightly falls open, and Lance breaths heavier. Lance is frozen by her image at the window. His thoughts twist as he thinks of her naked in his bed and then sitting across from him in the courtroom. Tortured by the fact that he never saw this coming, he reaches over and takes his switchblade out of his glove compartment; he flips open the blade. The sharp edge of the blade catches the streetlight, which flashes in his eyes.

Kira is sure someone is watching her. She walks to the window again. She cannot see the gold Ferrari outside on the street. She frowns and closes the drapes.

Soon a neighborhood patrol car drives by very slowly, looking at Lance. Seeing the patrol car, Lance closes the switchblade and slips the knife into his pocket. The patrol man goes past Lance and then circles back, coming back to park the patrol car across from Lance. Starting the Ferrari, Lance takes off. The patrol man jots down his license plate.

Kira takes her last sip of wine and climbs the stairs to go to bed, not knowing that everyone now knows who she is and where she can be found.

FBI Office

J IMMY DANIELS, A handsome, buff FBI agent, opens the door of the FBI office, downtown Los Angeles. He wears his identification badge on a tag around his neck with his badge hanging in clear sight out of his front pants pocket. He has gotten a call to report to his office—new information, just in on a case he follows. As he steps into his office, two investigators are reviewing a tape of the bank the day Kira met Lance. Jimmy is stunned when he sees Kira on the screen. He had lost touch with her and had been looking for her for weeks. She always has her way of slipping off and flying under the radar. She is like an electric eel in that way, slippery and then it shocks you.

"Recognize this girl?" one of the seated agents asks Jimmy. He stands stunned and speechless for a beat. Then the man continues. He goes in with the camera for a close-up on Kira's cleavage, which was very noticeable in the dress she had on that day.

"Now do you recognize her?"

The other agent sitting laughs. Jimmy says, "Yeah, now I know who she is."

"Thought you might like that."

"Well, it's good to see she is keeping busy. Who is her latest victim?"

"The guy is Lance McCann—totally slick real estate investor with ties to the Mexican cartel. He was tried and acquitted on laundering charges last year. Kira tagged him months ago, got acquainted with his schedule and found out he does his banking every Friday at 3:00 p.m. The dude never changes his steps. Kira goes in there in this swanky outfit and bingo. His dick is about as hard as this table." Both Jimmy and the other agent, Dave, crack up at this remark.

As they watch the bank surveillance tape, it shows Lance following Kira out of the building. They watch them talking and leaving together to the street.

"Anyway, now she has got him in court on rape and assault with intent to commit murder."

"Sweet. What does she get?"

"Twenty million, if she wins. But the bad part is this. She has been outed. A security guard picked up Lance's license plate sitting out in front of Kira's beach house in Santa Barbara. He ran the plate number though the FBI."

"That is trouble."

"Which is why we called you."

"I say we watch, see how the trial goes, and keep a close eye."

"It's your call."

"She is a busy beaver, if I must say so myself."

Jimmy quips back, "No surprises here."

Monday-Morning Courthouse

DEAD AIR HANGS like an iron curtain in the courtroom as everyone anxiously anticipates the jury's verdict. Dread on Lance's face oozes out his pores; Kira can smell it from across the room. She looks to signs on the juror's faces as they are called in for their verdict. There is eye contact from one, but is it confirmation or pity? Apprehension is growing in her stomach like mold. Prescott wears the stern mask of state judgement. Is it the bitter coldness coming from Dana sitting next to her? Or is Kira's angst real and a precursor for trouble ahead? Prescott calls the court to order.

"Has the jury arrived at a verdict?"

One of the jurors stands.

"Yes, Your Honor."

"Please read the verdict to the court."

"We, the jury, find Lance McCann guilty of rape and aggravated assault."

There are gasps in the courtroom. Dana looks surprised but relieved.

Lance is enraged with the verdict; fire is showing in his eyes, his face red with fierce anger. He explodes in a fiery rage. Jumping up from his chair, he lunges toward Kira. Kira screams out.

"Lying, backstabbing, mercenary slut! You will get yours, bitch!"

Dana stands up to shield Kira from Lance. A police officer from the court runs over to guard her, his hand on his gun. Another officer rushes to restrain Lance as he forces himself toward Kira further. Stan takes a firm hand and pushes him back in the chair as he is still fighting to get to Kira.

Prescott calls, "Order, order in the court!" while he is banging his gavel.

Everyone stunned at Lance's outburst. Kira is shaking in her chair.

Lance quiets down. Prescott continues.

"Since Mr. McCann has been found guilty and shows no remorse for this crime, because a gun was used, I have no other recourse than to impose the full penalty and award Ms. Michaels the full sum of twenty million dollars."

He bangs his gavel again.

"This court is now adjourned."

Kira stands up. Lance forces his way up again to charge her.

"You fucking fraudulent bitch! You better watch your back!"

Stan forces Lance back down once again. The police stand on guard.

Stan looks Lance in the face, yelling.

"Forget it! Just stop it right now! We will appeal! It's all right! Calm down."

Stan is still holding him down when Kira is escorted out of the courtroom. Dana and Tanya are following behind as the courtroom clears out.

Once out of the courtroom, Tanya catches up to Kira, throws her arms around her, and gives her a hug.

"Congratulations, Kira."

Kira hugs her back.

"Thanks, I will call you later."

Tanya tearfully says, "Please do."

She walks away to her car. Dana is parked very near to Kira. She is walking almost right next to her, close enough so that Kira can feel the tension wafting over to her. Kira looks over to Dana and says, "I guess I should say thank you."

"Forget it, Kira. I know all about you now. This isn't the first time you have done this. So how does it feel to be rich?"

"No, YOU FORGET IT, DANA! You may think that you know me, but that is just a drop in the bucket as to what I am all about. You don't know jack shit about me. If you did, you would have had a clue as to who I was before you stepped into that courtroom. And as a result, maybe I should ask you, how does it feel to be rich? You should be going home to celebrate, but you are not even that bright."

Dana's mouth drops open as Kira gets into a new Mercedes; she turns around and gets into the sleek, glamorous car. Dana stands stunned as Kira drives away, Kira giving her one last hard look as she goes.

Kira drives to her apartment in the Valley. This used to be a safe hiding place. She drives into her parking spot in the garage; she sits in the car for a moment, mourning the loss of yet another safe harbor. Strange because she would think this would be a triumphant day because of her win in court. Kira only sees it as another day of preserving herself with another layer of comfort.

She steps out of her car. She hears footsteps in the garage. She looks around but sees no one. Chills go down her spine, and she feels the chill of something sinister lurking close by. She rushes to the elevator, pushing the button multiple times. She hears the footsteps again, getting closer; she turns around and sees nothing in the total darkness. She pushes the button again and again frantically.

Finally, the door opens. She gets in, breathing a sigh of relief. Suddenly, with a jolt, the elevator stops. The lights go off. Kira tries to push the emergency button, but it does not work. She hears someone on the roof of the elevator, trying to get in. She sees a box in the elevator marked Emergency. Kira tries desperately to open it, but it is stuck.

On another floor, a couple waits for the elevator. Time is passing. They hear the banging coming from the elevator.

"What is taking so long?"

"I know. I have complained about this elevator. I wish someone would fix it already. I hear the banging. Maybe they are working on it."

Kira is still trying to open the emergency box inside. Just then the hatch on the top of the elevator starts to move. Someone is trying to pry it open. She sees the crowbar being used to lift the edges of the hatch. Then the crowbar extends into the elevator. Kira uses a karate kick to the box to try and get it open. The box opens, revealing a phone inside. Kira grabs the phone and dials 911. The phone is dead. She slams the phone down and starts to scream, kicking the elevator door.

"SOMEONE HELP ME, PLEASE!"

Hearing this, the woman waiting says, "Oh my god, someone is stuck in there."

The man standing there with the woman springs into action.

"I will take the stairs to the elevator shaft. Maybe I can help."

Kira, still stuck in the darkness of the elevator, looks up to see the hatch has been pried off. She looks up to see a man, and she screams again and again. The man drops the crowbar in on Kira. Kira quickly grabs up the crowbar and beats the man's hands with it as he is trying to climb in on Kira. Frantically screaming, she tries to fend off the attacker.

The man rushing to help Kira reaches the attic of the building. Inside he finds all the workings of the building. Finally stumbling on the switches to the elevator shaft, he finds they have been switched off. He turns them back on. Suddenly the lights go on in the elevator, and the elevator starts to rise, throwing the man on top over the side. He struggles to stay on but falls six stories. Kira can hear him scream on his long fall down and then a thud.

The elevator reaches Kira's floor, and she gets out. Trembling, she gets off the elevator and gets to her door. Kira gets inside and grabs up the phone.

"Tanya, oh my god! Someone just tried to kill me! I know Lance sent them! He said he would! I am so scared! Please come over here. I have another place we can go and hide from Lance. I have a place in Santa Barbara. Please bring your things and go with me. I can't be alone. I'll explain everything later."

"Good, I will pick you up. Be out front."

Hanging up the phone, she quickly checks the locks on her door. She can already see the emergency vehicle lights flashing on the windows of her apartment.

Kira immediately goes to the closet and takes out a suitcase and starts throwing clothes into it. She finishes up in the bathroom with her toiletries and then closes up the suitcase and is out the door. This time, she takes the stairs to the garage.

As she drives out of the garage, she sees the police and the fire trucks there with an ambulance. The man and woman who had been waiting at the elevator are talking to the police as other neighbors gather to watch. The paramedics roll out a stretcher with a body on it all covered up. Kira knows what that means and is no stranger to sights such as this.

Kira drives the short distance to Tanya's apartment.

Tanya is standing outside with her bag. Kira drives up to the curb, and Tanya jumps in the car.

LANCE'S HOUSE

ARRIVING HOME, LANCE is raging. Zeus runs up to meet him at the door and gets pushed away.

"Go on, get out of here." Losing the court battle has set him into a violent obsession to put an end to Kira. Owing Kira a small fortune is burning a hole into his brain as well as in his pocket. Maybe his animosity will be reprieved if he gets word that the hit man he sent to kill Kira is successful. The deal is not sealed yet since he has not paid out.

The phone rings; he picks it up.

"Stan, is the bitch dead?"

"No, the guy we sent to do her is dead. It ended up looking like an elevator accident. The police are still there. Kira was seen driving away, probably on her way to Santa Barbara."

"Fuck me!" Lance screams out as he tosses down a chair.

Stan quickly replies, "Don't do anything crazy. I am getting someone else to do the job."

"How the hell could he have fucked it up so bad?"

"Look, he is not a brain surgeon, man. You stay put. Don't get involved."

"All right, call me when you find someone." Lance hangs up. He will not stay put, though. He goes to his room, takes his knife, and puts it in his pocket. He loads a .45 with a clip and places it down his pants in front. If anyone is going to take Kira out, he is determined to be the one. He wants the thrill of watching her go down if it is the last thing he may ever do on this earth. It just might be.

KIRA'S SANTA
BARBARA RETREAT

T HE GIRLS ARRIVE at Kira's house in Santa Barbara. Tanya is amazed as they drive up to the mansion. She would have never known that Kira lived like this. The house sits way back on an expansive, perfectly manicured front lawn. It is a huge white stucco Mediterranean-style house with big archways and large arched windows in the front. The garden leading up to the house is lush with climbing roses going up the trellises to the balconies on the second floor. There are camellias and fragrant gardenias in the front as well. Several large pots holding lemon trees dotted the yard. Two large white plaster dogs sit at the front door to greet you as you arrive. Tanya is speechless as she steps out of the car and onto the Spanish-style tiles leading to the house. She is as speechless as she is impressed. Kira rushed ahead to unlock the front door.

Inside, there was a big white winding staircase. All the massive moldings were painted white. The walls shone with coats of soft pastels from aqua to lavender. There are fresh flowers in crystal vases everywhere. Although the interior had many French-style antiques, there were pieces of modern furniture and artwork mixed in very tastefully. How could this have been a secret for so long? Tanya was as awestruck as she was bewildered.

"Tanya, you can put your things in the guest room."

Kira leads Tanya down a hallway with wood floors, perfect moldings on the ceilings, and antique sconces on the walls. The guest room is painted in a pale pink. The bed is upholstered in white. There are arched french doors that lead out to a private garden. Tanya sets her bag down next to a soft pink velvet chair.

'Why don't you take some time and get comfortable? I will go and get us some cheese and wine and heat up the Jacuzzi. You brought a bathing suit, didn't you?'

"No, I did not. I was in such a rush and so worried."

"That's fine. I have plenty extra."

Tanya thinks, *Of course she does*. Then Kira goes away, coming back in a few minutes with a suit and a robe. She puts it down in the chair.

"Meet me in the kitchen in a few."

She leaves Tanya and goes into the kitchen.

Tanya goes into the guest bathroom to change. There is all-white marble, a golden-framed mirror, and a gorgeous footed tub. Could it get any more perfect than this? Just then Uriel, the kitten, breaks into the guest bathroom and purrs at Tanya's feet; now it is perfect. Tanya reaches down, picks up the kitten, and kisses her on the nose. Setting her down, she changes into the bathing suit and slips on the robe.

Tanya walks barefoot toward the kitchen; her footsteps echo in the expansive house. She wouldn't want a house this large for herself, but she understands why Kira needs it; she can get lost in here.

Kira is putting together a cheese and fruit platter in the kitchen. Two glasses of wine are already out on the counter. There is a massive center island in the room with leather stools around it. Crystal chandeliers hang above that dimly light the kitchen in a soft, romantic light. The sun is setting, and Kira lights some candles. Tanya takes a sip of wine from her glass.

"You must be feeling better now."

"I always feel better when I am here. It is my safe haven."

"Still, you need more security. Lance is a lunatic, all that ranting in the courtroom, and he definitely sent the person after you at the apartment."

"No doubt about it. I am sure it was him. But I do feel safe here. We have private security that patrol all the time."

"Still, I would feel better if you were gated and had a guard dog."

"Come on, don't we have something to celebrate? I won in court today."

Kira raises her glass to toast. Tanya smiles sheepishly and reluctantly raises her glass. The girls toast. Uriel runs around on the floor, chasing a small ball. Tanya's spirits are raised just a bit. The beauty of her surroundings is sinking in; she is feeling more comfortable. Kira's cares seemed to be cast away the second they set foot inside her abode, and so Tanya releases and decides to go with the flow.

Tanya takes a piece of cheese off the platter and sits in the chair across from Kira at the counter, nibbling the cheese. Kira grabs up a cluster of grapes.

"So how do you stand it? Living in such a shabby house? I mean, no dance hall, and where's your helicopter pad?"

"So you like it? I thought you might approve."

"Right, I could really get into this. It's so well furnished, it looks like something out of *Architectural Digest*. You must have lived here for a long time."

"Only four years. I had a decorator do the interior before I moved in. I love it. When I walk in, I feel transported to another place and another time."

"I saw that." Tanya picks up a slice of apple and bites into it.

"I feel badly I didn't tell you about it before. I have been trying to create a new life. I want to get the past behind me."

Kira sips her wine and takes another piece of cheese, wishfully looking out the back window to the patio.

"So you were fired from the FBI?"

Kira dodges the question.

"What do you say we go out and get in the Jacuzzi?"

Kira takes her wine in one hand and a candle in the other and walks to the back door. Tanya picks up her glass and follows behind.

As they step out to the back patio, there is seating and a fireplace. Beyond, there is a beautiful spanish-tile walkway that leads to the Jacuzzi, which is separate from the pool. The Jacuzzi is canopied with a trellis and wisteria vine in bloom hanging from it. There are boxwood hedges cut very neatly all around the Jacuzzi area, which make it very private. There is a Spanish-style fountain with a copper cherub spilling water from an urn. The sound of the water trickling is very soothing. Kira sets her wine down on the side of the Jacuzzi and steps in the steaming water. Tanya follows along.

Kira takes a sip of her wine, settling into the warm, bubbling water.

"I was fired by the FBI. I committed the carnal sin of sleeping with a man I was investigating. He was just too intriguing to me as a psychologist. When I profiled him, chills went down my spine. It became my obsession to meet him. After we met, the sexual attraction was undeniable. My desire for him overcame my logic. What could I do?"

"Did the relationship last for long?"

"No, he found out I worked for the FBI and was investigating him. He found a wire they made me wear. He was raging mad. He came after me and tried to kill me. It was devastating for me at that point. By then I was very much in love with him. I don't think I will ever get over it."

"He tried to kill you?"

"Right, when he found the wire, he tried to strangle me with it. The FBI was close by, broke in, and arrested him. He was being investigated for bank fraud, guilty of course. I still had to testify at his trial. It was heartrending and horrendous. I was fired and put into witness protection because he was part of a very powerful, dangerous group."

"You ended up suing him?"

"Right, attempted murder and bodily harm. In a separate civil case. Of course, I won."

The crickets in the night air are a soothing sound for the disturbing conversation. Tanya and Kira sip their wine as they speak.

Waves of uneasiness flow over Kira as she feels she is being watched. Is it real? Or have her life circumstances taught her to be paranoid?

"So you understand now why this has all been a secret."

"Yes, still, it is shocking."

"I was ruined, basically. My career was over, my love lost."

"But look at what you have now. If this is suffering, I want to suffer like you. That twenty million is not going to hurt either."

"These things can never make up for what I have lost. They only serve as a reminder of everything I have been through. Sometimes I feel like selling it all and starting over somewhere else. But I will never get away from my past. It will follow me wherever I go. The past lives on inside of your mind. You never get away from it."

Still feeling the uneasiness of someone listening in, Kira hears some rustling in the bushes; she looks over and sees nothing.

Uriel comes purring up to the girls.

"Uriel, my angel."

Kira reaches over and starts to pet Uriel.

"I am so glad you brought her to me. She is the best thing that has happened to me in a long time. It helps having her around. She cheers me up."

"I know. I love my cat, so I was sure you would feel the same way."

"Uriel, what is it honey? What do you want? I think she is hungry."

"Right, she has the little Friskies look in her eyes."

"I'll go feed her. You want a refill?" Kira says this as she picks up both wineglasses.

"Sure."

Kira takes the glasses, and Uriel follows her into the kitchen, her tail wagging as she goes.

Tanya can see Kira in the kitchen from the Jacuzzi as she looks though the cabinets for the cat food. She finds the food and pours it into the bowl, setting it on the floor for the kitten. She picks up the bottle of Chardonnay and pours two glasses. Just then the phone rings.

Kira goes to answer it.

"Hello, oh, hi, Jerry. Monday is not going to work for the delivery. I have had some delays because of a legal matter. Fortunately, it is behind me now."

Kira refills the wineglasses and looks for more snacks as she talks.

Tanya is enjoying the warm water and the sounds of the splashing water from the fountain. The bushes are moving, which go unnoticed by Tanya. A large predator emerges from behind the bushes. He slowly creeps up behind Tanya, his breathing getting heavier with each step he takes. He gets up right behind her, and then a hand goes over her mouth. At the same time, he puts a knife to her throat, then he slices it from ear to ear, the blood spurting from her neck. She was unable to even make a sound; she drifts down into the water to her death.

Lance is coming for his last revenge. Next it will be Kira.

Lance quickly moves up to the house and enters a sliding glass door at the rear of the house, unseen by Kira.

Kira is finishing up on the phone.

"Fine, Jerry, I will call to reschedule for a more convenient time."

Kira walks out with the two glasses of wine.

She shouts out to Tanya.

"Sorry about the phone call. I had to take it."

Suddenly, Kira realizes she does not see Tanya in the Jacuzzi. She walks over to the edge of the water, looking in. It is filled with blood! She sees Tanya floating. She opens her mouth and tries to scream, and nothing comes out, dropping the wineglasses and smashing them to chards of glass.

She collapses into a chair and is gasping for breath, hyperventilating. She is finally able to scream out, a horrible sound—part animal, part human, the sound of her deepest grief.

She knows that it must be Lance and that he is surely close by; she will be next. She takes some deep breaths; she must pull herself together to save her life. She runs into the house, locking the door behind her as she goes.

She runs though the kitchen, stepping on Uriel as she goes. The cat cries out, but Kira keeps on running through the house to the staircase. She hears footsteps; she knows Lance is in the house. She hears the cat cry out again; he is in the kitchen.

She runs into the bedroom, bolting the door behind her.

She frantically opens her drawers, throwing clothes out everywhere and looking for a weapon. Not finding one, she opens another drawer, searching that drawer and nothing. She goes to the next, clothes flying about, again nothing.

Kira hears Lance's footsteps on the stairs. His knife is pulled. He reaches the door. He starts to wiggle the doorknob to find it locked. He starts to kick in the door.

She finds a gun; she pops the chamber open—*no fucking bullets.*

The door is kicked wide open. There stands Lance in the doorway, the wild look of a madman in his eyes.

Kira stands stunned with the gun at her side.

Lance and Kira stand, staring at each other for a beat.

Then Lance speaks up.

"You stalked me. You hacked my computer. You got my financial records. I had it traced and found out it was you. You knew everything about me. Then you came after me. You had to ruin me. Why?"

"Because it was so easy, like taking candy from a baby. You were the easiest of all—your need to control, your fascination with women, the fact that you were neglected by your mother, your need to make up for the love you never had by overcompensating in business. You were like a toy, but then I got bored with you. And all that time, you thought you were in control."

Lance lunges forward, switchblade in his hand; his switchblade is opened with a deadly swish. He plunges the knife toward Kira's face. Kira points the gun at Lance's head.

Lance laughs.

"I was here earlier. There are no bullets in that gun. Now who is in control, little girl? The game is over, Kira. Now you die."

Lance runs at Kira with the knife held toward her face to rip it apart. Kira does an inside crescent karate kick and disarms Lance; the knife goes flying.

Lance jumps on Kira and tackles her to the floor. He gets on top of her and starts to strangle her. Kira reaches over to a burning candle and shoves into Lance's face; he screams out in agony. He grabs his face and releases Kira.

Kira breaks free and heads out of the room, running down the stairs.

Lance gets up and retrieves his knife. He runs down the stairs after her and grabs her from behind. They both roll down the stairs to the entry hall.

"Now you die, bitch!"

Kira gets up and Karate kicks Lance in the stomach. Lance goes down, holding his stomach and dropping the knife. Kira follows with two punches to the face. Blood trickles down Lance's face from his nose. Kira is fighting like a pro now.

Lance returns the punches to Kira's face and the stomach.

Kira falls to her knees and crawls away into the kitchen. Her arms and legs are burning with pain, but her adrenaline is driving her now. She is in pain but has the strength of a prize fighter.

Lance runs over to her, grabbing her by the hair. He drags her by the hair to the kitchen sink. Lance is holding Kira by the hair with one hand while plugging the sink with the other.

Kira is kicking and screaming in agony on the floor, her head burning in torment. She thinks, *This is really it. I am going to die.*

The sink now filled with water, Lance yanks her up by the hair and plunges her face into the sink. Kira kicks and flails her body, trying to get out of his grip. His strength overpowers Kira, and Kira is at his mercy.

Kira kicks so hard, she smashes the cabinet. Finally, she goes limp. She opens her eyes in the dark of the water.

This will be the last thing I ever see. Then her thoughts go to black. There is no more sink, no water, just black.

Lance drops her limp dead weight onto the kitchen floor. Covered in water and blood, Lance looks over at his victim, thinking for one second that he has succeeded in his grim task.

Suddenly Kira's eyes fly open. Then she gasps, followed by violent choking and coughing.

Lance quickly reaches over and grabs a kitchen knife off the counter. He instantaneously goes to plunge the knife into Kira's heart, his eyes filled with rage.

Kira only wishes she would have drowned, now rolling and still gagging on the water in her throat.

The front and back doors burst open. The room floods with dozens of FBI and SWAT teams, guns drawn.

"Drop the weapon, Lance!" one of the armed FBI men shouts to Lance.

Undeterred, Lance replies, "I will drop the weapon after the bitch is dead." He moves swiftly with the knife toward Kira.

"Give it up, Lance!" The FBI rush into Lance with several guns at his head.

Lance goes to plunge the knife into Kira.

Several guns go off with a deafening blast. Blood spatters all over Kira's face. Lance falls dead in a pool of his own blood.

Kira is screaming and sliding away from Lance's body on the floor, tracking the blood across the floor.

One FBI man rushes in and places his fingers on Lance's throat, feeling for a pulse. The others still hold their weapons pointed toward his head.

The FBI man nods and gives a signal that Lance is dead.

The FBI agent who had felt for a pulse rushes over to Kira, lifting her into a chair.

"Get an ambulance," he says as he takes his face mask off. Kira looks to see it is her ex-partner in the FBI, Jimmy.

"I am okay. Forget it," Kira says in a raspy whisper. Jimmy Daniels continues shouting orders louder now.

"We need some medical help over here!" He takes Kira's face lovingly in his hands with real concern. Kira shoves him away.

"I said I am fine. Stop it." She is still struggling to speak while choking on the water.

Jimmy can see she is in shock.

The other FBI are setting up the crime scene, starting to tape off. Some are hovering over Lance, trying to discover whose bullet must have killed him, looking over the body to count the entrance and exit wounds.

One guy runs in with a medic case and sets it at Kira's feet.

Jimmy tells the guy she's got multiple wounds to her neck and has apparently breathed in water.

The medic opens the case to get out a stethoscope.

"What? Are you deaf? I am fine." Her voice is getting stronger now.

"Don't be so hard-assed, Kira. Let him look at you."

"SHUT THE FUCK UP, JIMMY! WHY DON'T YOU LET THEM EXAMINE YOUR ASS? LET HIM TRY AND FIGURE OUT HOW SOMEONE WITHOUT A HEART CAN LIVE SO FUCKING LONG."

Kira's adrenaline is still surging.

"No gratitude at all? And I just saved your life. Better count your lucky stars, lady. Next time I could be a little late."

"EAT SHIT AND DIE! You let him kill Tanya! How long did you watch? You had to have known!"

"BULLSHIT! You know I would never do that. It's your fault Tanya is dead. You had to have known he was on the way. You of all people. Isn't that what you *used* to get paid for? Reading people's minds and knowing what their next move will be? *Or is it fucking* them? Tell me for the record, which is it?"

"SHUT UP! SHUT UP! I hate you, Jimmy! I hate your fucking guts!"

Jimmy breaks out laughing.

"Sticks and stones can break my bones—"

Jimmy gets cut off by a senior officer.

"Okay, that's enough. Stop it, you two. Do we have to go through this every time?"

"You won't go through this with me ever again. This time I am really out. You guys leave me the hell alone." Kira spits out some blood from a cut in her mouth.

"What a shame when we were having so much fun. Where else can you find a job with so much excitement, and just think of all the sex you will miss," Jimmy says very sarcastically.

Kira jumps up and goes to punch Jimmy. The senior officer blocks her and gets in her face.

"You settle down now! I am conducting a crime scene investigation here, and you are part of it!"

He forces her down into the chair.

"Don't move." Kira backs down, looking feverishly at Jimmy.

The FBI go on about making their reports. Jimmy walks away to check on part of the investigation while always looking back at Kira.

An officer who appears to be writing a report dictates to a recording device, "Lance was heavily involved in a South American drug cartel. He was laundering money through investments in real estate and the stock market. He was a powerful force in the underworld."

He then turns to Kira with the device off. "Lance was a bad guy. He had to go. We are sorry about Tanya. That was completely unexpected. We thought he was only after you."

"Only after me? So apparently, I am expendable."

"No, not exactly, Kira. We have been watching you for a while. You know too much for us to completely let you go. Actually, you are quite helpful. We have hacked your computer and watch who you are trailing. The guys you want, we want as well."

Jimmy quips in, "We will leave you alone the day you pick up on a normal guy, not a criminal, if that day ever comes."

Kira catches Jimmy's sarcastic remark and counters.

"Normal? You mean like you, Jimmy? You have to stop. You are about to make me vomit."

"Don't worry, Kira. You will never get that lucky again."

"JUST GET THE GODDAMN BODY AND GET THE HELL OUT!"

"Why don't you have a drink and try and calm down, missy? Isn't that your MO?"

The senior officer steps in again.

"Jimmy, that is enough." Then to Kira, he says, "We will clear out of here when we are finished with our investigation."

Kira gets up, staring a hole though Jimmy. She goes to the freezer and takes out a bottle of vodka. She goes to the cabinet and gets a glass, pouring it full of liquor. Looking over at Jimmy, she drinks it down.

He smirks at her, not impressed with her show of her defiant behavior, and goes back to the investigation. Kira pours another glass and goes out onto the front porch.

There is an outdoor seating area in the garden. Kira walks out there often to look at the stars and escape. She needs more than an escape tonight. She needs a flight to another planet, to another life.

Fucking Jimmy, not tonight. Not after the most horrifying experience of her life. She did not need him to come up and fly in her face about her catastrophes of the past, and there have been many.

One of the worst breakups of her life was with Jimmy, not just as her partner at the FBI, but they were also lovers. He was the most solid, normal man she had ever been with. She missed the comfort and security she felt with him.

She realized comfort and security was not what she was about.

Kira needed the roller coaster of life, living close to the bone. She likes it fast and furious or nothing at all. And so she sits in the front of her mansion in Santa Barbara, covered in blood with her glass of vodka. With two ex-lovers inside, one dead, one alive sorting out the details, is she the cause or the cure for all of this? She is not quite sure. Maybe it's fate. Maybe she will understand someday, or maybe she will never understand.

The coroner drives up in the driveway. Two men jump out and get a stretcher out of the van. Another coroner shows up, one for Lance, one for Tanya. Finally, the tears start to roll down her cheeks. Kira breaks down sobbing as she sees the stretchers go by her.

The police and FBI cars block the street. Red lights are flashing everywhere. Neighbors gather on the corner, but no one is allowed inside the crime zone. The entire street is cordoned off by police-line yellow tape.

Law enforcement rush in and out, and this continues until the wee hours of the morning. The fog and cold come rolling in off the ocean.

Jimmy steps out of the front door with a blanket for Kira, who is numb at this point. Without a word, he covers Kira with the blanket as if she were his child. Kira barely looks at him, but the gesture is comforting, as was having him for a partner in the FBI. So many bittersweet memories crowd in her head right now. Jimmy was always there for her like a faithful dog, always digging her out of her circumstances, there to catch her when she falls. Why couldn't he have saved Tanya last night? She wants to place the blame on Jimmy, and yet she realizes once again that it is all her fault. She will have to come to terms with it somehow.

In that moment, she forgives Jimmy in her heart. There is something there, something intangible, maybe even something magical.

At 4:00 a.m., the FBI team finally clears out. Kira is advised to spend the night in a hotel, which she declines. She walks back inside to the shambles of her beautiful house and sees the pool of blood in the kitchen. There are bullet holes in the walls, one of the cabinet doors is smashed, and windows are broken. Kira takes stock and thinks only one thing—she is alive—and with that, she wanders up the stairs to her room. Uriel comes out from her hiding place. She steps in the blood and tracks it up the stairs and to the bedroom and into the bed where Kira lies sleeping. She curls up next to Kira and purrs, giving her warmth and comfort through the night.

MIDDAY, FBI OFFICE

JIMMY AND DAVE are in their office that they share at the FBI headquarters, still doing the paperwork on the ongoing investigation of Tanya's murder and Lance's demise. The coffee is brewing close by. Jimmy gets up to get a cup.

Dave seems to be in deep thought about something as he is filling out yet another report. Dave looks over at Jimmy.

"I just wonder about Kira. What drives her to do it? I mean, after all the danger she has been in, all the destruction she has seen. When she has enough money to live out her life with, why does she continue to go after these guys?"

Jimmy thinks about Dave's contemplation and replies, "I think she is obsessed with the excitement part of it. She gets such an adrenaline rush from it and she needs that. It is in her heart. It is in her soul. She got hooked in the FBI. Now she can't put it away."

Dave walks over and pours himself a coffee, still reflecting, sitting on the edge of Jimmy's desk.

"Yeah, but how long before one of these guys takes her out? She is playing with fire, man. Sooner or later, she is going to get burned."

"You don't have to worry about Kira. She will always be one step ahead of the other guy. That woman knows exactly what she is doing."

Jimmy says that, and his mind drifts away to a better time, when he and Kira were a team. Looking out the window, he remembers waking up beside her. Maybe it was the taste of the coffee that reminded him—hot, sweet, and at the same time, bitter. He never saw all this coming down the road.

"Don't get me wrong, man. After everything that has been said and done, I really don't give a shit what she does. I don't know why I even bother to talk about it."

Dave walks back to his desk. He knows Jimmy is lying—covering up his feelings, manning up. There is a long silence between the two. Then Dave, in a consoling gesture, says, "Don't worry. Someday you will get over her. You will."

DAYS LATER, SANTA BARBARA HOUSE

KIRA IS COMING in from the garden with a handful of freshly cut roses, placing them in a vase. She is better rested now. All the police tape is down. The mess of blood has been cleaned up. The walls still have patches of plaster where the bullet holes have been covered. The cabinet door has been replaced but not yet painted. Still badly bruised but recovering, Kira goes to the refrigerator and pours a glass of tomato juice.

Her laptop is on the kitchen center island. She sits at her laptop, and sipping a glass of tomato juice, she starts working at her computer.

Her screen shows her accessing FBI files. She types in her password. The computer shows restricted access. Kira puts in another code, and she is in. She brings up five men's names: Mark Davies, Justin Hamilton, Taft Moore, Robert Hays, and Josh Baker.

After each man's name, she pulls up their financial records—real estate holdings, marital status, ages.

She now accesses their criminal files. She finds out why they are being investigated.

Mark Davies has had some shady dealings leading to his investigation for tax fraud.

Justin Hamilton is under investigation for dealing weapons. It is very lucrative, apparently, as it has earned him millions, which he invests in real estate.

Taft Moore, an investment banker, is being investigated for embezzling. He is suspected to have sent hundreds of millions into offshore banks.

Robert Hays has been forging legal documents for foreigners to stay in America and allowing them to get green cards.

Josh Baker formed an elaborate hacking ring that successfully hacked into hedge fund accounts, getting away with a fortune.

She is also searching their personality profiles based on FBI research.

She prints out the profiles so she can do an intense study on them.

Kira is narrowing down her search. Robert Hays and Josh Baker were shown to be married, so she has eliminated them. That will leave her with Mark Davies, Justin Hamilton, and Taft Moore to decide on.

FBI OFFICE, DAY

A DETECTIVE STEPS INTO Jimmy and Dave's office, where the two are sitting at their desk, on computers.

"We just picked up a trace on Kira's computer. She hacked into restricted access again."

Jimmy quickly switches on a flat screen, where they access the activity on Kira's computer.

They see her accessing classified files, digging into the suspects' backgrounds.

She finds out Mark Davies is currently incarcerated, so she passes on him. This is narrowing down to the final two, Justin Hamilton and Taft Moore. Kira does Google Images searches to find out more. Justin Hamilton is very handsome, with thick, wavy brown hair and dreamy green eyes, with an athletic build that Kira desires in a man. Taft Moore is what you expect of an investment banker, businessman type, conservative, short blond hair, and hazel eyes—this was going to be a hard call. Both are rich, successful criminals that Kira would love to take down.

Taft Moore lives in Connecticut with all the other rich investment bankers, where large stately mansions and lush greenery abound. Justin Hamilton is in West Palm Beach, Florida, where the rich go to play. There are white-sand beaches and lively nightlife on the coast. Must be convenient for shipping out weapons. It is even better for chasing down men who need to be brought down.

Kira chooses Hamilton. His dreamy big eyes and buff body are calling out to her. A vacation at the beach would serve her well. She goes to Spokeo; she gets his address in West Palm Beach. She finds he is unmarried and forty-four years old. She gets his pictures from Google; she prints them out and starts a file.

Kira immediately goes to an online travel site. She books a flight the following week. She needs the time to get the check from Stan Mays, who has been ordered to hand over the money to Kira. Apparently, there were partners of Lance's still trying to fight to keep the money, claiming it is theirs. Mexican drug lords hate losing money; now they hate Kira.

Kira chooses the flight time, also thinking that she will be looking better as the bruises go away. Her looks have always been her secret weapon and have served her well.

Kira searches the address of Justin Hamilton. She finds it on a map and then goes to check what hotel or house she can get close by.

Kira books a suite at the Breakers, a magnificent historical hotel on the beach for a long stay.

FBI OFFICES

J IMMY AND DAVE have been watching all of Kira's activities. They are rushing to keep her in their sights.

Dave goes over to his computer and makes travel plans for her and Jimmy.

"She chose a pricey spot. FBI won't be paying for us to stay in a place like that."

"There is a Hampton Inn close by, so not to worry."

"Just as long as there is air-conditioning."

"This is high-class. You get a refrigerator and a TV too. Cable is extra, though."

"Those bastards."

The travel plans have been made. Jimmy goes to his computer to brush up on the details on Justin Hamilton. He sees the guy's picture and makes a note of his good looks. A tinge of jealousy wells up in him. Of course she plans to have sex with him while Jimmy stands positioned to save her. His head starts to burn. Jimmy wonders, What has he done so wrong in life to deserve this? He really loves this woman. But he can't be with her for obvious reasons. Checking further into Justin's background, he sees the fortune Justin has amassed by selling weapons illegally overseas, probably to terrorists. So why would Kira choose a regular man like Jimmy with a government salary? The fact is she would not—too safe and too boring for Kira. The myriad of emotions spill over Jimmy as he thinks of her with Justin, with that another swarm of reasons that they can never be together, which just makes his heart burn hotter than his head. Jimmy turns off the computer; he looks over at Dave and says, "Let's go get a drink."

"I am ready," says Dave as he shuts off his computer too. They both pick up their jackets and head out.

Jimmy wants to get drunk and numb the pain he feels. He wants to block his brain from ever thinking about Kira again.

Next Day, Stan's Office

K IRA WALKS UP to the familiar office in Century City on Century Park East that Dana and Stan have offices in. Strange that she would be coming back here for a very different reason now. She is there to see Stan and get the cashier's check for twenty million dollars. She goes through the security desk; they send her on to the twenty-second floor. She steps off the elevator; her heart sinks as she passes by the office of Lance McCann, his name still on the door. She had no idea Stan and Lance had offices right next to each other. Her pulse quickens; she is already nervous, but this really sets her off to another level higher of anxiety. Her stomach is in knots as she opens the door to Stan's office. There is an attractive brunette at the reception area.

"Hello, what can I do for you today?"

"I am here to see Stan Mays."

"On what matter?"

"Twenty million dollars from Lance McCann's estate."

The receptionist quickly looks up at her, expression changing from pretentious to flustered.

She stammers a bit but then finally blurts out, "Ah, ah, your name, please?"

Of course, she must already know who Kira is.

"Kira Michaels."

The receptionist immediately picks up the phone and announces to Stan that Kira is there. She shows Kira to the door of Stan's office. There are pins and needles in Kira's stomach as she walks through the door to Stan's office. After all, she is the reason his good friend is dead. She knows that; Stan knows that. And here Kira is to pick up a check for twenty million, a fine day indeed.

Stan slowly looks up at Kira from across his desk. As Kira approaches him, he stares her down, starting at her feet and up to her face. Scrutinizing her shoes, clothes, and the way she walks, he seems to be balking at her boldness.

He folds his hands on top of his desk, still examining her. His piercing eyes meet hers. Kira continues to walk up to the desk and then takes a seat across the desk from Stan.

After an awkward silence, Stan decides to speak, "You could have waited. I would have sent the check to you through Fed-Ex. It is very brassy of you to want to appear in person. Lance was not just a client. He was my friend. It is really quite shameless of you."

"Sorry you lost your friend, Stan, but you really should be more careful of who you keep company with. He was a criminal, plain and simple. He was going to go down anyway. The FBI knew about him. It was a matter of time, really."

"Who benefits from all of this? It is just the cruel but beautiful Kira. How do you justify your actions? Do you think you deserve this fortune? You merely just fucked and fooled a man to death, literally to death. Yet you walk away unscathed. I hardly see that as justice. Who punishes you for being the mercenary little bitch that you are?"

"As I said, Lance was a criminal. He was a murderer. He slashed my best friend's neck. He got what he deserved, enabling the Mexican drug cartel and profiting enormously from it. He was running with a very dangerous crowd."

"But none as dangerous as Kira. Take your check, and get out."

Stan pushes the check across the desk to Kira with a steely look in his eyes.

Kira picks it up and opens the envelope to check and be sure it is correct.

"Lance raped me. He stalked me, cornered me, held me at gunpoint and assaulted me. He came to my house and slaughtered my friend. Don't think I haven't suffered. You have no idea the pain I have seen. This money doesn't even begin to ease the pain. It just buys me a nicer cage, a better ride. It doesn't heal the wounds. You have no right to judge me."

"I have a right to my opinion."

"That you do."

Kira spins on her heel and takes a quick exit out of Stan's office. She pauses at the door and glances back at Stan, whose parting words are "You will get yours."

At that Kira walks out of the office silently.

She thinks of Stan's last words to her: "You will get yours." It is the karma factor; her karma has already been served to her many times over.

I was bringing Lance to justice but on my terms, the terms of which most criminals never see, especially rich, successful ones. They buy the fancy attorney and skip away from the justice system. I make sure they pay. I didn't expect for him to die. I lost a friend I will never get back. Lance is exactly where he should be. His karma was served to him.

With that Kira puts the check into her purse and zips it tight. She has a short walk to the investment firm she banks with. She walks briskly as the wind is hitting her face. The streets are busy; businesspeople swarm the streets at lunchtime, all unaware of Kira's trauma. She loves getting lost in the crowd, the exhilarating feeling of being anonymous and blending in. She wishes she could just blend away where no one would find her. But that will never happen now; the FBI will see to that. Kira must stay on her mission. Someday maybe everyone will see she is not so bad after all. She must continue to be what she has become—a vigilante of justice, a badass female with a taste for reckless abandon. Maybe someday it will lead her to a safe place, or maybe someday it will lead to her demise.

She reaches her destination, Morgan Stanley, in Century City. Entering the Morgan Stanley building, she breathes a fresh breath of relief, feeling the worst is behind her now. After all, she is holding a twenty-million-dollar check she is about to deposit—a far cry from what she was paid at the FBI. Hard won, but she made it through, and now she is on the other side. The lights on the chandeliers look brighter. The marble floor sparkles back at her as she steps toward the receptionist. She never noticed the yellow silk brocade draperies in the windows before, and now this place looks beautiful to her, shiny, bright, and new.

Kira is greeted by the receptionist and ushered to the office of her agent, Eric Lee. He greets her warmly, getting up from behind his desk.

"Kim, so nice to see you. What brings you in?"

"I have a check to deposit."

With that, Kira unzips the purse and hands the check over to Eric. His eyes grow wide when he sees the extortionate amount of the check; he sits back at his desk.

"Congratulations, Kim, very nice. Clearly I am in the wrong business." And he laughs.

"Yes, well, I sold some real estate, family money actually."

"I see. Hope it wasn't due to a death in the family."

"There was a death."

"So sorry. I wish I would have known."

"It's all right. It was expected. I was prepared for it."

"Will you be putting this all into your money market account, stocks, divide it up, or what?"

He gets a work sheet out for her and passes it over.

"Why don't you write down how much to put into each account?"

"I will be taking some in cash. I will need some traveler's checks as well. Can you do that?"

"Yes, of course, whatever you need. Just fill in what you want."

Kira writes down the amounts on the work sheet.

"Can I get you some coffee or tea?"

"Tea, please, with honey if you have it."

"Absolutely."

Eric leaves as Kira continues to divide the money into accounts. Eric comes back with the steaming tea and sets it beside Kira. Kira takes a sip and hands over the work sheet.

Eric examines it and then signs off on it.

"Kim, will you please sign right here?"

Kira signs her alias name, Kim Daniels, which she is known by at Morgan Stanley. Her money is kept in secret accounts under an LLC. Eric picks up the work sheet and looks it over.

"Very good, then. I'll be right back."

Eric leaves to process the check and get Kira the money.

Kira sips the tea and savors it. She feels comfortable at Morgan Stanley; she feels comfortable with having the alias Kim Daniels, thinking how wonderful it could be to slip away and become Kim Daniels and never look back at any of this.

Eric returns with the cash and the traveler's checks for Kira. She receives it and places it into her bag, again zipping it securely.

"Thank you." She reaches out and shakes Eric's hand.

"Thank you, and let me know if there is anything else I can do for you," Eric says as Kira walks out the door. She smiles back and then exits the investment firm.

Feeling the relief of having the worst behind her, she feels as if a new chapter may be opening. This may be her biggest adventure yet, heading off to West Palm Beach, mingling with the old-money rich, is intriguing to Kira.

Kira walks back toward the Century Park East Towers to get her car. The cool breeze in her hair is uplifting her. The extra cash is not so bad either. She thinks about what she will be packing and decides to shop when she gets there. She has made plans with a pet sitter for Uriel and will need to get her over to the sitter by 9:00 a.m. She will be picked up at her house at 10:30 a.m. for a flight at 2:45 p.m. out of LAX to West Palm Beach.

Kira thinks how badly she needs to get out of the Santa Barbara house and out of Los Angeles for a vacation. She needs to let the memories of what happened there fade for a while. She knows, in her heart, the memories will haunt her forever. The past clings to you and becomes a part of you. Tanya's face, branded on her brain, appears time after time, sitting in the passenger seat next to Kira, always with a clever sarcastic remark, with her laugh, her smile, the warmth of her friendship. Flashing before her eyes is a more sinister image, Tanya facedown in the Jacuzzi, floating in her own blood.

Kira cringes at the thought. That was not something Kira had ever imagined would happen. It all seems so surreal now and, at the same time, too real, so real, she must flee.

Running from a memory that she knows will follow her forever.

NEXT DAY, LAX

K IRA IS GOING through security; she is dressed in a short denim skirt, heels, and a white lace top. She looks exquisite as always. Everyone stares down Kira as she makes her way through the line. Kira often wonders why. Even the women look her up and down. What is she, an alien? It is amusing and, at the same time, annoying.

She takes off her Christian Louboutin heels, belt, and Rolex watch and place them with her cell and iPad into a white plastic box. She hates walking barefoot though airport security, getting her feet all dirty.

Oh, thank you very much, Homeland Security. She walks through the metal-detection screen and *beep, beep, beep.* Kira is ushered over, where the TSA Agent has her hold her hands out and strokes a metal-detection device all down her sides and down her front. One *beep, beep* goes off as they stroke across her chest. The TSA agent thinks it may be her push-up bra and asks her to walk back though the x-ray screen. It was her bra, and she is given her white box to redress herself and retrieve her belongings. She thinks, *What a bogus hassle.* Then she goes to the waiting area for her flight. Kira is starving now from not eating all day, which is de rigueur for her. But at this point, she is about to faint.

She makes her way to the snack shop in hopes there will be something worth eating there. Kira picks up a bag of trail mix and a coffee. Maybe this will hold her over. Trying to juggle the coffee, purse, and a suitcase as she pays for the items, she spots a man in the airport shop, staring her up and down. She walks back to the waiting area for the plane, and the man follows behind her. She takes a seat and sips her coffee. The man sits directly across from her, never taking his eyes off her. He is starting to make Kira uncomfortable. Is he following her because she is under surveillance? Or does she know him? Could he be someone she once arrested or questioned as an FBI agent? He has a briefcase he keeps close by him, and it is in his lap. It could also have a hidden camera inside, recording Kira's every move. Has her life become this complicated? She is paranoid everywhere she goes. Maybe he is just a man hot to get a good look up Kira's skirt.

There is call for the plane to board. Kira's group gets called, and she takes her place in line. She watches closely as the others line up. The man of interest is well behind her, so she thinks, maybe she is in the clear.

She is hating every minute of boarding the plane. Being shuffled like cattle is not for Kira. Why doesn't she take private jets? More expensive but worth every penny.

She gets to the door of the plane and is greeted by the flight crew; there are smiles and pleasantries. She finds an aisle seat and takes it, stashing her carry-on in the overhead and placing her handbag on the seat next to her, hoping that she will get lucky and no one will sit there.

She is watching the passengers as they file in. Someone starts cramming their bag in with her carry-on in the overhead, knocking Kira in the head—yet another reason to fly in a private jet. Kira's focus has been taken off who is coming through the entrance of the plane. She thinks everyone is on board and seated when the curious man shows up to take the seat next to Kira. He is standing directly over her too closely, looking down on her.

"Is that seat taken?"

"No," Kira says, removing her purse from the seat.

"Thank you," says the man as he steps all over Kira, his crotch in her face as he gets into the seat.

Well, hello to you, sir, she thinks. Shit, why didn't she say the seat was taken? Something is up, and it is not just Kira's skirt. This man seems to have a plan; he is intensely focused on Kira. She can feel his eyes upon her, like a dull razor grating on her skin.

She briefly glances over at him while he fastens his seat belt.

Is that a gun in your pants, or are you just happy to see me? Smiling to herself as she takes another sip of coffee, she is thinking, *This is going to be a long flight.*

The plane is taxiing down the run way. Then it takes off; the lift pins Kira to her seat. She inhales deeply; takeoffs always make her nervous. It is one of the most dangerous times of the flight; a hundred things can go wrong.

The man looks out the passenger's window. It is a beautiful, clear day; Kira glimpses over and gets a shot of the skyline as she leaves Los Angeles.

The plane levels off, and the sun beams through the window, glaring into Kira's eyes. The man closes the window blind.

He smiles over at Kira.

"Do you take this flight a lot? I feel like I have seen you before."

Kira's head starts to burn; maybe he is someone she had under surveillance at the FBI. Damn, and she was thinking this was all because she is so irresistible.

"No, this is the first time I am taking this flight."

"Really, you look so familiar. You look like a movie star. Have you been on TV?"

Kira smiles.

"Yes, I have been on TV. Funny you should ask. I do stunts, and occasionally, I am pictured on a show."

"I knew I recognized you from somewhere."

"Why, do you take this flight often?" Kira asks the man.

"Actually, I do. I have accounts in West Palm Beach and Miami."

"Really? What do you do?"

"I deal in diamonds."

Suddenly, Kira thinks the man might not be so bad after all.

Could it be the rocks he has on board?

"Nice, do you have large stones?" Kira smiles devilishly.

"Very large." He smiles back.

He briefly pops open his case, opening it just enough that Kira can see a case filled with diamonds, unbelievably huge stones. Her eyes open wide.

No shit, he wasn't lying.

"That is quite a haul. Don't you need security when you are carrying such valuable stones?"

"I pack a gun, but it goes in the luggage. Airport security knows about it. I must disclose that it is in there. They also know what I am carrying. Security is pretty tight. I feel secure on the airlines."

"Where do your stones come from?"

"All good diamonds come from Israel."

He locks his briefcase securely and puts it down by his feet. He has wavy black hair and tan skin. Kira thinks he is probably Israeli; he speaks with an accent. He is dressed in a very nice black suit, and she notices his shoes are Italian. Kira really loves a sharply dressed man, among other things. She also notices a large diamond wedding ring.

"What is your name?"

Kira smiles and blushes a bit.

"Kira, what's yours?'

"Aaron." Kira confirms in her mind he is Israeli.

"Nice to meet you, Aaron."

Aaron smiles back.

The flight attendant comes by, asking for drink orders. Kira asks for a Bloody Mary; Aaron orders a diet Coke.

They put down their drink trays and are handed packages of peanuts.

"I noticed you walking through the airport. Couldn't help but look at those legs. Hope you don't mind if I say that. I also noticed that you don't wear a wedding ring, so you are not married. Do you have a boyfriend?"

"Not anyone in particular. I am going to meet someone in Florida."

"Sorry to hear that. I was hoping we could hook up. What is his name? Maybe I know him."

"I doubt that you would know him."

"Maybe I do. What is his name?"

"Justin Hamilton, he works on government contracts."

Kira looks over at Aaron as she says Justin's name. Something clicked. He is agitated; he looks disconcerted. She sees in his eyes. He looks out of the window quickly to hide his expression.

"What? Do you know him?"

Aaron looks back; she can see he is disquieted.

"No, that doesn't ring a bell." He pulls out his laptop and plugs in his earphones.

"Excuse me, just have some work to catch up on."

Kira smiles back. The flight attendant comes over with the drinks. She hands over the diet Coke to Aaron, handing Kira the Bloody Mary mix and vodka.

She is thinking how oddly Aaron reacted to Justin's name. She thinks there must be a connection. She is sure she is about to find out. She reaches up and turns off her light and closes her eyes for a little nap.

Time passes, Aaron still working on his laptop. The seat belt signs go on, and there is a signal. Kira opens her eyes and sits up. Aaron takes his earphones out and shuts down his laptop.

The captain announces that they are approaching West Palm Beach International Airport and will be touching down in ten minutes. Everyone puts their seat belts on. Some reach up to get their overhead luggage.

Aaron turns to Kira.

"You are a very pretty lady, but more than that, you are sexy. Sexy is very different from pretty. It is a rare quality that most women just do not have. But you have it. Do you know what is sexy about you?"

Kira answers, "No, what is it?"

"It's your essence, it is your soul, very sexy. Time can never change that."

Kira is not really sure how to take that interesting comment.

Aaron reaches in his pocket and pulls out a business card, handing it to Kira. She takes it and looks at Aaron.

"If you get bored of this guy, come and see me. I am staying at the Four Seasons. I can take care of you."

Kira slips the card into her purse as the plane is touching down.

"I am staying at the Breakers."

"How long will you be in town?"

"I am expecting to stay the week."

"I have a feeling I will be seeing you."

He smiles at her; she smiles back. He is sexy too, but she has a bigger fish to fry. She gets her bag down from the overhead just as they are opening the planes doors. She is going out the back; Aaron exits out of the front.

She is thinking, *What was that about? How does he know Justin? Was this a setup? Who is this guy, really?* She is thinking so much, she misses the car-rental office and tracks back though the airport.

She finally gets her car and steps out into the hot, humid air of Florida, tropical and sensuous. She looks out to the crystal-blue skies and breaths in the ocean air, soft and seductive.

She gets in the car and makes her way to the hotel. It is a very short drive from the airport to the Breakers. When she reaches the stately, palatial hotel, she drives up the long palm-lined driveway to the enormous entry. She is greeted by valets that take her car and bags. As she enters the hotel lobby, she is in awe of the immense entry and massive crystal chandeliers. There are cathedral ceilings that are all tiled and mosaic. Kira feels so small next to the hotel's enormity and yet aristocratic, having arrived at such a luxurious location. She truly belongs here. She feels comfortable and secure, which is a rare feeling for Kira; it is a feeling she relishes.

She approaches the front desk and is greeted by an attractive man who checks her in.

"You will have suite 277B, overlooking the ocean. I think you will be very pleased."

"I am sure I will."

"Would you want to book a massage in the room while you are staying, Ms. Michaels?"

"Will you be doing my massage?"

The front desk clerk is baffled and bedazzled by Kira's flirtatiousness; he blushes and laughs nervously.

"Well, I just book the massages. You can call the front desk and make a reservation anytime."

"Thank you, I will."

Kira winks at him and is escorted to her room by the bellman. They take the elevator up to the suite.

The bellman opens the door. Kira walks in to see the exquisite suite, washed in sunlight, with a balcony facing out to a view of the turquoise ocean and white-sand beach. The room is all white, with touches of turquoise that match the ocean and sky. It is Kira's personal heaven. She is so enthralled with the view, she barely notices the bellman putting her clothes in the closet.

"Can I get you some ice?"

He wakes her from her trance.

"Yes, please."

He takes the ice bucket and leaves the room. He comes back with the ice and puts it on the bar in the room.

Kira hands him a twenty as a tip.

"Thank you."

"Let me know if you will be needing anything else. Enjoy your stay."

He exits the room. Kira is standing out on the balcony, soaking in the sun and the seductive smells of the ocean. Seagulls are flying close by. From the balcony, she has a view far out into the ocean. She sees dolphins swimming in a group; occasionally they leap up to the ocean's surface, just enough so that you see them up and then back down, playing in the waves. Kira thinks, *What am I doing inside here? Get out there with them!*

She goes back in to get her suitcase. She looks again at the room. She has a full suite and a sitting room with a bar and fireplace with a little breakfast table. On the balcony is a café set. The bedroom also has a balcony looking out to the ocean. The wall behind the bed is mirrored. Too bad she is here alone. This would be the perfect romantic spot to make love with a passionate lover. Kira thinks she would like to have a relationship and share the intimacy that she deeply craves. The desire for intimacy has to be squelched for the time being. She has to focus on what she has to do and what she needs to accomplish.

There will be time for love; there has to be time for love. The thought of that satisfies Kira for now.

She gets her suitcase and pulls out the yellow bikini she bought with Tanya. The memories of that day come rolling back. Could she have saved her? Why didn't she take more precautions? She should have known what Lance was capable of. Was Jimmy right? Was it really Kira's fault?

Damn that Jimmy, will he ever go away?

She needs to stop thinking, put on that bathing suit, go to the beach, and swim with the dolphins.

Stepping out of the room in that yellow bikini, a sheer cover up, golden wedge sandals, and big sunglasses, Kira looks like a movie star. She takes the elevator down to the lobby. She walks past the man at the front desk, and he smiles as she passes by. She walks out the back of the hotel and down the steps to the bar and restaurant overlooking the beach. When she reaches the white-sand beach, she takes her sandals off to feel the soft, powdery sand between her toes, so soft and warm. She takes a seat at a cabana, lying back on a lounge chair. The waves are breaking gently on the sand. Children run at the water as it ebbs and flows. The ocean sparkles under the brilliant sun. Kira soaks it in as though it is healing light into her soul; she needs this.

"Can I get you a drink?"

The waiter comes by the cabana.

"A mojito please."

The waiter takes the order. Kira pulls out her cell phone and googles up Justin Hamilton.

She finds his address and a map to his house. He is very near the Breakers Hotel, which is why she chose the location.

Kira goes on his Facebook page; she sees he hangs out at a nearby club, Ta-Boo. Sounds good. That is the spot Kira will be going tonight.

The waiter brings over the mojito, setting it on the table next to Kira's cabana. She takes her first sip; it is perfect, sweet and strong, not too much sugar, perfect like the sun dancing on the ocean. Kira thinks that she would like to lock this picture in her mind forever and just stop time. She could live on this white-sand beach, watching the waves dancing forever. But life goes on, doesn't it? Maybe we live from moment to moment, and if that is the case, then this moment in her life is a roller-coaster ride at best.

Kira sips her mojito and revels in the view and her perfect setting. She feels the sun on her skin, warming her. She will be tan soon and look like she belongs here.

She gets a text on her phone; she picks it up to look at it. It is the man at the front desk, wanting to know if she wants that massage. She texts back; she will let him know tomorrow. Who knows what tonight might bring? At that thought, she dials the club Ta-Boo. They answer and she makes a reservation for one, at a table by the dance floor. Things are going to get hot tonight; Kira feels it in her bones. She finishes the mojito and heads back up to her room.

Going through her clothes, she is thinking, What dress will get her the most attention? She chooses out a dress with sparkling silver sequins on a beige mesh that fits her like a glove—short and sassy. With a clear look at her cleavage, this is the bomb.

She puts on lipstick and slides on the Louboutin heels. She is dressed to kill, literally. She walks out to the elevator and down to the lobby.

Out the front entrance to the hotel, cabs are waiting. Kira speaks to the valet. He blows the whistle and waves a limousine over. He opens the back door, and Kira slides in.

TA-BOO

A RRIVING AT THE club, Kira is impressed by the chic, elegant exterior. There is a line outside the club held back by velvet ropes—limousines, Bentleys, and Ferraris parked at the curb. Kira's limo is waved to the front by the valet. He opens the door for Kira; she slips out and goes directly to the front of the line. She speaks to the doorman, who automatically opens the rope to let Kira in. She is ushered to a table right in front of the dance floor. There is a jazz band playing sultry music. The lights are low, and a candle flickers a soft yellow flame at Kira's table.

She is taking in the scene. It is a crowded bar with a mix of well-heeled West Palm Beach natives and a few wannabes, just enough to pepper up the scene. She is thinking, *Justin Hamilton knows how to choose his clubs, music and vibe to entice and seduce.* At the table next to her is a couple getting cozy, smiling at each other. The man reaches over to touch the girl's hand; they kiss with their eyes. Kira looks away, and out of the corner of her eye, she catches a handsome man sitting at the bar, staring at her. She recognizes him as Justin Hamilton from his pictures she found on the web.

He is more handsome in person, with a huge white Cheshire cat smile. He is dressed perfectly and looks as if he just stepped out of a shower, so crisp, so clean. He makes eye contact with Kira, and it seems as if his smile is even brighter. His confidence and machismo fills the air, smelling like man fueled by lust, musky and delicious. Kira's heart dances with the flame. She wasn't expecting this, that he would take her breath away, but he does.

She sees him call over a waiter. He speaks to the waiter and hands him a bill from his pocket. Momentarily, the waiter brings out a bottle of champagne iced in a silver bucket and brings it to Kira.

"The gentleman at the bar sends you a bottle of champagne."

He lifts the bottle out of the bucket to show that it is Cristal, Kira's favorite.

"Thank you," says Kira and smiles back at Justin at the bar. The waiter puts down two champagne glasses and pops the bottle of champagne, pouring a glass for Kira and leaving the bottle in the bucket on the table. Kira lifts the glass as if to toast to Justin at the bar.

He takes her lead and walks over to her table. As he stands, she notices his perfect physique, tall and muscular. He walks very stern and straight, as though he is holding a crown on his head, a proud, if not cocky, stance. As he gets closer, she notices his face is strong and angular, with furrows in his forehead that echo thought and wisdom. He takes a seat at her table, and his eyes look into hers. They are a light green, big, clear, and glassy. Justin is smiling even wider now.

Kira says, "How did you know Cristal is my favorite?"

"Reading minds is just one of my many talents."

"Really? That sounds interesting. Just what are your other many talents?"

"I can read women by the way they walk."

"So what can you tell about me?"

"That you are a taker, you take a lot, you never give."

"Then I suppose you think I am a bad, bad girl."

"Yes, so bad, I can't wait to take you home, so that you can show me just how bad you are." He says this and sits back in his chair, flashing that Cheshire cat smile.

He pours himself a glass of champagne, and before he takes a sip, Kira quips in, "I'll drink to that."

They toast and sip. He moves in closer to Kira and puts his hand on her thigh, touching her softly and looking over at her.

Kira had no idea how good this would be—how much she wants him, desires him. He fuels her lust in a way that has never happened to her before. Did she choose him unwisely? Or is this exactly what she needs and has, for once, chosen correctly?

She feels a tingle go down her back as he grazes her thigh. Is it Justin or the champagne? All she knows is that it has suddenly gotten hot in here. She is not used to getting carried away. She likes feeling more in control. His hand slides up her thigh higher, almost at her crotch. She wants him to slide it all the way up; he would know then just how wet she is thinking of his lips on hers.

Justin reads her mind again; he leans over and gives her a delicious kiss. His lips are soft and warm. His tongue probes in her mouth, tasting of champagne. She wants his tongue all over her body at this moment.

Jimmy and Dave have been tracking Kira. They have a hack on her cell and know her every move. They walk into the crowded club. Jimmy scans the club, looking for Kira. She is not difficult to find. She shines out of a crowd as though there is a beam of light coming out of her head like a searchlight. He quickly spots her close to the dance floor. He sees her kissing Justin; he notices a lot of tongue and Justin's hand up her dress. Jimmy's mouth drops slightly when he sees Kira passionately embracing Justin, the two locked in a kiss.

Dave catches the look on Jimmy's face.

"Chill out. You are going to blow our cover."

The hostess walks up to the guys.

"Your table is ready. Follow me."

They follow her to a table where they are seated near enough to watch Kira. It is very difficult for Jimmy to watch. Especially knowing what he knows, Justin is no doubt armed, if not heavily armed. He is a very dangerous and wealthy criminal. He sells weapons on the black market, amassing a fortune. He has a lot to show for it and has made some nasty enemies along the way.

Kira is talking to Justin seductively, very close to his face. The two never take their eyes off each other; they seem to blend together.

Dave is watching Jimmy's face as he watches Kira. He really feels for the guy, but he has to reel him in; they have a job to do.

Kira is so caught up in Justin's powerful seduction that she is feeling overwhelmed. She slides her hand up his leg and whispers in his ear. She bites his earlobe slightly. She takes his hand and leads him onto the dance floor.

The jazz music is sensual and soothing; they rub their hips together as they dance slowly. Justin slides his large hands down Kira's naked back and down to her waist. Then he slides both hands lower, grabbing her by the ass and pulling her into him tight. Kira can feel him getting hard against her as he pulsates her on the dance floor; she wants it right now. She looks at him in the eye and kisses him very passionately.

Jimmy is getting sick watching this.

"I am going to give this guy one second to get his hands off her."

Dave quips back, "Sorry, bud, but there's going to be no saving her. She doesn't want to be saved if you ask me."

"Then I am getting the fuck out of here. This show is just too much for me."

"Sit down. We have a job to do. Just think of Kira as another agent we have to watch. She isn't your girlfriend anymore, and she sure as hell ain't your wife, so just stand down."

Justin gets up to leave. Fearing being discovered, Dave lets him go, not wanting to cause a scene. Jimmy heads toward the bar.

Justin and Kira take a break from their steamy dance routine and go back to the table. Kira's lips are smeared, and she is looking intoxicated—more with lust and desire than any champagne. Justin looks satisfied that he has her where he wants her, hungry for him. As they take their seat, Justin sits down and finishes off the bottle in their glasses. He toasts again to the lovely Kira, and they sip their champagne.

Just then a man walks up to their table. Dave is on guard; he seemed to come out of nowhere, a dark Middle Eastern type, black curly hair and brown eyes. He is dressed in a suit, so he blends in, except for now, as he stands at their table, all eyes on him.

He walks directly over to Justin. He stares him in the eyes.

"Are you Justin Hamilton?"

Justin answers back, "Who wants to know?'

"Your dear friend Ullah Khan." With that he pulls a gun out of his jacket and points it at Justin's face. Kira screams, and everyone's attention goes to Kira and Justin.

Someone else screams out, "He's got a gun!" Jimmy hears the screams, automatically pulls his gun, and turns back, running toward Kira. People are dropping to the floor. People are running out of the club. Dave throws the table over and uses it for cover as he pulls his gun out to take down the gun man. The gunman points the gun at Justin's face. Dave rises to shoot him down, pulling his badge and the blood begins to spill. Jimmy runs back to defend Dave.

"FBI, drop the gun." The gunman turns to Dave and fires off a shot, narrowly missing Dave. The bullet whizzes by, grazing Jimmy's ear. The whizzing sound almost deafens him. The grazing of the bullet burns his ear, and the blood begins to spill.

Jimmy, now standing right behind Dave, fires back, and the gunman drops.

Jimmy gets a clean shot at the gunman, right to his heart. He was dead when he hit the floor.

Someone calls 911. You can hear the sirens in the background.

Justin grabs Kira by the arm and flees the club. Everyone is running out of every exit. The club is in bedlam. Justin leads Kira out to his waiting Bentley, pops the door open, and lets her in. He gets behind the wheel and peels rubber as they make it out of there.

Sirens come flying out from everywhere. The club is quickly flooded and surrounded by law enforcement.

Kira turns around to watch. One ambulance goes speeding by.

Kira feels a sinking feeling she knows Jimmy and Dave were there to protect her. She has no idea if they are all right; guilt is pitting in her stomach. Just one ambulance, which is a good sign. She saw Jimmy take the shot; she thinks he is all right.

Justin is looking over at Kira, who seems dazed.

"Are you all right?"

"Shook up and stunned, I guess."

"I am sorry for all of that. My business has led me to the Middle East. It's a messed-up situation. I am sorry that had to happen. Everything was magical up to that point."

"Who is Ullah Kahn?"

"It's complicated, you know, business. I deal in foreign trade, importing. It was a deal in Afghanistan that went bad. I got paid, and my shipment that I sent got confiscated before it could get to him. He thinks I swindled him."

"Who is the guy with the gun?"

"Obviously, he works for Kahn. I have never seen him before. I don't have to worry about ever seeing him again."

"But there will be others."

"That's a cheerful thought."

"I am just saying, he tried to kill you once and did not succeed. He will probably send another hit, especially now. His hit man is dead."

"You seem to know a lot about this type of thing. What do you do?"

"I watch a lot of spy movies. I know how these things go. I don't work at a job. I'm an heiress."

"Really, how so?"

"My mother is a divorcee of the Koch family. I am her only child with Koch."

"Interesting story."

"I can see your mood has been changed. You need to loosen up. Come to my house, and we will relax and have a cocktail. I promise it will be very safe. It is a gunman-free zone."

"That sounds very enticing."

Kira smiles over to Justin. She places her hand on his thigh and rubs up to his groin. The mood is already getting better.

Back at Ta-Boo, the blood is being cleaned up and the body removed. Only law enforcement is left in the club. A few employees of the club are being interviewed by police. Jimmy and Dave remain to help to tie up the loose ends.

Jimmy's ear is all bandaged; the bleeding has stopped.

Jimmy has a chance to speak to the club manager.

"Have you seen the man who the gunman was after in the club before?"

"He is a regular, Justin Hamilton. He is in here all the time, always with a new blonde. The one from tonight, I had never seen before. She came in alone."

"What about the shooter? Have you seen him before?"

"No, I had never seen him before. Someone put him in on the guest list though, a regular named Abdul Hammad."

"I would like to get any information you have on him."

"Do you have any idea where Hamilton lives?"

"I heard he is at the Primavera Estates."

"Does he ever come in with friends? Or is it always a date?"

"Oh yes, he has his regular buddies always hanging with him. Tonight he was alone. Sometimes he just stops in for a drink. But then he got pulled in by the blonde. He bought her a nice bottle of champagne. Looks like it was worth it."

"If I come by with some pictures, do you think you can identify his friends?"

"Sure, come on by. That guy should be in here, thanking you for saving his life."

"It is all in a day's work."

Jimmy smiles and walks over to Dave, who looks tired.

"That's it. I'm done. Let's wrap it up."

The two walk out to the front of the club.

Jimmy sees an earring on the ground; he bends down to pick it up. He recognizes it as being Kira's. He slips it in his pocket.

"Looks like Cinderella is still at the ball."

JUSTIN HAMILTON'S WEST PALM BEACH MANSION

T HE COUPLE PULL up to the mansion on Worth Drive. Justin lives in the former Firestone Estate, which is next to the Breakers Resort, where Kira is staying. She could walk to the Breakers from here, but she won't. The electrical gates open at the mansion, and they drive in the Bentley up to the well-lit mansion. It shines out like a beacon in the night, with its big white pillars in front. It looks like an antebellum mansion, except for the palms, which let you know that you are in paradise, somewhere. There is a huge fountain in the middle of the driveway. The electric gates close behind them.

Justin drives up to the entrance. He gets out and opens the car door for Kira. Stepping out of the car, Kira is greeted by a German shepherd guard dog, who sniffs her closely. There are four other guard dogs in the yard.

"Don't worry. They are well trained. He will not hurt you. They attack only on command."

The guard dog sits tolerantly but keeps his eye on Kira as Justin and Kira walk the staircase up to the door.

Justin opens the door to the house. It is more opulent than Kira had ever expected. Huge iron doors open to a winding dual staircase that is lit by a huge crystal chandelier. There are gold and black marble floors with oversized black pots set about that each hold a palm tree. Off to the left, she could see an expansive living room lavishly furnished with huge french doors that opened to a patio and an infinity pool that looks out on the ocean.

Kira was almost dizzy from the grandeur of the house, or is it the champagne? She was not quite sure. She steps into the living room breathlessly taking it all in. Justin follows her in;

"Sit down." He steps behind the bar and grabbing up a bottle of Bourbon, throws some ice in a glass and asks: "Can I get you a drink?"

"Sure, I will have whatever you are having."

Justin pours them both a bourbon on the rocks and comes over to Kira and pulls a chair in across from her. He puts her drink on the coffee table next to Kira. He takes his bourbon and sips the drink, putting it down and staring into Kira's eyes. He deeply inhales as if he can breathe her in. He slips his hands up and down Kira's silky long legs. He pulls one of her Louboutin heels and starts massaging her foot deliciously. Kira closes her eyes and throws her hair back off her face. She opens her eyes and looks at Justin as he starts to slowly kiss her foot where he has been massaging. He takes his tongue and licks slowly up Kira's foot to her toes. He starts to circle her toes with his tongue.

Kira starts to imagine what that would be like on her clitoris. She feels herself getting wet at the thought of it. Justin's soft green cat eyes stare up at her as he erotically licks her toes. He then starts to make his way slowly up her leg, licking, kissing, and nibbling as he gets closer and closer to her thighs. Reaching her thighs, he licks sensuously all over the inside of her thighs. Kira is wiggling with anticipation and urging him on. He reaches up her dress and slowly, sensuously pulls her black lace panties down her legs and off. He grabs her by the rear and pulls his face into her soaking wet vagina and circles her clitoris with his tongue. Kira is moaning and pushing herself into his tongue, her wantonness growing to a fervor. Her orgasm builds like an itch that only Justin can scratch with his tongue growing stronger inside her. He puts two fingers into her aching vagina and touches off an orgasm that totally consumes her. She is left whimpering after the aftershocks of her intense orgasm.

Kira drops to her knees on the plush carpeted floor with Justin and deeply kisses him as she tastes her juices on his mouth. They are kissing into a fervor as Kira unbuttons Justin's pants and takes them down. She is excited to see his huge penis. She hungrily goes down on it, taking it into her mouth as far as she can without gaging. It is the best thing she has ever tasted; she circles his penis with her tongue until he pulls her head away. Pulling her up and propping her back on the chair, Justin gets in between Kira's legs and gets inside her. Nothing has ever felt this good to her as he completely fills her vagina with his hard penis. Justin starts to drive himself in and out of her and then goes deeper, making her scream and moan as passion overtakes her. She wraps her legs around his back as he deliciously penetrates her. Kira's excitement is growing stronger as she feels another orgasm building, moaning and urging Justin on to take her as deeply as he can. He starts to thrust into her deeply; his breathing is harder and deeper. Kira lets go with another earth-shattering orgasm. Justin releases a huge groan and clenches his teeth and drives his erection in deeper as he comes intensely inside of Kira.

They both lie in the floor in each other's arms as their breathing gets back to normal. Justin brushes hair out of her eyes and kisses her deeply again. He reaches over and finishes the bourbon he poured. He looks over at Kira and rubs her arm softly, embracing her tenderly like a child in his arms. Kira feels transported to a breathless dream world.

Is this what falling in love feels like? she thinks as her head is reeling out of control. There can be no other explanation for what she is feeling right now. Strange that she always wanted to feel this way. But she feels more afraid now than facing down any dangerous criminal. Because facing down a criminal made her feel strong and invincible, this feeling that has overtaken her makes her feel weak and vulnerable. She would run, but she knows she can't. The feeling is inside her, and it is not likely to let her go. And so she breaths deep and hopes that it can last forever, because if it does not, it is going to take her down.

Justin stands up and takes Kira by the hand. He leads her though some french doors at the end of the living room into the plush master suite. His bed is a large black lacquer with high post that holds up a canopy. There are gorgeous velvet draperies tied back on the bed. Justin pulls back the blankets for Kira. Kira sinks into the bed. Justin goes into the closet and brings out one of his shirts for Kira to sleep in.

"Put it on. I don't want you to get cold." Kira puts it on, feeling the softness of the fabric on her skin. It smells like Justin, a wonderful masculine musk. She never wants to take it off. She slips in under the blankets, and Justin slips in around her, cradling her in his arms. The feeling of full and complete comfort enveloped her. She fell asleep and had never slept so sound. Her dreams were of Justin with his face next to hers.

She wakes to the morning light trickling in, looking over at Justin, still sleeping. He opens up his eyes for one second to see her. He embraces her tightly, and they both fall back into a deep sleep.

The french doors to Justin's room fly open. Kira is startled, and she gasps and quickly sits up in bed. Justin wakes up and turns over. An elderly man carries a silver tray with breakfast, sets the tray down on the bed close to Justin, and hands him a paper.

"Good morning, James," Justin says, groggily.

Kira calms down when she sees it is his butler. He seems very blasé about seeing Kira in the bed. He goes to his work, pouring the coffee from a silver coffee pot. Kira looks at the tray to see that there is an array of toast and jams, fresh juice, and sliced fruit—a proper english breakfast. He puts down a cup of coffee for Kira on the side table on her side of the bed.

"Do you take cream and sugar?" James asks.

"Just cream."

He gets the cream dispenser and pours cream into Kira's coffee.

He turns around and says "Enjoy" as he walks out of the room.

Kira sips the coffee; it is perfect. She looks over at Justin, who has his glasses on reading the paper. She leans over and hugs Justin. She is feeling a bit awkward having just met his butler. Thank God, she had the shirt on.

"Would you like some fresh mango juice?" Justin says while still reading.

"Yes, I would."

Justin pours her a mango juice and says, "Try it with a squeeze of lime. That is how I like mine, cuts the sweetness."

Justin squeezes the lime into the juice and hands it over to Kira. She takes the glass and tastes the juice.

Justin is watching her drink it.

"Good, right?"

"Delicious." Kira drinks the juice and fixes herself a piece of toast with jam. Justin is emerged in the *Wall Street Journal* and the stock market. Interesting that he does not read it online. He then reaches over to his laptop and opens up his email.

James taps at the door and then walks back into the room with Kira's purse and clothes that were left on the floor last night.

"I assume these are yours." He lays her things down on the foot of the bed.

Justin says, "Thank you, James."

Kira's face is blushing, really embarrassed to have the butler carry her panties from last night and put them on the bed in front of her face.

Justin smiles over at Kira.

"It's okay. He doesn't even notice. Nothing fazes James. Just relax.

Kira shakes her head and reaches into her handbag to get her cell phone. Justin is back at his emails. She opens her cell phone to see she has several texts from Jimmy last night. Damn! He shouldn't be texting her. What the hell? She opens the texts:

What happened?
Call me now
Where are you?
WTF?

Kira is steaming; her text could be followed. He should never be reaching out to her like this. He is totally wrong in every way. Kira is seething. She finishes her coffee and gets out of bed, grabbing up her things. She heads into the bathroom just across from the bed.

Justin looks up.

"There are extra toothbrushes in the bathroom. Help yourself to anything you need."

Kira turns and smiles at him and heads back into the bathroom.

It is all white marble and has a sunk-in tub. The wallpaper is black with a silky fabric texture. A chandelier hangs over the tub. Kira pulls open a drawer to find several brand-new toothbrushes still in packages and an array of toiletries. Kira opens a toothbrush and brushes her teeth.

Looking in the mirror, she brushes her hair and cleans up her smeared eye makeup from last night.

Justin come in the bathroom. He looks adorable in his baggy shorts and black thick-rimmed glasses; his body is all buff with amazing abs.

"I see you found everything. Don't worry about James. He has been with me forever, since my childhood. He came here with me from England, hence the english breakfast."

"Oh, you are from the UK?"

"Right, I've been in the United States since college."

"Harvard?"

"Right. What about you? Where do you live?"

"I live in Los Angeles, California. I am staying at the Breakers."

"Right, I wondered why I have never seen you before. That explains it. On vacation all alone?"

"Yes, I needed some time of rest and relaxation. Just really needed to get out of Los Angeles."

"Not much rest and relaxation with what happened last night. Sorry you were dragged in that mess. It is very strange about the FBI just conveniently being there. They must have had that character under surveillance."

"Who knows? Just lucky for you they were there."

"How long will you be in town?"

"I was only planning on a week."

"I have business to do today, but can I take you to dinner tonight?"

"I would love that."

Kira is slipping on her clothes from last night. She hands the Justin's shirt back to him.

"You don't want to keep it?"

Kira laughs and holds it back to her face and breaths in deep.

"Yes, I do. I was hoping you would say that."

Justin hugs her tight.

"I will get James to drive you back to the Breakers."

Justin leaves the room to get James, and Kira slips back on the Louboutins.

Feeling grungy in last night's clothes, she wishes she had something clean and comfortable to slip on. James follows Justin back into the room.

"I will be driving you to the Breakers."

"Thank you," says Kira as she grabs up her bag. James leads the way to the front door. Justin opens the door for Kira to walk through. James goes directly to the car; he holds the back door to the Bentley open for Kira to get in. Justin stops her at the door and gives her a kiss goodbye. His kiss is like no other. His lips are soft and wet. His tongue rolls around in her mouth so perfectly and deliciously, she never wants the kiss to end. He pulls away and, looking into her eyes, says, "To be continued tonight."

Kira smiles and walks toward the car. She is thinking she would go back in and have Justin on the floor with his clothes off in one hot second. She gets into the car, and James drives down the driveway. Kira dreads going back to the Breakers and taking the walk of shame to her suite. She is so obviously in her evening clothes from the night before.

THE MANSION

JUSTIN WALKS BACK into the house goes into his office and closes the door. Two rough-looking guys show up at the door and ring the doorbell. Justin sees that they are Matt and Tony, who work for him; he lets them in. They are ushered into his office for a meeting. Justin wants answers on the shooter last night, and he wants them now. The two are Justin's personal detectives on the street. They want the details. Matt starts the questioning.

"Who was the chick you were with last night? Are you sure she had nothing to do with it?"

"Of course, I am sure. She could have been killed too," Justin answers.

"I am just saying, FBI just being there? Sounds too convenient for me."

"No, no way, it's not about her. The guy was sent by Ullah Kahn. Find out where Ullah is. We need to take him out."

"We do for sure. I will run a full investigation on the shooter and everyone who was involved. I'll leave no stones unturned. By the way, what is the girl's name?"

"Kira Michaels, she is an heiress of the Koch family."

Tony adds, "Nice. She is hot and rich, some guys have all the luck. Okay, we will get back to you."

Justin sees them to the door.

IN THE BENTLEY

THE DRIVE IS very short. When she arrives, the doorman from the Breakers opens the door to help her out. Kira looks back inside and thanks James for the ride. Kira is thinking, *Not too bad, actually, to be stepping out of a Bentley and into this grand hotel.* Kira notices the color better in the light now; it's a royal blue with white leather interior. Justin has impeccable taste.

She starts the walk of shame through the elegant lobby of the Breakers. Walking past the hottie at the desk, he looks up and smiles at her; she shyly smiles back. Her sequined dress sparkles hotter in the day. It seems to be screaming out, "This is the dress from last night." She is getting glares from all the matronly ladies as Kira traipses by in the skintight absurdly short sequined dress. So Kira carries herself a little taller and sticks her breast out just a little more for the show.

Here it is. Get a good look. Finally, she gets into the elevator. *Please let the next stop be my floor.* But no, the elevator stops at the next floor. A small bald guy gets in. The door closes; he is eyeing Kira up and down.

"You out this early?" the guy says to her, obviously mistaking Kira for a hooker. She is fuming as she looks over the top of his bald head.

When the door opens to her floor, she turns to the short chubby bald guy and says, "Better get some sunscreen on that head." The guy frowns back. The elevator door closes as Kira slips her key into the door; she is laughing now. The guy's expression was priceless. Kind of mean of her but worth it for the laugh. Kira is happy to step into her suite. The light fills the room. She throws the balcony doors open and breathes in the sweet, salty air. She steps back inside and starts peeling off the slinky dress. She strips down to her bra and panties and throws herself on the plush bed.

Oh my god, Justin. He is all she can think of. His eyes are seared into her brain. His eyes, his lips, his body. She wants to remember and savor every second of it. What is she going to do? Does she have to take him down? She is thinking maybe not, maybe not this time. This may be her only chance at real love. What will she do if she ruins him? Could life pass her by with no other loves? Would she end up lonely and always searching? Wanting something she just can't have, is love really that rare? Or can it come around often? Kira has never had to worry about getting a man. She has always had more than her share of attention from men. But love, well, that is different. Feelings like this don't come around that often, in fact, hardly ever. The chemistry between the two of them could be cut with a knife; it is so thick with lust and passion. Kira thinks back on all her lovers from the past. She knows this one is different. It's like Kira has been in a locked box. Justin just held the key that unlocked the box. Kira feels alive and so intensely aware. She feels different, changed, and somehow better. She realizes she feels something she has never felt before. It is scary and, at the same time, exhilarating. Her gut is telling her she must go with it, to see where it leads her. It could hurt her, but it is not the type of pain you die from.

Just then, there is a text on her phone. Jimmy again? What the hell?

"Are you still breathing?"

Her text back: "What the hell do you think you are doing?"

Jimmy gets back: "Sorry for giving a damn. Obviously, you are all right."

Kira replies, "Stop texting. You know this can be traced."

HAMPTON INN

J IMMY THROWS THE phone down on the bed in his cramped room at the Hampton Inn. Jimmy thinks, of course, she is all right. She is the invincible Kira.

How would she ever be interested in me? She does not care even though it could have been him taking the bullet in that club. He was there to watch out for her, and she doesn't even give a shit about him. She didn't even look back when she walked away and he was hit. *What the fuck? How the hell can you love this girl?* He hates himself for being so blind to all that Kira really is. There should be a pill you could take that could kill love and wash it away, clear that person out of your heart forever, because Jimmy would be first in line to take it. His heart aches for her always. You would think that someone could be so cruel that the love inside you just dies. That is what Jimmy would hope for. But the love does not die, and perhaps it just grows stronger with every breath he takes.

Dave walks into the room.

"We got the call from the manager at the club. He is ready to ID some people for us. Just got the pictures in an email. We have got to hit it."

Jimmy picks up the phone, and the two head out.

AT THE BREAKERS

KIRA ERASES ALL the text off the phone. She is thinking of dumping the cell and getting a new one. That way she can shake Jimmy and Dave. She knows they have a trace on her and can watch her every move though the tracking. But should she do it? Of course, she should. She can take care of herself; she doesn't need them. Thinking again, she decides to plant the phone somewhere and go get another. If she destroys her phone altogether, they will know. This way she will throw them off track.

Perfect, she thinks, *that is the plan*. She takes her bra and panties off and jumps into the shower, rejuvenated at her brilliance.

Kira reemerges from her room, showered and dressed. She is wearing a black silk slip dress with high-heeled black sandals. She looks sexy and sophisticated. She gets on the elevator, and seconds later, she is walking through the lobby.

She sees a young couple, obviously on their honeymoon. They are leaning on the balcony overlooking the pool, caught in an embrace and looking into each other's eyes. Kira is wondering, Will she ever be that blissfully happy? Could Justin be the one? Or will he rip her heart to shreds and leave her with a nasty scar? A scar that never fades away and she shall never recover.

Spotting the young guy at the front desk, she stops off to say hello. His huge grin tells her he is glad to see her.

"Are you enjoying your stay?"

"So far it has been wonderful. Still have to book for that massage." Now she knows she is teasing him.

He says, "Anytime."

"Sorry, I never caught your name."

"I am Trevor."

"Nice to meet you, Trevor. Would you mind doing me a favor?"

"Anything, Ms. Michaels."

"Could you please hold on to my cell phone for me? I didn't want to leave it in the room, and Verizon has promised to pick it up for me at the front desk. It needs some work. I can tell them to talk to you."

"Absolutely, I will take good care of it." Trevor slips the cell phone in his back pocket.

"Perfect, thank you!"

Walking out to the front of the hotel. She sees two magnificent cranes walking together on the lush lawn of the Breakers. Kira takes seeing the cranes as a sign. That all in nature has a mate, now with Justin, she may have found hers. She must wait to see as fate will play out its mystical journey. She feels this time with Justin, she has been dealt an ace and she is going to play it for the final jackpot.

At that she strolls up to the valet, who whistles over for a cab. He holds the door open for her, and she gets in.

"Where are you going?" the cabbie asks.

Kira says, "Do you know where the nearest Boost Mobile store is?

"Sure," says the cabbie, and they are on their way. Minutes later they pull up at a Boost Mobile, and Kira has the cabbie wait for her. She goes in and reemerges with her prepaid phone. That will be untraceable to the FBI and, most importantly, Jimmy. She has to make a clean break from him.

Kira gets back into the cab.

"Where to now?"

"Henry Morrison Flagler Museum."

Kira texts Justin: "What time tonight? Where?"

Justin texts back: "Who is this? I don't recognize the number."

"It's Kira, I lost my cell, had to get a new one."

"Ristorante Santucci at 8:00 p.m."

Kira looks at her watch and sees it is six thirty; that is plenty of time to see the museum and make it over to the restaurant.

Kira texts back: "Perfect :)"

They reach the museum. The cab driver whisks over to the curb. Kira gets out of the cab, looking up, in awe of the magnificent museum. She turns back to the cab driver.

"Would you mind to wait? I won't be too long, and I must be at Ristorante Santucci by 8:00 p.m."

"That is fine. I can wait."

Kira walks up the long palm-lined sidewalk to the expansive mansion, owned by Henry Flagler, founder of Standard Oil and a railroad mogul, built in the 1900s by the builders who built the Ponce De Leon Hotel. It is very reminiscent of the Breakers Hotel in grandeur. It was hailed as more wonderful than any palace in Europe, and at the time in the 1900s, it was the most magnificent private dwelling in the world.

THE FLAGLER MUSEUM

KIRA IS IMMERSED in the elaborate mansion. She walks up to the huge marble stairs up to the entrance of the museum. She is dwarfed by the immense white columns at the entrance.

She walks in to see the grandest domed entrance. It has murals on the ceilings with heavy gilding all about. She thinks what it would have been like to have lived in those times. She imagines herself as the grand lady of the mansion, visualizing the splendid parties she would have hosted, the gowns she would have worn. She imagines she could hear the music playing as she walks down the hallways and views room after room. She loves the way she could hear the echo of her steps as she walks the hallway.

The mansion was built to evoke the sense of the temple to Apollo, the Greek sun god. There are references to the sun in the architecture. The grand columns in the entrance were molded after a temple to Apollo. There are lions' heads at the entrance as well, which is the Greeks' ancient symbol of the sun.

She steps out into the atrium and the lush formal gardens. There is a three-layer fountain in the center of the garden with a beautiful Venus in the center. It is a classical paradise filled with tropical plants. Kira feels that she has just beheld a piece of Heaven sent by the sun god straight to her.

She flashes on the Venus and remembers Lance's gift to her of the statue. All his fascinations with Greek mythology, even his dog was named Zeus. Who would care for Zeus now? She shudders at her thoughts. Did she come here to be reminded of Lance? He will forever haunt her with his memory. Thinking of Lance leads her straight to thinking of Tanya. How she wishes Tanya could be standing here to see this magnificent place. She sent flowers to her mother but could not attend the funeral, held in Texas where Tanya was from. The tears start to roll down her cheeks as she stares into the water cascading down the beautiful Venus. The tears flow in unison with the flowing water over Venus, washing all the memories back into Kira's head until they over flow and come out in tears. Her heart aches for her lost friend. What would Tanya say to Kira when Kira would tell her she is in love? Finally, really, definitely in love. She would wipe her tears away. At that last thought, Kira turns to leave this historical place and gets back into the cab and on to see her lover.

In the cab Kira tells the driver, "Santucci restaurant, please." The drive is very brief, only a couple of blocks away. The outside of the restaurant is not extremely impressive—an arched walkway and two clay urns are the entrance to the restaurant. As she walks in, she is surprised and dazzled with the elegant interior, all white satin walls, tables dressed in white satin tablecloth, sparkling crystal and china settings, set off by brilliant chandeliers over each table. She imagines heaven would look this way, sparkling white and dazzling. She doubts heaven would have the rising aroma of garlic and pasta, which in comparison would make this restaurant even better than heaven. She could almost taste the food already by the aroma. There are views of the city skyscrapers lit up all around in huge picture windows. And right next to one of those sweeping city views, she sees Justin. His eyes meet hers from across the room. He is dressed in a crisp white shirt and black blazer; he looks chic and elegant, a great match for the atmosphere. Her heart starts to beat faster. She is actually nervous and feeling quite giddy. It reminds her of how she felt at her first high school dance. It is the kind of nervousness that tells you, "Get ready. This is something important."

He smiles over at her as he sees her approach. He stands to greet her and leans over to kiss her as she arrives. He already has ordered a bottle of pinot grigio, and it has been poured. Kira sits down across from Justin.

"You look stunning, enticing, and hot, all at the same time."

Justin takes a sip of the wine and says, "That's it. Let's get out of here."

Kira laughs at his playfulness, knowing that he means, "Let's get straight to having sex." Actually, that sounds perfect to Kira too, except for those delicious smells coming from the kitchen that have certainly sparked her appetite.

The waiter brings over a couple of menus.

"Our specials tonight are sea bass with a garlic cream pesto and a softshell crab in caper sauce over linguini."

Kira says, "I love softshell crab. I will have that."

Justin says, "I'll have the rib eye ravioli."

The waiter says, "Perfect, I will have those right out."

The waiter leaves, and Kira reaches over the table and touches Justin's hand.

"This place is fantastic. You have such great taste."

Justin kisses her hand.

"I have the best taste in women."

Kira smiles back at him and sips her wine.

"I had a fabulous day touring the Flagler Museum."

"It's been so long since I have been there. Isn't it magnificent?"

"Yes, it is, a real trip back in time. They don't build mansions like that anymore."

"Well, could you imagine the cost of that today? Just the land value would be enormous. So glad that the family preserved it. At one point, they were going to tear it down and redevelop the land."

"What a travesty that would have been."

"Did you see the private mural Flagler made for his wife on their twenty-fifth anniversary?"

"No, I missed that."

"It's a cherub flying over Venus on a big heart in pink stone and solid gold writing. 'You are my sun and my stars, my night, my day. Of glory and sustenance, all might be divine. My alpha and my omega, and all that was ever mine.'"

"That is beautiful. Sorry I missed that."

"Well, you will just have to go back."

"This time with you."

Justin raises an eyebrow in an expression that said, "Yes, of course," and Kira agrees.

She looks out to the lights of the city.

"I did not expect West Palm Beach to be so built up. I was expecting oceans and mansions as far as the eye can see."

"Oh no, we have a huge metropolis now. It's a giant seaport as well, lots of large corporations with a huge trades market. I love this city. It has a little of everything."

"Yes, I could certainly see myself living here."

"Could you?" Justin smiles at her, raising his eyebrow in a different way.

Kira takes this as if to say, "I could see it too," but she can't say for sure just yet.

She peers back out the window, imagining that they are two years in the future, married at the Flagler museum in the garden. She pictures herself in a glistening wedding gown, standing in the garden and facing Justin. He places an enormous diamond ring on her finger. She looks into his creamy green eyes and melts into his kiss as they say, "I do."

They would release hundreds of fluttering butterflies to encircle the guests gathered there. It is then when all of Kira's past pain would melt into the ground and be washed away into the ocean forever. No wonder the sea is so moody, holding a multitude of tears such as Kira's.

Justin smiles at her as she is deep in thought. He has an inquisitive look on his face, wondering what she is thinking. But he doesn't ask he lets her savor her thoughts.

"Do you enjoy sailboating?"

"I love it!"

"I have a sixty-five-foot sailboat I keep at the marina. I would like to take you out on it tomorrow. Are you down for that?'

"Sounds divine."

"It is supposed to be a real calm day at sea, perfect weather, not too much wind. We could do an easy sail, just around the marina."

"I love the sound of that that."

"I could even get James to come along. He could help sail the boat if we should decide to go below deck."

Justin smiles brightly.

"Now we are talking, really nice day."

"I don't know. I may have to think about James going. I may want to be completely alone with you."

Kira raises her glass, and they toast to that.

The waiter brings their entrees. Kira breaths in the aroma of the garlic and caper sauce. She twirls her fork into the linguini and taste the first bite. It seems to explode with flavor in her mouth. Perfectly cooked, obviously fresh, handmade pasta. The dish is perfection, and the pairing with the pinot grigio could not be better. Justin savors his ravioli and calls for more parmesan on top. The waiter quickly comes over and tops the dish with a fresh coat of parmesan.

Justin tastes his and smiles. His next bite, he holds on his fork and leans across the table to give it to Kira. She takes the bite of the ravioli and savors the rich, deep tomato and meat bolognese sauce; it is heavenly.

Justin looks past Kira at the bar and frowns for some reason. Kira looks over at the bar to see what Justin is looking at; she sees two rough-looking men staring back at them. Kira's heart skips a beat, remembering the last time she saw those men was at the nightclub. What would she do right now if one of them pulled a gun? She is totally unarmed, so stupid of her. She is cursing herself in her mind. How can she be so unprepared? She can hardly expect for Jimmy and Dave to come crashing in to save the day.

"I am sorry. I need to go speak to someone. Excuse me."

Justin gets up and walks over to the two guys at the bar.

They look like they are discussing something very serious. She cannot make out the words they are saying. They seem to be standing very near to each other to keep their conversation very secretive. One of the guys leans over the bar to order a drink from the bartender.

Just then his jacket falls open, and Kira can see a handgun in a shoulder holster.

Chills run down her spine; her heart begins to race. Her head is spinning; she is thinking of an escape route or a way to save Justin should they pull the gun. She starts to sweat; she can feel it trickle and slide down her back. There is a deep dampness between her breast. There is no jumping over a balcony; they are at least three floors up. The only way out may be though the kitchen.

She would have to save Justin. All she has on her side is her karate experience and one steak knife at the next table, and that is looking pretty good. Taking out two really buff guys would not be so easy. Now even her legs are sweating and sticking to the chair. Each second he is standing with them, Kira grows more and more anxious. She sees Justin clenching his teeth as he speaks, raising his voice. One guy puts a hand in his pocket. This is it; Kira stands and faces them.

The guys look over at her like, "Are you crazy?" Justin brushes them off and comes back to sit with Kira, who is now in a full-on fight-or-flight mode; her breathing is short, and she is visibly shaken.

Justin still has an anguished look on his face.

"It's okay, sit down, sit down."

"Who are those guys?"

"I said it's okay. They work for me. Just annoying that they interrupt us with troubling news. They are a pain in the ass."

"I was freaking out."

"I saw that. What the hell were you going to do?'

"I was thinking of something, like hitting them with a chair."

"That's nuts."

"One of them has a gun."

"They both have guns. I am in the arms business, remember? It's a dangerous business, and there is a crazy world out there. You must always remember this—I am in control here. You do not intervene on my business under any circumstances. Understand that?"

Justin looks her right in the eye, and he is very strenuous in his voice. He has totally changed in his demeanor from just minutes before. His words send shock waves through her stomach and grab her core. She feels a cold chill run down the side of her head when her brain registers; he is still a criminal. Have you forgotten that? And yes, temporarily she did, wanting him to be something more, something better—a prince in shining armor, blowing out of the water her rational mind and replacing it with a fairy tale.

"I understand," Kira says sheepishly, like a little girl who just got caught coloring on the wall. Her storybook painting was so much better than reality. Back to black-and-white.

Justin takes a deep breath and then chugs his wine, calls the waiter over, and asks for a shot of tequila. He looks to Kira.

"I'll have a Ketel One martini up with two olives."

What she really needs is a shower.

Justin takes two more bites of the ravioli and pushes the plate aside.

The waiter brings the drinks, and Justin shoots down the shot. His hand is shaking; Kira could see it. Now she has to know what that was all about. But she doesn't dare to ask. Justin is definitely on edge.

Kira takes a big gulp of the martini, wishing she had a Xanax to take with the swig of vodka. Her breathing still not back to normal, she takes another big sip.

"Excuse me, I have to go to the ladies' room."

Justin looks at her and grabs her arm as she stands up.

"I am sorry my guys frightened you."

"After last night, what do you expect?"

"You are right."

Justin drops her arm, and Kira goes to the ladies' room. She heaves a big sigh of relief, standing in the vanity mirror. She takes a tissue and mops the sweat off her brow. She tidies up her face with some powder and lipstick. Breathing really deeply again, she feels almost human.

As she walks back to the table, she notices the men still at the bar. They look over at Kira and check her out as she walks to the table. Little do they know, she could take them out. And she won't be without her gun again.

Kira musters a smile at Justin. He is so damn handsome after all. Criminal or not, she wants to get him naked.

He seems to have calmed down. The waiter comes to collect their plates.

"Can I get you anything else?"

"Just the bill," says Justin.

The waiter brings the bill, and Justin throws a card down.

The two men are still at the bar, and they periodically look over at Kira and Justin. Kira is starting to think that they may be there to protect Justin, thinking of her as a possible spy. Otherwise, why would they continue to linger and watch. Kira's mind is running wild; it is probably not about her at all.

The waiter brings the bill over to sign, and Justin puts his signature on. Kira admires his writing style, large and dramatic, so true to his character.

They are going to have to walk right past the two at the bar to get to the door. As they stand, Kira grows increasingly tense. She feels fear and anger but really doesn't know why. It's her gut reaction; her instincts are kicking in the door to her brain.

They stand to leave; Kira is getting more anxious with every step she takes toward them. Her reasoning is telling her not to even look their way and pass by them without noticing their existence.

Getting closer, Kira looks straight at the door. Suddenly Justin stops; Kira walks on. Justin grabs her arm, pulling her back.

"Kira, I would like you to meet Matt and Tony.

Kira is forced to look at them; her face reddens.

"Nice to meet you." Her lips, tight and white, are conveying something else not so nice.

"Yeah, nice to meet you too," says Tony, looking her up and down, like he is undressing her with his eyes. Kira finds him repulsive and looks at the floor.

"You look familiar. Haven't we met before?" says Matt. "What did you say your name was?"

"Kira."

"Right, but Kira what?" Kira has to think for a minute.

"Kira Koch."

Kira's breathing goes shallow, she feels panic setting in like an unwelcome guest. Could these be criminals she has tracked or even arrested when she was with the FBI? Her thoughts go racing though her head.

"No, I don't believe so." Matt eyes her up and down now too but in a very different way. He seems as if he does actually know her, and recognizing this, Kira's head starts to burn as if it were on fire.

"Yes, it was from the club Ta-Boo last night. You were there."

"Right, that must be it."

"Funny, it just seems like I know you."

Kira musters a stiff smile, her body frozen in trepidation.

Justin says, "Don't get too drunk, guys. Let's talk on Monday." He takes Kira's hand and leads her out of the door.

Kira is grateful for the cool evening breeze hitting her face. She breathes in deep, hoping she was not so obviously shaken by meeting the two thugs.

Justin's car is brought around, and the valet holds open the door for Kira. Justin's face registers concern as he gets in the driver's seat.

They take off toward Justin's house. Kira decides to change the subject and not to mention Matt and Tony the rest of the night.

Justin flips on the stereo in the car and turns up the music loud.

They drive up to the huge ornate iron gates to Justin's house. The gates automatically open as Justin's car arrives. Kira notices cameras at the entry.

The German shepherds scatter as the Bentley rolls in.

This time Justin drives into the garage, which opens automatically as well. He walks around to Kira's door and opens it. As soon as Kira rises out of the car, Justin pins her against the door and holds her arms over her head as he kisses her passionately. Kira is caught up in his forceful machismo and leans into him. His tongue deep in her mouth, his hands slip under her dress, squeezing her breast hard. He pinches her nipple with a perfect pressure that starts her juices turning. Her panties getting wet, she wiggles under his restraint. He slides his hand down into her underwear and takes them down; he slides his fingers in and out of her vagina. She is withering in ecstasy.

Justin says through clenched teeth, "Baby, you are so wet." His tongue still in her mouth, she moans as he pushes two fingers in her vagina and touches her perfectly; she is almost ready to orgasm now.

Justin drops his pants, and pinning her up against the car, he gets inside her. Lifting her up, she wraps her legs around him as he drives deeper inside her. She feels lost in the fervor. She lies down on the hood of the car and Justin has her with both legs in the air. He goes in so deep and hard. He releases and with a huge moan he goes deep and hard for the last time. Then he rests his head, all wet with sweat on Kira's stomach. Kira rubs his head. How can someone so bad be so damn good? She wants him more than ever before. She wants him now and forever.

A Diner in West Palm Beach

J IMMY AND DAVE are having dinner. This is later than usual for them, but they had hit the beach that day, it being a Saturday. Jimmy is feeling very tense as they have not gotten a fix on Kira in hours. Jimmy's sixth sense is telling him something is in disarray. He is deeply sensing Kira is caught up in some mayhem. He sits fidgeting with his food, rearranging it on his plate. Dave looks over at him, knowing he is thinking of Kira; he feels his unrest.

"Are you going to eat that? Because if not, pass it over."

Jimmy pushes his plate over to Dave, who quickly digs into the chicken pot pie.

"Why aren't you eating this? It's so good."

Jimmy stares out the window. It is night now, and he knows Kira is out there somewhere; he has got to find her.

Just then he gets a notification on his phone. He looks at it and seems relieved.

"What is it? What is going on?"

"We just got a line on Kira." Her GPS has come up on Jimmy's radar.

"She is out at a club, the Pawn Shop. I have got a feeling something is going down. Let's get out of here."

They pay at the register and jump in their car parked at the curb and whiz off to this hot spot.

Pulling up, it was not what Jimmy expected. Kira is used to the finer things in life. This looked like a typical dive, painted in a bright yellow and actually looked like a pawn shop. Walking in, the dark club lit only by cobalt blue lights shining through the bar, passing by girls scantily dressed, Jimmy is scanning the crowd for Kira. The waitresses are lit up too and wear glow-in-the-dark neckties. There are neon lights on the dance floor, which is packed to the gills with gyrating bodies. Not Jimmy's kind of thing, but here they are.

Jimmy looks at Kira's GPS being picked up on his cell. It is showing her to be on the dance floor. But he does not see her. He hands his cell phone over to Dave.

"What do you think this is?" Dave takes a look.

"She is here, probably disguised." They scan the crowd closer. They take a table close to the dance floor to watch and see if the GPS tracking moves. It is moving, but it is a man. Jimmy zeros in on a man on the dance floor. The GPS on Kira's phone is coming from him. He passes the phone to Dave. Dave nods and agrees it is the man Jimmy pointed out. Jimmy fears the worst, thinking that the man could have abducted Kira. He is dancing with a girl in black lingerie on the dance floor. Several women are in the club on a bachelorette party, all dressed in black sexy dominatrix attire. How the man with Kira's phone got so lucky to be on the dance floor with so many women, Jimmy would like to know. He knows he is about to lose his luck when Jimmy barrels down on him.

He could be an accomplice of Justin's, and they are holding Kira somewhere. Jimmy is careful not to take his eyes off of the man on the floor. The girls are sandwiching the man and getting sexy with their moves. They are dancing the twerk on steroids. It's getting pretty heated. He sees the waitress go over to their table and set down a round of shots. The man on the dance floor goes over, and two girls follow. They shoot down their shots, sitting for a rest. The man starts deeply kissing one of the girls. The other girl joins in, rubbing his back and shoulders.

Jimmy is thinking this guy won't last much longer. He will have to take one or both of them home with him. Surprisingly, he breaks away from the girls, excusing himself to go to the men's room.

Jimmy nudges Dave, and they follow him into the bathroom. As soon as the man turns his back to them to use the urinal, Jimmy and Dave bolt the door and pull their guns.

"Hands up, FBI." They flash their badges.

"What the fuck?" Jimmy turns around, still unzipped, shocked to see the two detectives with guns pointed at him. He falls against the wall.

"Give me the cell phone that is in your pocket," Jimmy commands him.

"What the fuck? What cell phone? Are you guys crazy?"

"You have got a cell phone in your pocket. Hand it over."

The man tosses out the cell phone.

"Where did you get this?"

"It's some girl's phone that is staying at the Breakers. She told me to hold on to it. I forgot I had it in my pocket."

"What is your name?"

"Trevor Belden, I work at the Breakers. I had no idea the phone was stolen."

Jimmy takes the phone and looks it over.

"She looks like a normal girl. Her name is Kira."

Jimmy and Dave look at each other in disgust. Jimmy believes Trevor's story. He is sorry for making such a fool of themselves. They both put their guns away. Jimmy hands the phone back to Trevor.

"It's not stolen. Make sure she gets it back."

Trevor is still in shock as they unlock the door and leave the bathroom.

Jimmy and Dave immediately leave the club. Walking out to their car parked at the curb, Jimmy pounds his fist down on the car.

"Fucking bitch."

"For once you are right," Dave says as he leans back on the car beside Jimmy.

"She purposely fucked us over, dumping her cell phone to throw us off. Stupid slut, we are the ones that save her life every time.

And I am going to tell you my gut says she is running straight toward disaster."

"She really may damn well deserve it, did you ever think of that?"

"In a ludicrous twist, it is our job to make sure Kira lands safe and sound. The bad boys she chases get behind bars where they belong, so suck it up."

"She won't beat us. We will find her."

"Look up where this guy Justin Hamilton lives."

Dave goes on his cell and comes back with "Eighty-Five Lake View Drive, in the Primavera Estates."

"Let's go."

Jimmy and Dave get in the car and set the GPS for the address and take off. They speed though the West Palm Beach streets, passing palm trees and chic boutiques.

They reach the exclusive enclave of a neighborhood where Justin lives and see there are guard gates.

Jimmy stops the car and gets out of it to look through the gates. The frogs and the crickets singing in the hot balmy night air seem to be mocking him. Stopped again in his quest to find Kira, Justin looks out at the beautiful palm-lined streets and at the well-lit mansions. He knows she is in there. And there is literally nothing he can do about it.

Jimmy gets back in the car. He swings it in reverse and backs out back onto the street.

"I knew we were not going to catch up to her. Kira wins again."

"We are going to find her. Tomorrow is another day, and we will find a way."

NEXT MORNING, 85 LAKE VIEW DRIVE

M ORNING LIGHT COMES streaming in. Justin rolls over and kisses Kira all over her back and shoulders, waking her up.

She turns over and kisses him all over his neck and chest. They start to get heated as Justin starts fondling Kira's breast under the silk sheets.

There is a knock on the door. Justin moans, "Not now, James."

James calls out from the other side of the door, "I've got my special macadamia nut pancakes with coconut syrup."

Kira says, "Mmmm, sounds really good."

Justin says, "Bring them in."

James comes in with the bed tray and sets them down, handing the paper to Justin. He pours the coffee for Kira and puts the cream in. He carries it over and sets it on the table beside the bed, closest to her.

He says, "Enjoy," and walks out of the room, closing the door behind him. Kira picks up a plate of pancakes and bites into it. The taste of the sweet coconut syrup and macadamia nuts blend deliciously together, one of the most delectable things Kira has ever tasted. Justin has a few bites as he picks up his laptop and goes through his email. His face looks distressed as he reads one.

Kira says, "What's wrong?"

Justin says, "Just more from Matt and Tony."

"Those two look like a couple of gangsters."

"You sure were agitated with them. Why were you so disturbed?"

"I saw they had a gun. I thought they were going to shoot you, just like what happened the other night at the club."

"You should have known it was all right. I went over and talked to them. You seemed to be very on guard. Are you sure you had never seen them before? Matt seemed sure that you had met."

"I was being protective. I really never met him before in my life. I live in California. Where would I have seen him?"

"It was more like vigilante. I had never seen a woman become so militant. It was like you turned into a completely different person. Have you been through some difficult altercations?"

"I have had a few confrontations, nothing out of the ordinary."

"Interesting, you need to chill out. A sailboat ride will be just what the doctor ordered."

Kira pops out of bed and goes into the bathroom; she is brushing her teeth and freshening up. Justin slips on some shorts and flip-flops. He walks into the bathroom as Kira is brushing her hair.

"Can James drive me over to the Breakers? I will need to get my bathing suit and a few things."

"I will get him to drive you there, I want you to pack all of your things and bring them back with you."

"Of course."

Justin walks out to get James. Kira gets dressed and grabs her purse. She walks out and kisses Justin goodbye as she walks out to the car.

"Don't take too long. I would like to get to the Marina before noon. It gets so crowded."

Kira smiles.

"Sure."

She gets into the car and is whisked away by James.

THE BREAKERS

KIRA MAKES HER way through the Breakers, walking past Trevor at the front desk. He looks at her and quickly puts his head down to avoid her glance. Kira thinks this is awkward. She is in a hurry and quickly moves on. She enters her room and immediately finds her cell phone, which has been pushed under the door. Now it seems even more bizarre with the way Trevor was obviously avoiding her and now the phone being pushed under the door. She knows something happened, but what?

She quickly jumps in the shower. As the water is washes down her back and steam fills the room, she goes though the scenarios in her mind of what must have happened with the cell phone. The story she told him was obviously a fake because the Verizon people never picked it up, and he just politely returned it. Or was Jimmy texting her and Trevor receiving the text? So many possibilities. Never mind the possibilities. She will put the phone in the safe in her hotel room and leave it there. This way the phone will not be on her, the FBI can't track her whereabouts, and she is free at last.

She jumps out of the shower and wraps herself in a towel. She gets out her yellow bikini, the one she bought with Tanya. Tanya's face flashes in her mind, like a big red-light flashing-stop! You are running into danger." For a fleeting second, streams of angst run though Kira's body like a lightning storm. Is this a real premonition?

Or has she just learned to live in terror, constantly afraid of what lurks around every corner? Paranoia stuns her mind. Her breathing gets shallow. Her heart starts to pound, her legs start to shake, she feels faint. Her PTSD is kicking in the door to her brain, from her many brushes with death. She grabs for her bottle of Xanax with shaking hands and washes one down with a glass of water. She will feel better in a few, she reminds herself.

She makes a strong effort to just forget these thoughts and go on about getting ready. She puts on the yellow bikini and throws on a white dress over it. She grabs up a small bag and packs it with things for a few nights. She goes into the bathroom to blow dry her hair and put some makeup on. Slipping on some white sandals, she is ready to walk out the door. Just before she leaves, she goes to the safe in the room and activates a code. She slips her cell phone in and locks the door on it.

Getting into the elevator, she realizes she has calmed down and returned to her rational mind. She pushes the button to go to the lobby. As she is slowly lowering down, she can see the ocean though the glass elevator. Soon she will be out there and so far away from all her cares and worries.

She is nearing the front desk. Should she stop and talk to Trevor? It will be so awkward if she doesn't. He has his back turned to her as she walks up. Kira calls out his name, "Trevor."

He turns and looks at her and immediately looks away awkwardly. She knows something has happened.

"Thank you for returning my phone. Did the Verizon people come at all?"

"No, not the Verizon people. It wasn't them." Kira senses from Trevor's reaction, that it was Jimmy, but what could he have done?

"Oh, well, I thought they would have come." Kira tried to make excuses, knowing full well now, it was something much worse by the look on Trevor's face.

"Can we talk about this another time? Now is not a good time for me."

Astonished and uneasy, Kira says, "Sure."

"Maybe coffee on Monday. I will be working all weekend."

"That will be good. We will set something up."

Trevor looks dismayed and suspicious. Kira knows something bad went down. But now is not the time, so she continues making her way out to the car that is waiting.

She jumps into the back seat, and James takes off. She watches as the beautiful fountains and the palm trees of the Breakers drift into the background. Will this be the best trip of her life? Or the last trip of her life? That is a question the Kira always faces. She actually likes the fact that she just does not know. Life is a game, and she is a player. She plays to win. The stakes are high.

SAILING AWAY

J USTIN'S MANSION IS only minutes away. As they pull up in front, Justin is already waiting in the driveway. The German shepherds lay in the shade of a large tree, getting respite from the hot Florida sun. It is near one hundred degrees with at least 90 percent humidity.

Justin opens the door to a bright-yellow Porsche Carrera convertible. Kira gets out of the Bentley and hops into the Porsche. Justin gets behind the wheel, and they take off. Kira's hair blows in the wind on the way. Kira leans over and kisses Justin as he drives, taking in how handsome he looks in his nautical shorts and red shirt. Everyone stares at the couple as they pass in the hot sports car. Kira thinks it is the real reason anyone would own a Porsche is to get the attention one gets from driving such a car.

Nearing the marina, Kira looks out on the beautiful sailboats docked there. Justin takes a parking space facing his boat.

They get out of the car and walk up to the gate to the boat dock. Justin unlocks it, and they are standing at Justin's most impressive sailboat; it is a sixty-five-foot Oyster. It is all white with teakwood decks, two sails, and two steering wheels, and Justin flies a British flag. On the side, Kira reads the name *Stairway to Heaven*. The boat is certainly appropriately named.

Justin steps on board and takes Kira's hand to help her in. Justin says, "So what do you think?"

"She is beautiful."

"I love this boat," he says. "It was custom-made. The British make the finest sailboats."

"Clearly they do," Kira says as Justin goes around the boat opening the hatches and untying the sails, getting it ready to go out on the ocean.

Justin unties the boat from the dock and lifts up the anchor. He turns on the power and starts to taxi out of the port. Kira takes a comfortable seat at the back of the boat behind Justin at the wheel. The breeze picks up and blows her hair as they taxi out. The Florida sun is brighter than ever. Kira peels off her dress and lays back soaking in the rays, her well-toned body getting bronzed in the sun. Justin takes off his shirt, revealing his cut physique. They look like models in a Ralph Lauren ad. Kira breaths in the misty salt air. She loves the sea mist on her body, cooling it from the heat of the sun.

The day looked like a picture on a postcard—the translucent aquamarine ocean below the white stallion of a sailing vessel, the summer sun shining brightly and reflecting off the water like stars rising up from the sea, sea lions seeming to wave and smile as they pass by.

Justin clears the port and rolls up the sails; there is one red and one white sail. They look glorious filled with the wind, like a proud bird with a puffed-up chest. They are now in a full sail. Justin comes over briefly and sits by Kira.

"How great is this? Have you done much sailing?"

"I have been several times but never in Florida. The water is so much clearer here, and the sea seems milder."

"Be right back." Justin goes down into the galley and comes up with a chilled bottle of white wine and two glasses. He sets it in an ice bucket and pours Kira and himself a glass.

Kira sips the wine. It is perfect and crisp like the day. She looks back at the shoreline fading in the distance. She knows Jimmy is out there somewhere, looking for her. She is filled with a yearning to keep on sailing so far away from everything that she has known. And yet there is a tinge in her stomach. Is she sailing into dangerous tides?

Justin breaks her train of thought when he sees a school of dolphins playing in the water. They periodically leap out of the water playfully. Cackling and laughing as they go. Justin takes up the binoculars and looks closely at the sea mammals. He hands them over to Kira to get a look. She sees that they look like a family. They could be a mother and father with two calves.

They swim closer to the boat and raise their heads to get a closer look at Kira and Justin. They seem to be jumping and swimming along with the boat. Justin takes out his cell phone and snaps a picture of the dolphins at play. He turns and snaps one of Kira lying out on the deck. He jumps in close by and slips an arm around her and takes a selfie of the two of them. Kira says, "Send it to me," which Justin does; for that minute, she is sorry not to have her own cell. Even if she did, who would she share the picture with? Justin reaches over and touches Kira's face. As he looks into her eyes and places his mouth over hers, Kira opens her mouth to his tongue sliding into hers. They melt together skin on skin, like blended flesh. He is forceful with his tongue and his body, taking over Kira with hot passion only matched by the sun. Kira's mind drifts to Apollo, the Greek sun god she saw so much of at the museum. Perhaps Justin is a close match for Apollo's image, fiery and strong.

Justin ties the wheel and lets down the sails. He takes Kira's hand and leads her down below. The boat is like a house—beautiful, plush upholstered sofas, gleaming teak floors and walls, a kitchen with granite countertops, a stainless steel stove and refrigerator. It is impressive and expansive, much more than Kira had expected. Justin leads her to the bedroom. There is a bed on a wooden pedestal, with cabinets all about and mirrors on two walls facing the bed.

Justin kisses Kira deeply; she feels herself pulling into him as if they are melting together. He slowly slips off her bikini top as he lifts her onto the bed. He gently kisses her down her neck. When he gets to her breasts, he encircles each nipple with his tongue. Then he gently bites her nipple, sending shock waves into her vagina, making her yearn for him to be inside. Kira wiggles her hips as he continues to lick, caress, and bite her breast. She feels herself getting so wet with desire. Justin slips off Kira's bikini bottoms. He moves down between Kira's legs and spreads them wide. He buries his tongue inside her vagina and flicks it across her clitoris, causing Kira to grind into him. He is moving his tongue slowly and rhythmically around Kira's clitoris. Kira gives away with a euphoric orgasm. She lies wiggling and convulsing on the bed. Kira is halfway in a trance when she sees Justin open the drawer next to the bed. She briefly looks in the drawer and sees a handgun in there. Justin pulls out some silk ties and bounds them to her wrist, tying her wrists together. Raising her hands over her head, he ties her to the bedpost. Kira is breathing heavily in anticipation as to what Justin will do next.

He gets between her legs and pulls them wider apart, holding them up in the air. He enters Kira deeper than she has ever had a man before; she is screaming out in ecstasy. He starts to pound into her harder and harder. Kira's head starts banging on the headboard. His fervor is growing ever stronger, deeply thrusting into Kira. She starts to whimper and beg him to stop. Justin picks up the speed.

"Tell me I own you."

Kira screams out in her delirium, "You own me. Take me all the way. Take me so deep."

Justin grinds into her deeply one more time before he pulls out of her vagina and stuffs himself into her mouth. Kira feels him let go into her mouth. The taste is salty and pungent, and it is thick sliding down her throat; she gags a little. He pulls out of her and collapses on her breast, breathing heavily and covered in sweat. Her arms are aching from being tied up. Justin reaches up and unties her, resting back on her breast. He looks into her eyes and deeply kisses her. Kira is surprised as he is tasting his own semen. He licks around her mouth and deeply kisses her again.

He loves the taste of himself on Kira's lips. Kira embraces Justin and runs her fingers though his hair as he rests on her breast.

So many thoughts go rushing though Kira's head. How many women have been where she is now? Did he want to "own" them too? He was very skilled and talented in his sexual prowess.

There must be many before her. His strength and animal magnetism is easy to succumb to, it is almost frightening but also thrilling and exhilarating at the same time. If this is just a taste of what he is capable of, what lies ahead? Her thoughts roll in her head in unison with the swells of the sea, her heart rocking on the inside like the sailboat on the ocean. Will she sink or swim? Or drown in the tidal wave of her emotions? Only time will tell.

Justin starts to tickle her stomach, softly running his fingers up and down her abdomen and up between her breast. He smiles at her and kisses her again. He rises and goes to the bathroom, closing the door. Kira hears the water go on and the toilet flush. He opens the door and Kira goes into the bathroom as Justin comes out. She closes the door, rinses her face off, and swishes some water though her mouth. She gets into the shower and turns it on. Standing under the warm wash of water, she finds it hard to steady herself as the boat rocks with the current, so she rinses quickly then steps out to dry off. She comes back out and finds her bikini on the bed. She slips it on and goes back up to join Justin on the deck.

The sun is starting to set. The sky is a perfect shade of crystal blue; the clouds are bright pink and look like bellows of pink feathers in the sky. Justin has prepared a platter of cheeses and fruits. He opens another bottle of wine. This one is a rich and robust red zinfandel, one of her favorites. Justin takes his wine and goes to the wheel; he flips the sails around, and they head back toward the marina, the brilliant sun setting lower and sending sparkles across the ocean.

SIMULTANEOUSLY IN
THE POLICE STATION

J IMMY AND DAVE have a meeting with the chief of police of West Palm Beach. They enter the busy station and identify themselves at the desk. They are shown into the police chief's office. It is overly neat, his many awards and accolades clearly displayed on stark white walls. He is Chief Newhause; he has been in command twelve years. He makes it his business to keep track of any and all criminal activity in his precinct. Jimmy and Dave introduce themselves, and there are traditional handshakes all around. Chief Newhause starts the conversation.

"What brings the FBI to West Palm Beach?"

Jimmy says, "We have Justin Hamilton under surveillance." Jimmy hands over a picture of Justin to the chief. The chief takes it, looks at it, and raises an eyebrow.

"Do you know him?" Jimmy asks.

"Yes, he is an exporter, importer of sorts. He is a weapons dealer, but he has a legal license to sell guns and ammo. I became aware of him when we have had some trouble with some robberies at his warehouse. There was a shooting there about two years ago. Someone shot the guard in order to get access to the warehouse. It's a messy business to be in."

Dave speaks up, "It gets even messier. We have information linking him to terrorist groups and selling to enemies of the United States. He apparently botched a deal with a Pakistani terrorist group, claiming to have a shipment stolen en route to them. They now want him dead."

Jimmy adds, "There was a shooting at the Ta-Boo night club only days ago. It was a suspected member of that terrorist group who did the shooting."

"So that is why you were on the scene there?" Chief Newhause asks.

"We have reason to suspect he will soon send another shipment to the Pakistani group, under pressure to make good on the deal. Otherwise they will kill him," Dave includes.

"I understand," replies Chief Newhause.

"We want to intercept the shipment and shut down the supply of guns to the terrorist once and for all. We want to arrest Hamilton and prosecute him to the full extent of the law," concludes Jimmy.

"I want you to know, you have my full cooperation on this. In fact, I will assign some of my detectives to work with you."

Jimmy says, "Thank you, Chief, we appreciate that. What would really be helpful for us right now would be if we can get some street surveillance footage to track his whereabouts. We had a tracker on a cooperative who is close to him, and now we have lost the trace."

"Lost the trace?" The chief seems concerned.

"It is a female ex–FBI officer. She may have purposely stopped the trace." Jimmy continues, "She likes to go rogue."

"Interesting," the Chief notes.

"We would like to check dates at the Ta-Boo club and streets around it for the night of the shooting. We also want surveillance video around the Breakers hotel where our cooperative is staying."

"I can let you see those, all that we have. You may need a warrant to get inside the Breaker's surveillance to see what goes on with your cooperative. I can get you that."

Dave says, "Thanks, Chief."

The chief stands up and ushers the guys out of the office and down the hall to a surveillance camera room. There is a room there with multiple monitors that access many cameras though out the city. They can access data from all over the West Palm Beach area. The chief introduces them to the head of the surveillance room, Clinton Cox. They are instant friends. Jimmy and Dave sit down to check the dates and what is on camera.

Pulling up data from the Ta-Boo club shooting, they are able to get footage of the shooter going in. He is dropped off in a cab. They are able to get footage of Kira being dropped off and going into the club. Sometime later the shot is of Justin arriving in his Bentley, which gets carefully parked at the curb.

After the shooting, they are able to see Kira leave with Justin in his Bentley. They are able to follow their route back to the Primavera Estates. The camera footage will only take them up to the gates. They see Kira go in the gates with Justin in his car.

Next they check for camera surveillance around the Breakers Hotel. They are able to see Kira leaving in the limo on her way to Ta-Boo the night of the shooting. They see her return the next day with James in the Bentley. They watch her leave later and follow her to the museum and later to the restaurant where she meets Justin for dinner. They note the restaurant as they think it may be a favorite. They follow the surveillance as Kira and Justin leave the restaurant and go back to the Primavera Estates. Kira leaves the next day again with James. The camera records Kira returning to the Breakers and later leaving again with James back to the Primavera Estates. They later see Kira and Justin leave in the Porsche and follow them to the Marina. The camera clocks in at about 10:45 a.m. Most importantly, it looks in at the marina and finds the Porsche still parked in the Marina at 6:45 p.m.

Jimmy looks at his watch, and it is 6:45 p.m. He looks over to Dave instantly and says, "That's it. We have to go." He bounds out of his seat and makes his way to the door.

Dave jumps up and says, "Thank you, Clinton, we will be back in contact with you."

The two partners bolt out to their car.

Jimmy says, "I hope we get there before they get back to the car. Let's put a tracer on the Porsche."

"Exactly what I was thinking," Dave agrees.

They get in the car and race away toward the marina with no time to waste.

It is a short drive to the marina from the police station, and Jimmy is driving recklessly to make it even shorter, going through red lights, cutting in and out of traffic, narrowly missing a pedestrian in the crosswalk.

"Jesus, God, Jimmy, you don't have to kill us!

"The sun is going down. They are not going to be sailing after dark. I can't miss this opportunity."

"We will make it! Just slow down."

Jimmy revs up the motor again, passing a slow driver and barreling though another red light. Nearing the marina, he has to slow down as they get behind a truck pulling a boat. Jimmy is huffing and puffing behind the wheel, cursing the truck driver with the boat. Finally they enter the driveway at the marina. The sun is going down; they have only minutes to locate the Porsche in the light. Dave spots it close to the dock. They park several spaces away and walk over to the Porsche. Dave gets on the ground and rolls himself under the car. He pulls the tracking device from his pocket and affixes it to the underside of the car. He has a small flashlight he uses as he works swiftly to get it done.

Dave looks up and sees the *Stairway to Heaven* dropping its sails and pulling up to the dock. He kneels down and, in a hushed voice, says, "They are back. We have to hustle."

Jimmy finishes the work in the nick of time. They are tying up the boat, and Justin jumps out. He holds Kira's hand, lifting her to the dock. Kira is happy to get her feet on solid ground. She still feels the waves of the ocean in her legs.

Jimmy and Dave walk at a normal pace back to their car. Kira looks to see Jimmy walking though the parking lot; she is stunned for a second. She almost gasps but then catches herself.

"What's wrong? Are you all right?"

"No, no worries, I am fine. Just a little dizzy, still trying to get my sea legs."

Justin put his arm around her and looks concerned as they walk out to the Porsche. Justin points his key at the car and unlocks it; the car lights up. Justin sees Jimmy and Dave walking to their car; he watches them for a moment, looking intensely and acting anxiously. As soon as they get in their car and turn on the motor, he excuses them as nonthreatening. He opens the car door for Kira; she gets in. Jimmy and Dave drive by before Justin gets in on the driver's side. Justin looks right at the two guys driving by. Jimmy gives him a hard look back and then drives away.

Justin gets in the car.

"What the fuck was that?"

"What do you mean?"

"I think I have seen those guys before, the ones who just drove by."

"What guys?"

"You saw them. Aren't they the ones from Ta-Boo? Aren't they the FBI Guys?"

"Are you kidding? I didn't get that close of a look."

"Fucking shit, they are after me."

Justin pounds his fist on the steering wheel.

"Maybe that wasn't them. It is really dark. How could you have gotten that close of a look?"

"The guy looked right at me. I know it was him."

Justin starts the car, clearly extremely agitated. He drives away, looking all around, and then floors it to get out of there in a hurry, continuously checking the rear-view mirror to see if he is being followed.

"I will fucking kill those guys. They are not going to take me down. They have no idea who they are messing with."

"Just calm down. It is probably not who you think it is. We will just keep an eye out for them.

"No way, I am not waiting for them to make a move on me. The best defense is an offense."

Kira looks out the passenger-side window; she tries to hide her rage inside. Everything was going so damn well. Will she have to worry about Jimmy and Dave trailing her the rest of her life? Always ruining and stepping on the new life she is fledging, what the fuck were they doing? Kira thinks for seconds before she realizes there is a tracer on the car. Should she tell Justin? But no, then he will know that she knows who the men were; that would not be good. She needs to think this out slowly; she decides to keep it to herself.

They arrive at the gates of the Primavera Estates. Justin rolls down his window and speaks to the guard at the gate.

The guard steps out of the guard post as Justin stops the car.

"I need extra security tonight. I believe I was being followed. There are two men in a black Ford sedan. So be on the lookout, and I want some drive-by security."

"Sure thing, Mr. Hamilton, I will be here until seven in the morning. I have got you covered."

Justin drives up to his own electric gates. They open, and the guard dogs follow the car in as the gates close behind.

Kira turns to Justin.

"We are fine. You have got guarded security gates, electric gates at your home, and four potentially ferocious guard dogs. Who is going to get through all of this?"

"Plus an arsenal of weapons. I know, no way, right?" Justin answers.

"Right."

"But don't forget it is the friggin' FBI. If they come with a warrant, there is nothing anyone can do."

"You are way ahead of yourself. None of this is going to happen. Let's try and not jump to conclusions."

Justin lets it go, getting out of the car and opening the door for Kira. They walk inside the house.

FBI Vehicle

S IMULTANEOUSLY THE BLACK sedan drives through the streets of Florida. They pick up a trace on Justin's Porsche. They know that Kira and Justin are back at Justin's house behind the gates. Suddenly Jimmy whips a U-turn.

"What are you doing?" Dave asks.

"Going back to the marina. I am going to put a tracer on his boat too. I know they will be going back out in that. We especially have to watch when he takes the boat out. He could be meeting another boat on the sea and exchanging weapons, out of sight of any law enforcement."

Jimmy drives at a killing pace back to the marina. They park right in front of Justin's boat in his parking for the Porsche. They get out of the car and climb over the security gate, onto the dock. The ocean is flat, no swells in sight. A couple of sea lions have crawled onto the boat next to Justin's. They bark out as Jimmy and Dave walk up the boardwalk. Jimmy shines a flashlight on them, and they jump back into the ocean. Jimmy quickly goes to work affixing a tracking device to a hidden place on the side of the ship inside a porthole. He makes sure it is securely in place. They climb back over the security gate and walk to their car. Security drives by in a golf cart, stopping right in front of them.

"Everything all right?" the security guard questions them, shining a flashlight on them.

"Everything is fine. We just came back to look for a wallet we lost earlier today." Jimmy smiles wide and pulls his wallet from his back pocket. "Found it!"

The security guard smiles back.

"Okay then." He drives on, confident that they mean no harm.

Jimmy and Dave get back into the car. Jimmy starts it up and they drive away.

As they drive away, Dave is wondering how much of this is about apprehending Justin Hamilton. And how much of it is Jimmy's way of keeping track of Kira? He really hopes, for Jimmy's sake, he will just move on. There is never going to be a reconciliation between the two of them. Kira is just bad to the bone. The sooner Jimmy realizes that, the better for him.

The sun rises on the mansion on the beach. Kira lies dreaming in bed next to Justin. In the dream, Kira is in bed with Jimmy; they are naked, and he is kissing her. Justin stands outside the door of the room; she can hear his hand on the doorknob. Kira tells Jimmy that they have to stop because Justin is coming in. Jimmy will not stop. He continues to kiss her. Kira wants him very badly; she wants him inside of her. Jimmy gets on top of Kira and enters her. It is intense and deeply sensual. Wanting him more Kira grinds into him. Justin enters the room with a gun.

Startled, Kira wakes up. She sits straight up in bed and looks over at Justin, still sleeping. Kira is very shaken up about the dream. Why did she dream that? She doesn't want Jimmy. She gets up, puts on a robe, and steps into her flip-flops; she wanders out of the french doors. Just outside his room, there is a stately patio with a fireplace and comfortable seating. Bold blue pots hold huge succulents that accent the patio. She breathes in the cool salty air. The sun is just rising, and it breaks through the clouds with golden glimmers of light. Kira strolls out to the garden path. The light hits the flowers and the rosebushes; it seems to highlight them. The path is lined in violets all in bloom. It is a cobbled path that has moss growing around each stone. There is a small koi pond with lily pads floating. Kira stops to look at the koi. One brightly colored koi swims up to look at Kira, who believes she has made a new friend. Just beyond the path, there is a patch of grass with two chairs facing out to the ocean. Kira winds her way over to one of the chairs and enjoys the view of the sun rising on the ocean.

She is deeply disturbed by the dream. What could it mean? Is she afraid of Justin? What was she doing in bed with Jimmy? The dream mystifies her; she can't stop thinking about it. She thinks it is just because she had seen Jimmy the night before. She knows he is lurking out there to try and apprehend Justin; will he succeed? Although Justin has given Kira no reason to fear him, the fear must be there. She knows he is a criminal and potentially dangerous. Kira likes the danger; the thrill of it excites her. It drives her vigilance to capture criminals. The exhilaration of the danger pushes her forward. But have the tables turned, and has she been captured? Maybe this one is too tough to be taken down, and maybe she has lost her will, giving in to her lust and desire for Justin. Or is she temporarily blinded by it? Lust is an extreme driving force. It always has been For Kira. It can temporarily blind you with hope of love and passion. Confused and dazed, Kira continues to gaze at the ocean and the sky.

Seagulls glide above and land on the beach. The waves lap softly on the sand. The ocean is peaceful. The sun is rising higher; the clouds give away. Kira is washed in its warm light. What if Justin really knew Kira? If he knew the truth of who she is, he would kill her, she is certain that he would. The dream was a warning. With that she rises and walks back into the house. She goes into the doors leading to the kitchen area. She finds a teapot and fills it with water. She sets it on the stove and turns it on.

James comes in and is surprised to see Kira in the kitchen.

"Well, good morning," he says in an interesting way, as if to say "What are you doing here? This is my territory."

"I was going to bring you your breakfast."

"I woke up early, I had a bad dream. It's okay. I can help myself, I am a big girl. I know how to do these things."

James goes about his business, fixing a tray for Justin. The pot boils, and Kira pulls a cup and a saucer from the cabinet and puts a tea bag in the hot boiling water, watching water turn a golden brown as the tea bag seeps.

James pours the mango juice and sets the lime perfectly on the edge of the glass. Toast pops out of the toaster, and James places it in the bone china. He puts jellies and butter in dishes. He picks up the tray and takes it into Justin's room. Kira puts some honey in her tea and takes a sip. Tea is healing, it is good for the soul, just what Kira needs right now.

Kira breaths in the sweet aroma of the tea and sips some more. She picks up her glass and carries it into Justin's room. He is sitting up with the tray on the bed. Reading the paper, with his tablet is on the bedside table, he looks at it simultaneously. He briefly looks up at her.

"What gets you up so early? I felt you get up around six."

"I know. I had a bad dream. I woke up and could not get back to sleep."

"It wasn't about me, was it?"

"No, that would be a good dream." Then Kira smiles. She sips her tea and goes into the bathroom to brush her teeth.

"What is wrong? Why don't you come back to bed?" Justin calls from the other room. Kira gets a ping in her heart. And when by *ping*, it means pain. Although it hurts her, she knows now what she must do. She walks out and smiles at Justin.

"Haven't you had enough of me?"

"I can never get enough of you."

Kira picks up her cup of tea, sipping it to the bedside. Putting it down on a table close to the bed, she slides in beside Justin. He unties the robe and starts kissing her neck and breast. She is tingling all down her shoulders and all the way to her vagina. He bites softly on her neck, sending shock waves through her. He puts his mouth on hers and kisses her so passionately, she is wiggling beneath him as he crawls on top of her. He enters her and pushes himself in so deep. Kira gasp at his hugeness. He pulls her legs wide apart and lunges into her, each lunge causing her deep tremors of warm seduction. Her orgasm rises up in her. She is moaning, and Justin thrust his tongue in her mouth, stifling her moans. He thrusts deeper, digging his hands under her butt cheeks and clenching them in his fingers. He releases into her with a huge thrust. He tightens every muscle in his body as he does. Kira looks at his chest; the sweat on his body amplifies his well-defined muscles. He gives away and lies back onto his pillow. He is breathing deeply and looking up to the ceiling.

"You are amazing. You really are. You sure that dream wasn't about me?"

"Of course I am sure." Kira rolls over and rests her head on Justin's chest. She rubs her hand on his stomach. They lie there holding each other, and then Justin's phone begins to ring. Justin breaks away to pick up the phone.

"Justin Hamilton. Yes, what is it, Matt? More information? So tell me now. Meeting? Let's do lunch. Meet at Two Georges Water Front Grill."

He ends the phone call, gets out of bed, and pulls on some shorts.

"I am meeting the guys for lunch. I will get James to drive you back to the Breakers."

"No, I am fine. I want to walk. It is just down the beach."

"You sure?"

"Of course, I am fine."

Justin goes into the bathroom and closes the door. Kira gets on her bikini in case she decides to go for a swim in the ocean. She steps into her flip-flops and throws a loose shirt over her. She steps back out of the french doors and makes her way through the back garden. She follows the path down to the beach, and soon she is on the warm, white, sandy beach with the sun on her face.

THE BREAKERS

J IMMY AND DAVE enter the Breakers Hotel. Trevor sits at the front desk, watching them approach. His knees start to shake as he recognizes them from the bathroom in the club the other night. He doesn't know if he should run and hide or what. What could they want with him? Jimmy and Dave are standing right in front of Trevor now.

"Can I help you?" Trevor asks with a quiver in his voice.

"We would like to speak to the manager," Jimmy says, looking at Trevor with a strange look, noticing how nervous he is. Finally, he recognizes him from the club.

"No worries, we are not after you."

"Good to know," says Trevor. "I will page Mr. Riley."

Trevor picks up the phone and steps away.

Jimmy looks at Dave, smiling.

"That guy almost shit a brick when he saw us coming."

Dave just laughs and looks away.

"Mr. Riley will be right with you. Please have a seat in the lobby," Trevor says as he points over to the very elegant and expansive lobby area. Jimmy walks to a plush sofa and takes a seat. Dave sits in a chair across from him. Soon they are greeted by Mr. Riley.

"What can I do for you?" Jimmy is surprised to see that he is six-foot-five at least with a rather impressive build, just not what he was expecting for a hotel manager.

"Yes, sir, we are from the FBI." Jimmy discreetly slips his badge out of his pocket to show it to Riley.

"This is Special Detective Dave Watson, and I am Special Agent Jimmy Trevino."

"Nice to meet you, please step into my office."

Riley takes them past the front desk. Trevor's eyes grow wide as they approach, but they pass him by. They walk into a plush office that overlooks the tropical pool area and, beyond that, the white sandy beach and turquoise ocean.

"Your office is much nicer than mine." Jimmy smiles as he talks.

"Not too shabby, I can deal with it."

"Makes you really want to come to work every day," Dave says.

"Go ahead, sit down," says Riley. Jimmy looks around and takes a seat across from Riley's desk. Dave sits on a comfortable sofa away from the other two.

"What brings you in?"

"We are doing surveillance on a guest in your hotel who may be a girlfriend to a man most wanted by the FBI. It's not the girl we want. It is the man. It would be very helpful to us if we could access your security cameras for information on who may be meeting with her here, possibly seeing her as she goes and comes."

"I can't allow you to have open access to our security room. Normally we would only let law enforcement into our business files if a crime has been committed."

"Sir, I know this is unusual. But I assure you the person we are trying to apprehend is a huge threat to the United States, and it is my personal pledge to apprehend this man in any way possible. I am extremely dedicated to this cause and promise not to disturb your guest in any way. We will be extremely discreet."

"I could let you look at some of our past footage. Do you have the dates that you want to look at?"

Jimmy hands over a paper with dates and times they want to look at. It has Kira's name down as the registered guest. The request is in writing on FBI letterhead. They are asking access to cameras outside Kira's room. Riley reads the paper over quietly then looks up at Jimmy.

"I am only going to give you access for the dates written here and for cameras in public areas exclusively. Obviously, I do not want my guest disturbed."

"Don't worry, sir. We will be very discreet." Riley rises from the desk, walks to the door, and holds it open for the agents to pass through.

They walk through the hotel to a back room, which is the security room. The room is large and has many screens reflecting all the workings of the hotel—front entrances, back exits, every restaurant, bar, pool and every floor. Jimmy and Dave are very impressed with the sophisticated system. Riley introduces them to the security chief.

"Paul, this is Jimmy Trevino and Dave Watson from the FBI. They need to look at certain cameras and have some dates for you." Jimmy and Dave shake hands and greet Paul. Riley hands Paul the sheet with the dates, and he goes back though the footage. They are able to get close-ups on Kira being picked up and returned. Most importantly, they get a license plate on the Bentley so they can get the information on the registration.

BACK ON THE BEACH

B ACK ON THE beach, Kira is having a glorious day. She walks on the soft white sand at the beach and feels it sifting between her toes. She passes by several immense beach houses on her way. There are a couple smaller private hotels as well. As she passes one, she notices a lively crowd at a swim-up bar in the pool. She decides to get a closer look. Walking up the steps to the posh hotel, she makes note of the bright-yellow umbrellas and pool lounges. Kira blends in well in her yellow bikini. She puts down her beach towel from her bag on one of the lounges. She tosses her bag down on top of it and walks down the steps into the pool. She swims across to the bar. There is just one stool left at the bar; Kira takes it. She notices a very athletic-looking man sitting next to her. His tan skin told her he had spent a lot of time in the sun. A tennis pro or a golfer? Kira is not sure, but she thinks she has seen him before. The bartender notices Kira.

"What will it be?"

Kira says, "Mojito, please."

The man next to her says, "My favorite drink, he makes a good one." He has an Australian accent. His eyes are as blue as the ocean. Against his almost-black skin, they are mesmerizing. Kira could get lost in those eyes.

She smiles at him.

"I know I have seen you before."

"Really? Do you follow golf?"

"Not that much. Why, are you a player?"

"Right, I am on the pro circuit. I am Garry Nelson. I have played in many televised games, so you might recognize me from that."

"I am sure that is it. My name is Kira." He smiles a great, devilish grin; his perfect white teeth stand out even more with his tan. She is served her mojito, and she takes a sip while admiring Mr. Golf's powerful pecs and ripped stomach.

Kira knows in the back of her mind, she could be running into trouble here. She has plenty of trouble to deal with right now.

"You from around here?" His Australian accent is so alluring.

"No, I am a California girl."

"I love California. Played at the Riviera Country Club recently. Do you ever get over there?"

"Yes, I have been to the Riviera. You are from Australia, no doubt."

"My Aussie accent gave me away. Yes, but I spend a lot of time in the States. Are you in Florida on vacation?"

"Yes, staying at the Breakers." Kira sips on her drink and looks into his eyes.

"I only have a couple more days here before I move on with the PGA. Next game at the Barclays in New Jersey."

"Too bad you have to leave so soon. It would be nice to get to know you."

"Yes, it would be." He smiles again, his blue eyes lighting up even more. Kira looks into his eyes and thinks she sees the sky and the stars.

Kira is finishing her drink.

She turns to her new friend and says, "So nice to have met you. Good luck in that tournament."

"Kira, what is your last name?" Kira reply's "Michaels."

"Kira Michaels, I will look you up when I am in California."

"Nice." She smiles and thinks as she walks away that he is a true born winner. He could be in the top ten in her playbook, maybe even the top three. Kira steps down from the stool and swims back to the steps, getting out of the pool. Her hot golfer friend watches her as she gets out. She picks up her towel and her bag and makes her way down the beach to the Breakers. The sand is getting hot as she reaches the beach behind the hotel. She puts her towel down on the sand and runs to take a dip in the ocean.

She enters the water, and a wave flips up on her. The water is soft and warm. It feels like swimming in the bathtub. It is so nice, she goes in up to her waist. She dips down to wet her entire body. Kira gets pulled along by the current and dreams of floating away, never to return to this life, letting the ocean completely wash away all of her cares and worries of the future. She would go wherever the currents take her. What was going to become of her and Justin? Where would their relationship lead? Is she slipping into dangerous waters? Is she in over her head? The thoughts swell in her head and roll out of her eyes in tears. She has so many questions but still no real answers. She must continue forward, watching her steps as she goes.

BACK TO THE BREAKERS

A T THAT KIRA comes out of her daydream and out of the surf. She picks up her towel off the beach and climbs the stairs up to the Breakers pool deck.

Jimmy is still sitting at the security desk, watching through the cameras. They catch sight of Kira on the pool deck. Jimmy asks to zoom in on the girl in the yellow bikini.

The camera gets a perfect shot of Kira up close to her face and breast, her cleavage wet and slick from the ocean. Her skin looks gorgeous and bronzed now from her walk on the beach. Jimmy gets shock waves through his core. Kira still affects him. There is just no denying it. Dave looks over to Jimmy.

"Maybe we should get moving along." He thinks it is best they get out of there before Kira knows they have her in their sights.

"Yeah, we should move on. Thanks for all your help," Jimmy says to the security guard as they get up to leave.

"Glad that we could help," the security guard assures him.

Jimmy and Dave head quickly though the lobby as they are heading toward the door.

Kira is entering the lobby at the same time. She passes right by without noticing them. Sitting at the front desk, Trevor sees Kira. He feels he must warn her, and he needs an explanation as to what is going on. He hesitates as he does not want the FBI to see him move toward Kira. He waits for them to pass him before he runs after her.

Kira hears the footsteps running fast on her heels and turns to see Trevor. Just beyond Trevor, she sees the backs of Jimmy and Dave exiting the hotel. They are completely out of the door when she notices the fear on Trevor's face. He looks white, his color all drained away. It has been a rough couple of days for Trevor since he got shaken down at the club.

"What's wrong? What is going on?" Kira says, seeing his disturbed look.

"I have to talk to you. It is really important."

"Can it wait? I just popped out of the ocean. I need a shower."

"Right, I am working now, but I am off at three. Can we meet for coffee?"

"Sure, how about the café on the roof?"

"No, it can't be in the hotel." Kira looks surprised when she notes the urgency in Trevor's voice; he knows something.

"All right, where then?"

"There is a Starbucks at the corner. Meet me over there, about three fifteen."

"Sure." Kira's heart drops as she walks away. She knows that drama is about to ensue her. She could see it in Trevor's eyes. There is a story there; she is about to get hit with it.

She contemplates what must have happened with Trevor. She knows Jimmy and Dave were involved since they were leaving the hotel. Did they reveal Kira's true identity? They couldn't have; they are sworn and under oath. How could they be doing this to her? Kira's mind is in a swirl of tangling thoughts. She almost does not remember how she gets back to her hotel room. Once inside she takes a seat on the balcony overlooking the ocean to contemplate further what to do about her daunting situation.

Her thoughts of drifting away in the ocean seem so valid to her now. How much easier would that be? Is this really the life that she chooses to live? Or has she been set out on a treadmill that she is tethered to? This path she has chosen was supposed to be leading to her transformation, resurrection and the control of her own life. Instead, she is feeling trapped by her circumstances. She needs to make some changes, like moving your king around on a chessboard, only she is a queen who is feeling more like a pawn.

TWO GEORGES

J USTIN SITS WITH Matt and Tony at the Two Georges restaurant on the ocean front. The restaurant is a replica of an Irish Pub. Red leather booths and black floors reflect the lights on the floor-to-ceiling bar. They have a great scotch collection, but Justin and the guys are enjoying the microbrewed beers the restaurant is famous for. The guys sit hunched over the table in intense conversation.

"I have done a background check on Kira Koch. First thing you need to know, there is no Kira Koch. The Koch family heirs are all well documented, and none of them are named Kira. There is nothing on Google, Facebook, or any public record anywhere with someone with that name. So clearly she is not who she claims to be." Matt is adamant in his assessment."

"So who is she?" Tony throws in.

"How do you know she is not an illegitimate child of one of them? There could be a feasible explanation for her not showing up in their family archives." Justin is trying to stay positive.

"Not showing up in any public records, though."

"The whole thing about you being shot at that first night you met her. None of that has settled right with me. Could she be working for Ullah Kahn? It's all too convenient," Matt rattles on.

"That doesn't make sense. Why would Ullah Kahn send a woman to infiltrate me the same night he sends a hit man to kill me? It's crazy. It just doesn't add up."

"The fact is she is lying about who she is, why?"

"I think it is much more likely that she just is some woman out for adventure and just wants to get laid anonymously. Probably married so she is lying about who she is."

"I think you can't be too sure about that. I think we need to find out more about her. There is that part about you being followed by the FBI too. What about that?"

"That is crazy. The FBI would know about me anyway. I am a weapons dealer. I am watched by law enforcement night and day. We need to disconnect me with Ullah Kahn. We need a reputable company that can vouch for me saying we made the shipment to them, you guys get me that. Don't worry about Kira. Get that off your minds. She is just a hot piece of ass. I can take care of her."

"I'll get on that boss," Tony says.

Matt does not want to back down. He has got a gut feeling about this, and he is sticking with it.

"Still find out what her real name is. Ask some questions."

"The fuck am I going to say? 'Look, you lying bitch, what's your real name'? That is really going to mess with my game."

"Isn't there some way though the hotel that we can check what name she is registered as?" Tony throws in.

"Look in her handbag for some ID when she is not looking," Matt says.

"What kind of pussy goes looking though a ladies' handbag? You are kidding me, right?"

"I am just saying we need to turn over every stone. We need to know more."

"This is a waste of my time. I am tired of talking about it. You two get productive and get me the lead on a legitimate company we shipped those guns to. Get it ASAP."

Justin stands up, chugs the last of his brew, and walks out.

As he walks to his car, his mind drifts to Kira. Who is she really?

WEST PALM BEACH BOARDWALK

KIRA WALKS UP to the Starbucks. The street is busy with traffic. Kids whiz by her on skateboards, pushing her out toward the curb. She is in white cotton sundress; she will be meeting with Justin later and is dressed to seduce, as is always the case with Kira. She spots Trevor sitting at a sidewalk table. He already has ordered her a latte and has it waiting. She takes a seat across from him. Taking the latte in her hands, she says "Thank you" to Trevor.

He smiles briefly at her, then his expression changes to distressed.

"What is wrong? You seem so tense," Kira says, knowing full well that Trevor has seen something to rouse his suspicions.

"I was accosted by two FBI guys at a club last night. They friggin' held a gun to my head. I thought they were going to kill me. They wanted your phone."

Kira looks surprised. She had no idea about the shakedown. *Jimmy must be getting desperate*, she thinks.

"What the hell? Did you give it to them?"

"Yes, but they gave it right back."

"So you slipped it back under my door."

"Right. What is going on? What are you into? Why involve me with this?"

"First of all, I had no intention of drawing you into anything. I needed to ditch the phone. That is how they track me. There is no way I could have known that the FBI would do that to you."

"Why are they after you? What have you done?"

"It is complicated. I have been seeing a person that is on the FBI's watch list. They think if they track my every move, they will know what he is doing."

"It seems like there is more than that. They were at the Breakers today. They had a meeting with the manager. I saw them go to the security room. They were there for a long time. Are you sure it is not you they want?"

"I said it is complicated."

"That's it? It is complicated? That is all you have to say to me after I almost got killed for having your cell phone?"

"I said I am sorry. What do you think? I told them to do that? I had no idea!"

"But there has to be more to it. Why are you seeing someone who is so dangerous, he is wanted by the FBI? I mean, my god, you seem so bright to me. That is just stupid to put yourself in danger, for what? There are so many guys out there that would want you. Why choose a criminal?"

"There is so much that I am just not at liberty to say. I promise never to involve you again. That was a senseless mistake on my part."

"All I am saying is, walk away, leave this guy. A guy like that is going to get you killed."

"I am well aware of the consequences. I am up to the task. Don't worry about me."

"So I am right, there is more about you. There is history there. I see it in your eyes."

"You are just seeing your own reflection in my eyes. My history is sealed in stone. I have to go."

"Right, well, see you around. Just remember what I told you, no dude is worth dying for."

Kira finishes her coffee and gets up from the table. She starts walking back toward the Breakers, leaving Trevor at Starbucks. She really did not have to leave, but he was getting too intense. She is not about to give up her story to anyone. The last person she did that for is now dead.

Kira pulls out the ominous cell phone, and just to shake things up more, she calls Justin on it.

Kira's picture appears on his phone as it starts ringing. He sees her and picks up.

"Hey, gorgeous. I was just thinking of you."

"Good thoughts, right?"

"Hot, steamy, arousing thoughts. Getting hard just thinking of you."

"Where are you now?"

"Outside Two Georges."

Just then Jimmy gets a signal Kira is on her phone. They have a tap on it. Jimmy signals Dave, and they listen in.

"Who were you meeting there?"

"Matt and Tony."

"Those two thugs? You should lose those two."

"They work for me. They are some of the best intelligence guys out there. Plus, they know too much about me. If I let them go, I would have to kill them," Justin says, and then he laughs.

Jimmy is getting all of this recorded; Kira prods him on.

"You could do better on your own."

"They know important people, though, the ones I need to get to."

"You could get to them yourself just as easily."

"Right, but then when would I have time for you?"

"Who are these people you want them to find?" Kira asks the leading question. Then Justin hesitates; sensing she is leading him, he changes the subject.

"Why are we talking on the phone? Let's meet. You are planning to be with me this evening, aren't you?"

"Of course."

"Meet me at the marina. Let's take the boat out for a sunset sail around the bay."

"Sounds good."

"See you in twenty then."

Kira hangs up her phone. She walks back to the breakers and hails a cab at the valet's desk.

Jimmy is confused as to why Kira picked the phone back up and made such a specific phone call. He knows Kira all too well; she is up to something. He will soon find out, like it or not.

Kira makes her way to the marina in the cab; she stares out of the back-passenger window. The sun is starting to set, and the sky takes on a pink glow. Big clouds turning to the blush of an angel and then almost to crimson in places. The sky tries to compete with their beauty, poking through crystal blue where it can. Kira thinks, red sky at night, sailor's delight. But there is something more sinister about this sky and this shade of crimson. Almost like blood, it is a sailors warning. There are sharks in the water, tasting the blood as the sky bleeds into it.

The cab reaches the Marina. Kira tells the driver to pull into the parking space next to Justin's Porsche. She pays the driver and he leaves her there. Justin is already aboard the *Stairway to Heaven*, untying the sails and getting ready to go out on the ocean. He stops to watch Kira walk toward the vessel. He reaches out a hand to help her in. Then he playfully puts his hands up the back of her dress, pulling her up by the buttocks. Kira giggles and wraps her legs around Justin, and they have a soft, deep kiss. He breaks away and sets her to the ground.

"I missed you," says Kira.

"Missed you too."

Justin unties the ship and starts the engine. He gets behind the wheel of the sailboat, and they start to taxi out of the slip through the marina, passing others as they go. Kira goes below deck and comes back with a bottle of wine and two glasses. She pours the glasses full of wine and hands one to Justin; he sips it as they move out to the open sea.

The sun is setting lower now, almost looking as if it is falling into the ocean. The light reflects on the water with a blinding light cutting through, Kira thinks when it finally reaches the water it will boil the ocean.

Kira lets her head hang over the side of the boat as Justin turns it onto its side as he lifts the sail. He a good sailor, handling the boat with such precision.

They sail off into the sunset, literally. Once out to the open sea, Justin ties the wheel and comes to sit next to Kira.

He sips his wine and looks out to the ocean, putting his arm around Kira. He looks over at her and bites her gently on the ear then kisses her neck, looking into her eyes now.

"So what is it like to grow up as a Koch?" Justin says as he fondles her hand.

He looks over at Kira, and she instantly sees the doubt in his eyes. The tone of his voice tells her; she better have a plausible story. Kira takes a deep breath and begins the fabricated tale.

"My mother was divorced from my father since I was a baby. I was very removed from the Koch lifestyle. I really rarely saw my father, except on certain holidays. Then my mother moved to the West Coast with me. I hardly saw him at all. He paid child support and my college. That is what I know about him, just some distant memories." She pauses, considering that the story is true; that was her life. Only the name had been changed.

"Where did you go to college?"

"We were living in Brentwood in a condo really close to UCLA, so I went there. I was very removed from school, though. I did not live on campus or join a sorority."

"What did you take?"

"Believe it or not, criminal justice." As this comes out of her mouth, Kira realizes that what she said is too close to the bone. Her face turns as crimson as the sunset. Justin notices. Kira thinks, how stupid of her. She should have gone in another direction. The silence that follows is awkward. Then Kira follows that with "Right, I was thinking of being an attorney, criminal law. I soon changed, though, to a theater arts major."

"That is very different. It seems more like you, though. You are clearly an actress." He says this and looks deep into her eyes as if to say he knows she is lying. Kira looks back at Justin, deadpan. Checking for his reaction, he looks away.

An actress? She thinks he is onto something. Was that meant to be snide? She is not sure but tries to change the subject.

"I really did not like school. I would rather learn from life experience."

"So when did you change your name?"

"What do you mean?"

"Well, you are not Kira Koch anymore. You signed into the hotel as Kira Michaels. When did you change your name?"

Flustered now, knowing Justin has checked up on her and has suspicions, Kira answers, "My mother remarried, and I took on her new married name. It was just easier for schools and all to try and explain we were just one happy family."

"Makes sense, right? Who would want to be a Koch?" Justin is sarcastic. Kira is nervous with his line of questioning. She is better than this, though; she is trained to control. She has to get a hold on her trepidations.

"Actually, you are right. I did not want to be a Koch. I was not really part of the family. My father, William Koch, was the black sheep of the family. After the divorce, my mother was a complete outcast to the family. So I actually wanted to have a real family, which I found when my mother remarried. A name is not really everything. Family comes from the heart. I wanted a real family."

Justin smirks or smiles; Kira is not sure which.

Justin knows it is a really good performance. Still he is thinking, *Who is Kira really?*

He takes a big gulp of his wine and pours more into his glass. Kira thinks he seems to be satisfied with her answer.

Eager to move away from the line of questioning, Kira moves in for a deep, hot kiss. Justin takes the lead over and lays Kira down on the cushioned seat, spilling her wine over the side and dropping her glass in the ocean. In the back of her mind, she fears that is where she will end up.

Justin pulls up her white cotton dress and reveals her tiny white lace panties with her vagina showing though. Justin circles his hand over the panties, feeling the moistness of her vagina. That is all it takes to get him hard. Kira sees his penis bulging though his nautical shorts. She wants him, danger or not.

Justin rips her panties down. Then he slips her straps off her shoulders, revealing her perfect breasts. The sun is setting lower, and the pink glow seems to take over her body. Her passion starts flowing over her in waves like the ocean. Justin opens his mouth wide and takes her breast almost completely in his mouth, circling her nipple with his tongue.

Kira is moaning and withering under Justin's bravado. Justin reaches down to caress her vagina, which is now dripping wet. This makes him even harder. Feeling he may tear though his shorts, Justin unzips his shorts, taking out his huge penis. Kira reaches down to stroke his swollen member, noticing how hard it is but how soft the outer skin is. She strokes it until she can feel a small oozing of fluid. Instead of stroking it more, she grabs him by the testicles and thrusts his penis inside of her.

Justin goes in deep, killing the yearning inside of Kira's vagina, spreading it so far open, she gasps in deep, lustful ecstasy. He drives deeper and deeper still, causing Kira to grab his butt cheeks, pulling him even deeper inside her.

Justin is on his knees while Kira is perched on the sailboat bench, her legs spread well apart. Justin, lost in his fervor, pounds into Kira with his penis. Kira is screaming out and looks into Justin's eyes to see if it is passion or anger that fuels him. His eyes are glassed over in euphoria. She knows he is intoxicated and lost in the passion.

Kira starts to move her vagina in circular motions to meet Justin's fervor. Justin gasps and grabs Kira by the butt cheeks, and with a deep final thrust, he empties a full load of semen in her wanton vagina. Kira pulls him out and finishes the last drops in her mouth, sucking and swallowing it down.

A huge yacht in the distance blows its horn. Kira and Justin look over to see it is passing by.

Uncaring of the passing vessel, Justin kisses Kira deeply as he pulls up his pants. Kira lets her legs down and takes a huge gulp of Justin's wine, washing it all down.

The sun has fully set, and an evening breeze blows over them in a welcomed relief from the intensity and the heat between the two.

Justin runs his fingers though his hair, lifting it off his face. It is wet with sweat but is drying in the cool night breezes. Kira stands up and pulls her straps back on, smoothing out her dress.

Justin unties the wheel and takes back over at the helm.

Kira's passions has been satisfied. But have Justin's questions been answered? Kira fears there is more to come. She needs an exit plan.

She is usually in control, but she has let the situation get out of hand, fueled by passion. She needs to get her wits about her.

Justin turns the sail, and they are headed back to port.

Apartment on the Ocean

T ONY AND MATT share an apartment overlooking the harbor. This night they are working diligently on Justin's case. They are on a mission, and Justin is their only client. They have to come through for him; he pays them well. They are both mystified by Kira and, at the same time, leery of who she is.

The room is dark, lit only by one illuminated computer screen. It has been particularly hot and humid the last few days. They have all the windows open and fans blowing to cool them off. Even that is not enough to make a dent in the hot, steamy Florida weather.

This night, Matt and Tony ruminate about Kira. Tony is fast at work on his computer as they try and find out as much as possible on Kira.

"What the fuck did he say her name was that she gave to the hotel?" said Tony, punching away at the computer.

"Kira Michaels," says Matt, and Tony types it in.

"She is not on Facebook, LinkedIn, or Instagram. It's like she does not exist."

"Come on, not everyone is on social media. Look for jobs. Look for schools," Matt continues. Tony is googling madly. He goes to Images in her name, and nothing that resembles Kira comes up. Tony is exasperated.

"The answer is Kira Michaels is not her name. That is the only explanation," Tony reasons. "We have got to get to her real name, but how?"

"There is a search engine called Face Search. You can access photos of people under any given name. You can look through the photos to see what names are associated with that face. Go to that. Check it out," Matt says and then moves to look over Tony's shoulder at the computer screen.

Tony goes on the search engine and puts in Kira Michaels's name. Immediately pictures of several girls come up matching that name. Finally, they find a picture of Kira associated with Kira Michaels. It came up on a IMDb file; she apparently keeps a profile on the website to help her get acting jobs.

As they go through a dozen photos, something turns up.

"Wait a minute, stop, back up. Isn't that Kira?" says Matt.

Tony, still going through the pictures, had passed up one that Matt recognizes as a much younger Kira.

Tony points to the picture of the girl in the photo, and the name Kira Daniels comes up. "Oh my god! It is her. She is really young here!

"Quick, google up Kira Daniels. See what we find."

Tony is fast on the draw and quickly goes to Google and types in Kira Daniels.

This brings up the very picture they just spotted. Clicking on the picture, they find an article associated with that picture.

It is a graduation photo from Dartmouth University, and it highlights Kira as graduating at the top of her class in psychology. The article goes on to say she will pursue a career in law enforcement.

"Son of a bitch. Do you see that? What is she? A fucking cop?" says Tony.

"Goddamn it, I knew something was up. But going to Dartmouth and then becoming a cop? That is a rich-bitch school. She has to be rich and fucking brilliant to graduate at a top of a class there. Something tells me she wasn't a street cop."

"This has to prove to Justin that she is not who she says she is. I will send this over to him so that he can see it for himself."

Tony emails the picture and the article to Justin. He writes, "Check out this picture. I think you know this girl. But you really don't know this girl. Call us in the morning."

He sends the email feeling satisfied that Matt and Tony's suspicions were correct. It is actually more than a coincidence that Justin met Kira.

The *Stairway to Heaven* pulls into dock at Justin's slip. The water has gotten choppy, and it is difficult for Justin to navigate the vessel into the slip. He gets it in and the boat is rocking hard. He helps Kira out of the boat and she is glad to get onto dry land.

She thinks about California and how she misses the cool night air in Santa Barbara. Maybe this trip was a mistake; she hasn't met her goal. She knows she has allowed her emotions to overrule her mind. Now she will have to choose, will it be her heart or her head? It is a question that is futile; the heart usually always wins this one.

Justin puts a cover on the exposed portion of the boat and snaps it to be secure, the boat seeming to fight him in the rocking motions. He finishes his task, and he takes Kira by the hand. They get into the Porsche and drive away.

Sitting in the parking lot are Jimmy and Dave. They have recorded exactly where Kira and Justin have been by the tracking device on the boat. They are watching to see if anyone else is watching or approaching Justin.

Jimmy gets a familiar pain in his heart, watching Kira drive away with Justin. Just knowing that he is having her is eating away at him. There is no one in the world right now that Jimmy would want to bust more than Justin. He is dying for the right break in this case, like a dog for a juicy steak that he just can't get to. He can almost taste the bitterness he feels. How sweet will it be when he gets to bust Justin Hamilton? He can almost taste that too.

MANSION AT THE PRIMAVERA ESTATES

THE SUN RISES on the ocean the next morning. Kira cannot sleep and has had a restless night sleeping with Justin. He tossed and turned, keeping her awake. Kira thinks the lost shipment to Ullah Kahn is really getting to him. She stops trying to sleep and gets up to see the sunrise.

She goes into the kitchen and makes a cup of tea to take with her, stepping out onto the patio and on the garden path to the lounge chairs overlooking the ocean.

The sky is moody with dark-purple and gray clouds blocking the sun. Is it a sign of autumn approaching? Or a sign of dark days to come? Maybe a night of no sleep is tainting her brain. Her intuition has always been the one thing she can always rely on. It has kept her alive through the most perilous times. The dark is creeping up on her again.

The sun breaks through the clouds, lighting up the ocean. The wind comes up, and the palms wave briskly, making crackling noises all around her. The chill makes her walk back to the house. This time she walks back into the house though the french doors to Justin's room.

She finds Justin sitting up in bed with his laptop open. He is going through his emails. Kira walks in, and he does not look up.

"You are awake early," Kira says.

Justin does not answer, seeming very intense about his emails. Kira goes to the bathroom and shuts the door.

Justin has read the email from Tony; his blood is boiling. He knows now Kira has lied from the first day he met her. He has been betrayed and, worse, defrauded by a deceitful bitch, smiling in his face, ready to put a knife in his back. He knows at least to look out for his enemy Ullah Kahn. Never knowing someone worse was in his house and sleeping in his bed.

Quickly Justin emails back to Tony: "Find out more. She told me she went to UCLA and studied criminal justice. Check UCLA for any records. Check for more aliases, and meet me at the house."

Justin pushes the bathroom door open with such strength that it punctures the wall as it bursts open.

"WHO THE HELL ARE YOU?" he screams in Kira's face.

Kira turns to face him from the sink and falls back on it in shock.

Streams of terror are going through her. She wasn't expecting this, not today. Kira takes some slow, deep breaths, staring at Justin, thinking of her next move.

"I said I am Kira. That is the truth."

"Who are you really, and what are you trying to do to me?"

"I am not trying to do anything to you. If I was, I would have already done it. Believe me. Don't try me. I am capable of so much more than you can ever expect."

"You don't scare me, you filthy lying bitch. You don't have to tell me who you are. I will find out. You just met your match."

Justin grabs her purse, takes out her cell phone, and stomps on it, breaking it to pieces on the bathroom floor. He throws the pieces in the toilet and flushes them down.

Kira stands stunned, watching him.

"There it goes, bitch. No way to reach your FBI buddies now."

"What are you talking about?"

"You know what I am talking about. I found the device they put on my boat last night. There will be no way they are going to be able to reach you now."

Justin rips though her purse, throwing all her things out on the bathroom floor. Lipsticks and compacts go crashing to the floor, breaking into shards of plastic and glass. When her wallet spills, he picks it up and rummages through, looking for ID. He finds her driver's license and takes it out. He reads that it says Kira Michaels.

"I'll take this too. You won't be needing it." He slips the license into his pocket. He looks into her money pocket, finds six hundred, and takes that too.

Kira is shaking and terrified now. He has an arsenal of loaded weapons in the house, and she is now his worst hated enemy.

James comes into the room, hearing the fracas. He sees into the bathroom from the open door, looking at the debris on the floor, and knows there is a problem.

"Everything all right?"

Justin storms out of the bedroom and goes to a drawer, opens it, and takes out a loaded pistol; he hands it to James.

"Take this and make sure you keep a watch on Kira. Make sure she does not leave. It's like a baby-sitting job, except if this baby gets out of the crib, you shoot it."

James takes the gun and looks over at Kira.

The doorbell rings; Justin goes to the door. Matt and Tony have arrived, and they all go into Justin's office and close the door. Kira looks at James holding the gun.

She stands speechless for a moment. She focuses on the wreckage on the floor and bends down to see what she can salvage. She starts throwing the ruined pieces in the trash. James sits down in a chair in the bedroom, where he can still see Kira. When Kira is done cleaning the mess, she steps out of the bathroom, looking at James.

"Would it be all right if I took a bath?"

James steps back into the bathroom to check it out. He looks at the windows and decides it is secure enough.

"Go ahead, but don't lock the door." He steps out of the bath, and Kira closes the door and turns on the bath water.

Still shaking from the startling blow, Kira strips down and gets into the warm bath. Sinking down into it, she feels this may be her last. She was so unprepared for this. She has never let her guard down this much. Her thoughts stray to the thought of what it would be like to just slip down under the water and just breath it in, letting the water fill her lungs and just float away to her death in the warmth of the bath. So much better than the violent death she is sure to meet at the hands of Matt and Tony, Justin's thugs.

Moments Later, Justin's Office

I N JUSTIN'S OFFICE, Tony and Matt are going over how to handle Kira.

"We know she went to Dartmouth University, not UCLA as she said. Graduated at the top of her class with a degree in psychology. She has to be a fucking genius to graduate with honors from that school. She apparently went from school to police work in some fashion. We can't find out much about that," Tony is telling Justin after his investigation.

"I found a tracking device planted on the *Stairway to Heaven*. I am sure the FBI followed us there," Justin adds, now relinquishing to them that their suspicions are most likely true.

"There is definitely a connection. I knew that the first night you met her. Just too convenient that the FBI were there too. Strange coincidence an assassin catches up to you in the same night," Matt throws in.

"I took away her cell phone and destroyed it in case that is the way they are tracking her," Justin shares with his tribe.

"She's got a lot of aliases—Kira Daniels, Kira Michaels, Kim Daniels, Kim Matthews. She has been a busy girl. But why?" says Matt.

"She could be a double spy; did you think of that? She might actually be working for Ullah Kahn. She could be a 'honey pot.' That is what they call the female spy they get to seduce the men so that they get the inside information," Tony explains.

"That does make sense," Justin says, feeling good that he is finally seeing the light.

"What do we do with her now? We can't just kill her. They are no doubt wanting her back," Matt reasons.

"We have to hold her captive. That way we can use her as leverage. We make a deal, you let us go, we give you the girl back. If we kill her, we have got nothing. This is how we will find which side she is on." Justin has come up with a plan.

"So we have to hide her, but where?"

"We take her to the warehouse. It is secured like Fort Knox. There is a room with a bathroom and beds. No one can get in, she can't get out."

Justin disagrees, "That is the first place they would look. It is so obvious. They all know where the warehouse is. Take her to the harbor house with you two. That way one of you can always stay home and watch her."

"No way, she will hear all our conversations. She is going to know our every move." Matt does not want her in his personal space.

Tony goes back to the warehouse idea. "The warehouse is perfect. It has cameras everywhere. We can watch her every move, and she will not have any idea what we are doing. Come on with twenty-foot gates and barbed wire. No one is going in, no one is going out. Simple perfection."

"All right, I am going with Tony on the warehouse—at least just temporarily, until we know more about who she is."

"That's a plan then."

Justin says, "I am going to let you guys take her without me. They will be watching if I am the one driving her."

With that they open the door to the office and go in to get Kira.

Justin throws open the door in the bedroom, startling James.

"Where is she?"

"In the bath," says James.

Justin throws open the bathroom door, and Kira is aghast.

"Get out of the tub, Princess. You are going to take a ride."

Kira is terrified, but she stands up, gets out of the tub, grabs a towel, and wraps herself up.

Justin turns to the guys.

"Go ahead, take a break. I will bring her out to you."

James, Matt, and Tony clear the room. Kira finishes drying herself off. Still wrapped in the towel, she walks into the bedroom where Justin sits.

She lets her towel fall. She walks slowly past him to the closet to get her clothes. She puts on some panties and turns around to see Justin standing over her.

He grabs her by the face and looks deep into her eyes.

"Why don't you just tell me who you are and spare me from finding you out and then having to kill you? The truth may set you free."

"In this case, it won't," says Kira, deadpan.

Justin lets go of her face and lets his hand slide down her breast slowly down her thigh, looking deep into her eyes.

"Fine, we will do it the hard way. It won't be pretty."

"I like it hard." Kira is unwavering.

He walks away and goes and lies on the bed as Kira finishes dressing.

She walks into the room wearing the white cotton dress from the night before, thinking how crazy it is that just yesterday they were making passionate love on a sailboat. Now they have nothing but disdain for one another. How can love turn into hate and hate into despise in a matter of hours? It is unimaginable but true.

"You will go with Matt and Tony."

"Are they going to take me to the hotel to get my things?"

"That's insane. Of course not. You won't be needing your things where you are going."

"They will notice I haven't checked out. You know they will come looking for you. We have been seen everywhere together."

"So let them come. I will be ready for them."

Kira picks up her bag. Justin opens the door to the bedroom and pushes her along. Matt and Tony are sitting in the living room. They stand up and walk to the garage door. They step out into the garage, getting into a Mercedes with blacked-out windows. Tony climbs behind the wheel, and Matt gets into the passenger seat. Justin has a firm grip on Kira's arm, and he pulls her to the car. He opens the backseat door to the car and sits Kira inside, pushing her head down.

"Keep your head down."

"That's not going to work. We need to blindfold and cuff her. Remember, she is trained."

"Right," Justin says and goes back into the house. He comes back minutes later with handcuffs and a handkerchief. He gets Kira back out of the car, turns her around, and cuffs her, locking them tight on her wrist behind her back. He then ties a handkerchief over her eyes and pushes her back down, face-first on the backseat of the car. He slams the door.

"Come right back after you are done," Justin tells Matt and Tony.

Tony starts the car, and they are in motion. Kira's breath is forming moisture on the seat, making her face wet. She turns her face so that she can breathe. Her arms ache from the pain of being in this position. It is not nearly as bad as the pain in her heart, the knife from Justin slowly twisting through her heart. The intensity of the pain going through her core makes the pain in her arms feel like respite. She really loved Justin; how could he do this to her?

Kira tries to pull her attention away from her pain to her currently desperate situation. Her efforts are futile, her mind and heart struggling against one another.

The car ride goes on for what seems like forever. Every stop, every turn, every breath she takes she fears may be her last.

Kira finally breaks down and cries—not the fearful tears, the gut-wrenching tears. The deep ones will come out of your soul and rip through your body before they explode out of your eyes. The tears that take your breath away like someone has socked you in the stomach.

She cries this way not just for herself and the position she is in. It is because of all of the times she forgot to cry, for her mother she never sees, the family she does not have, and Tanya who is dead and gone, the life she once had in the FBI and the friendships left behind, the heartbreak of Justin, the utter loneliness in her life, the piece of light she thought she found in Justin.

It is all flowing out in her tears.

Matt turns on the radio and blasts some music to drown out the sobs.

The paradox of the music playing in contrast to the pain in her core is the extreme she never knew could happen.

"Clap your hands if you feel like a room without a roof, because I am happy."

The car comes to a final stop. There is total darkness. The car door opens. Matt pulls her to her feet. They are in a garage; she can feel it. She can smell the fumes from cars and gasoline. There is must and mold in the air. They are close to the ocean in an old building; her senses are heightening.

Matt pulls her by the arm through a door; lights are turned on. Matt pulls the blindfold from her eyes. She can barely see from the light glaring in her eyes. Kira squints as they pull her into a room. They sit her down on a chair. Kira looks around the room that is all white and sterile, just a bed a TV and four blank walls.

"You can uncuff her now," Tony says to Matt.

"It's more fun this way," says Matt, smiling an evil smile at Kira, looking at her like he would like to take her clothes off and thinking he should give it to her good.

"No, you aren't." Tony says back to Matt, reading his mind.

"Why not have a little fun?"

"Forget it, Matt. It's not going to happen."

Kira starts to think of what to do if he approaches her to try and rape her. She has a sinking feeling in her stomach. She is afraid of what they may do to her if she kicks their ass, which she is totally prepared to do.

Tony says, "Give me the keys!" to Matt, who reaches in his pocket and tosses the keys over to Tony.

"You are no fun," Matt says to Tony.

"This is a job, not a playground.

Tony goes behind her and unlocks the cuffs. Kira gets her wrist free and rubs her wrist with her hands, trying to rub the pain away.

"This is where you are going to stay," Tony says to Kira.

"There is no way out, so don't even try. There are twenty-foot fences with barbed wire. The whole place is videotaped, and we are at the other end of the cameras. You have got a bed, bathroom, TV. There is a kitchenette. He shows her in the closet. There is a mini refrigerator, a sink, some water, and some food.

"We will bring in more food. So make yourself at home."

"What is going on? What are you planning to do with me?"

"Using you for bait," says Tony.

"Shark bait," Matt chimes in.

This makes Kira thinks they are planning to throw her from the sailboat out in the deep ocean.

"We are not going to share details with you. We will be back," Tony replies.

"Can I ask you for something?"

"What?"

"Bring me back some cigarettes? I need something to do, sitting here all alone."

"What kind do you like?"

"Virginia Slims, menthol."

"Fine, I'll get you some."

"I need some jeans and some socks. It's cold in here."

"I'll look around. I'll see what I can find."

They walk out the door. Kira hears the locks bolt as they lock her in. She is in a cell, like so many criminals she has put away.

THE HAMPTON INN

J IMMY LEANS BACK in his chair at the hotel, a cup of coffee on
the table in front of him, his cell phone right next to it. Staring out
of the window, pondering his current circumstances, Dave is at the
computer and quickly grabs up his cell phone, looking at it in shock.

"What is it?" Jimmy responds

"We lost Kira," Dave answers. Jimmy vaults up out of the chair.

"What the hell? She just started making contact with us again."
Dave looks alarmed. "This is not good, and the signal has been
completely destroyed. Either Kira did it, or it was done to her by
Hamilton or his group."

"We need to check in at the Breakers, find out the last time she
was in," Jimmy says as he simultaneously picks up his cell and puts it
in his back pocket. They both bolt for the door.

At the Breakers, Trevor is jolted when he sees the two FBI investigators back. He strongly fears something bad has happened to Kira,
just as he had warned her.

"What can I do for you today, gentlemen?" Trevor asks politely,
masking the fear inside.

"We need to speak to Mr. Riley."

"Of course, one minute." Trevor picks up the phone and dials.
He hangs up the phone. "He will be with you momentarily. Please
have a seat in the lobby." Jimmy and Dave walk over and take a

comfortable seat in the opulent lobby. Jimmy nervously taps his feet. Dave glances over with an annoyed look. Jimmy takes the cue and stops like a child being corrected by a parent. Riley approaches the two.

"Gentlemen, please come with me to the security room." Walking briskly toward the back of the lobby, they follow Riley.

"I know why you two are here. I have taken it upon myself to make note of Ms. Michaels's adventures. I noticed she hasn't been to her room for at least three days. The housekeepers have been in, and there are no changes. So you are looking for her?"

Jimmy quickly answers, "That is right, sir. We fear for her safety."

"Understandable. Let's check out the security tapes." The men walk in the room and greet Paul, who is watching twelve screens in the room. "Turn the cameras back to three days ago, on suite 312." Turning the cameras back, they see Kira enter the room and, speeding the footage up, see her coming back out two hours later. They focus on the outdoor valet area now and see Kira get into a yellow cab; they note the cab number, 56. Jimmy writes it down. They check back at the room for the next consecutive days and see only the housekeepers going in and out. "That is it. That's all we have got," says Riley. "I hope that helps."

"That is a great help, sir. We will be checking with the cab company," says Dave.

"Please call us ASAP if there is any activity at all, anyone comes and goes from her room, any calls to her room, anything."

"Absolutely," says Riley. Jimmy and Dave step out of the security room, walking back through the lobby to the valet area.

Trevor shudders as he sees them pass. He has frightening visions of Kira buried or hidden. He does not know which or why he thinks this.

The detectives do not look Trevor's way; clearly, they are on a mission. Once in the car, Dave calls Yellow Cab to inquire about cab number 56 and where it drove Kira to on that night. They confirm that the trip was to the Marina. They know it was on Justin's sailboat.

WEST PALM BEACH POLICE STATION

J IMMY AND DAVE walk into the police station, showing their badges at the desk, they are escorted to Captain Newhause's office. The chief greets them with a handshake, and they sit again in his cold, sterile office.

Jimmy starts with "Chief, we may need your assistance. Kira Michaels, who is with the person of interest, Justin Hamilton, has not been seen for three days. Suspicions are rising that she could have been abducted and is being held against her will."

"She could just be shacked up with Hamilton," says the chief.

"Except her cell phone that we had tracers on has been destroyed," Dave adds.

"We were in full contact with her just prior," Jimmy throws in. "That sounds bad but still not enough for a search warrant. What if I send a car over just to question him on when he saw her last? They can sniff it out if it smells bad. I will get you the warrant."

"Sounds good," says Dave. The chief makes a call to the desk, and they put out an order to go to the Primavera Estates to question Hamilton. Jimmy is anxiously waiting to see what will happen.

PRIMAVERA ESTATES

THE SQUAD CAR rolls up to the gates at the Primavera Estates. The police stop at the security gate. They are questioned by the guard. They confirm that they are going to the Hamilton house to conduct police business. The guard has to let them in. He calls ahead to let Justin know they are on their way. They park on the street outside the electric gate and walk up to the bell. Cameras face them down as the gate opens up. As they advance to the front door, the officers ring the bell. James opens the door.

"Won't you come in, Officers?" James shuffles the officers into Justin's office, where Justin is sitting at the desk. "What can I do for you, Officers?"

"I am Joe Parelli from the West Palm Beach Station. This is Officer Thomas Andrews. We are here to ask about Kira Michaels. We understand that she was dropped off by Yellow Cab at your boat Tuesday night. She has been missing for three days. Do you have any idea where she might be?" Officer Parelli passes a picture of Kira to Justin. He looks at it and raises an eyebrow.

Undeterred, he says, "We went for a sailboat ride that night. She came back to my house and spent the night. She left the next day, which would be Wednesday, and said she was going to see a friend. The strange thing is, I have tried to reach her, and she is not answering her cell phone. So I really have no idea where she is."

"Did she say who the friend was?"

"No, she was really vague. Can't imagine who she knows here. She is from California."

"She met you in a hurry."

"That she did."

"Did she leave any of her belongings behind? Something that she may be coming back for?" asks Anderson.

"None that I have seen, but you know women. They always seem to leave something behind."

Justin adds, "Mind if we have a look around?"

"Not at all, Officers," says Justin, then he asks James to show them around. They walk around the gorgeous mansion, mostly marveling at its grandeur but also making mental notes. Any blood splashes, broken windows, signs of struggle? They look with a particular interest in the bedroom. There was a hair band on the nightstand, left behind obviously by a woman. Parelli picks it up to find a long blond hair in it. He quickly slips it into his pocket for the DNA evidence. They step inside the bathroom, and one officer notes that the doorknob was crashed through the wall behind the door. Parelli looks in the trash to see the broken shards of mirrors and cosmetics left behind. He looks over to Anderson and points to the evidence. They nod to one another, seeing the signs of a struggle. Anderson lifts a lipstick from the trash container for another DNA sample. They silently step out of the bathroom. James shows them to the door. They pass by Justin's office on the way out. Officer Parelli steps in and hands Justin a card.

"Please call us if you hear from Kira."

"Absolutely, I will, no problem," says Justin. "We will be in touch if there is anything further." Parelli gives him a hard, cold look, as if he knows there will be further. He knows; some things you feel in your bones.

Just as the police are walking out to their car, Matt and Tony are driving up the drive. Matt and Tony get out of the car and exchange glances with the police before they go inside the house. They enter Justin's office, showing some concern.

"So the heat is on," says Matt.

"It certainly looks that way," Justin answers.

"She is where they will never find her," says Tony

"We have to work fast. I got a message from Ullah Kahn. They want a meeting on Skype in ten minutes. I know he will ask for a replacement shipment. We got Kira out of the way just in time. We can't have anyone in our way if we are going to pull this off. Our lives actually depend on it. We have to satisfy this guy and give him what he wants." Justin gives the directions. "There can be no fuckups this time. We will need backup guards to get the shipment through. It can't be done with just us three."

"Count me out. The police and FBI will be watching me too closely. It will be you two and maybe three others to pack up and man the ship. You will load the weapons into a rented U-Haul truck and get them to the marina. I will get a small cargo ship and have it waiting at the dock. I want you to pack the guns in unmarked cardboard boxes."

The computer is already set up to go for the meeting. Skype rings through. Justin opens it up, and the screen comes on. It is Ullah Kahn and his staff. Matt and Tony move behind Justin to appear on the screen.

Ullah Kahn starts.

"Mr. Hamilton, I am very disappointed in doing business with you. You have cost me a lot of money, lives, and lost time. I was so furious with you, I sent a hit man to kill you. But I have thought about it. I am giving you one more chance to make good on the deal. You send me the load of AKCs, the ammo, the grenades, and the explosives, and we let you live."

"Thank you, I appreciate your generosity," Justin says with a touch of sarcasm. "But what you do not seem to understand is that I had no control over the fact that the last shipment was stolen. My men were clearly outnumbered. We tried to get you the guns. I can order another ship to carry the goods, but I also need the manpower."

"I will put up the funds for a ship to carry them over. I can send some of my men to help with the transfer," Ullah Kahn replies.

"I am going to need some consideration for the guns and ammo. The fact is that the stolen guns were a loss to me as well, one that was very costly."

"We paid you sixteen million dollars and did not get our goods. I will pay you half that this time to make up for the loss. But I had better get my guns."

"I need three days to get the shipment together." Justin is adamant about this.

"I expect to have it done in three days then. I expect another meeting Sunday morning, 10:00 a.m., to be sure you are on track."

"Talk to you then." They cancel the Skype meeting. Justin looks over at Matt and Tony.

"You have to get back to the warehouse and start packing the shipment. You should wait until late so you can be under the cover of darkness."

"What about the girl?" Asks Tony.

"What about her? Obviously, she is hooked up with the FBI. Ullah did not ask about her. I would say kill her and we can drop her body at sea when we do the shipment, except the police are already on it and suspect me."

"There would be no proof, though, no body, no crime," Matt reasons.

"I say we keep her right now. We may need her in case anything happens, and we need a plea deal," Tony adds.

"That's what I am thinking. We hold off for the time being," Justin says. "I am still not sure about Kira's identity."

"She asked for some warmer clothes," Tony adds.

"Look in the guest room. We have some things the maid left."

Tony goes out to the guest room and looks though the closet and some drawers. He finds some jeans and a sweater for Kira. He packs them in a bag and goes back to the office.

"That's it. Let's get going," Tony says to Matt, and they head out of the door.

WEST PALM BEACH POLICE STATION

J IMMY AND DAVE have taken over a vacant office at the police station. They hear some commotion going on and look to see that Parelli and Anderson are back in. They go behind closed doors with the chief.

Jimmy is on edge, wondering if they found out anything about Kira. He grows tenser each second that she is not accounted for. He thinks of her in a cold, dark basement and shudders at the thought. They have got to find her alive. Their phone gets buzzed; it is the chief calling them to his office. They go to the chief's office, where Parelli and Anderson are; the doors are closed. The police chief starts.

"Parelli and Anderson found evidence of a struggle at Hamilton's house. I am going to get a search warrant for both of his properties, his house at the Primavera Estates and at his warehouse. I am sure we will turn up something. I can smell the smoke from the fire."

"We recovered this in the trash." Anderson pulls out the lipstick from the trash bin and places it on the chief's desk. "It is good for DNA. We can prove it was Kira's."

Jimmy gets chills from the thought.

Are we reducing her to just some DNA now? He wants Kira back alive. He admonishes the thought of just checking for DNA evidence; he wants the whole Kira.

The chief continues, "I want you two to be in on this. My officers will back you up."

"Thank you, Chief," Jimmy says. The team of officers sense his timorous feeling and are fueled to get Kira back more than ever.

"I will go and get the paperwork started," Anderson says and leaves the room. Jimmy and Dave go back to their makeshift office as the paperwork gets done.

KIRA AT THE WAREHOUSE

L YING ON THE bed and looking at the ceiling, Kira is angry with herself for being in this predicament. She is better than that; she is well trained and competent. She should have guarded her heart better. She let her heart fool her into something her head already knew could never be right. She curses herself for being vulnerable, tearing her soul out to have a look at what is inside, how love tricked her into twisting her fate. So what is this thing called love that can blind you with its light? Is it a hoax on the human condition? Or is it a journey worth suffering for, no matter the cost? Will she ever understand the mystery that love is? So many questions yet to be answered. What is clear is that this is the hand she has been dealt; she has no aces. With the hurt and the loss comes enlightenment. This is when Kira sees what she must do to overcome her circumstances. Even through the darkest night there comes the dawn.

Feeling an urging to draw all of her strength together, Kira hurtles off the bed. She examines the room without any windows. There is block wall all around with just one door. The door has a small window toward the top of it. Kira goes to jiggle the doorknob; the door is solid and is locked and bolted. She goes into the kitchenette area, looking through drawers. She pulls them all, open examining the contents. Forks, knives, spoons, what can she use? She finds nothing that she can make a tool with to try and pick the lock. She walks back into the bedroom and goes for the nightstand, which has a drawer. She opens it up to find some magazines, definitely not helpful. Pushing around the contents of the drawer, she finds a large paper clip and a letter opener. Kira uses her police training to do a trick known by many criminals. She straightens out the paper clip to be a wire. She goes to the door with the wire and the letter opener to try and work on the lock. Jamming the wire into the lock and working the letter opener to twist the lock, she hears a click and the knob turns. The door remains bolted; this will be harder. She sticks the letter opener in as far as it will go, twisting it left and right. It is a rusty lock, years of moist air, being close to the ocean, has melded it together. She gets an idea to use some cooking oil out of the kitchen to loosen it up. Just when she thought she would have no use for some Crisco oil, there it was, looking like her hero. She pours some of the oil into the lock and tries to chisel her way through the rust. She sees the muddy mess dripping down the doorway as the rust breaks away. She hears a click as she again inserts the letter opener into the lock. The bolt turns, and she opens the door; on the other side of the door, there is only pitch dark. She feels her way down the wall of the next room, finding a switch. She flips it on, and there is light.

As the light fills the room, she looks around to see that it is an office. There is a desk with a light and a computer. There are several compartmented rooms separated by chain-link fence to the ceiling. She finds a flashlight on the desk. She uses it to explore the space, finding that all the doors are secured and there are no windows. She appears to be in a warehouse. She shines a flashlight on the ceiling, showing that there are fire sprinklers. Walking back into the office, she turns on the computer. The power goes on; she can see it trying to boot up. The seconds seem like hours. Then she hears a rolling door open. She quickly tries to switch off the computer, but it is not cooperating. With the computer in stall mode, she clicks it off several times before she unplugs it from the wall. Hearing footsteps, she runs back to the prisonlike bedroom and locks the door. Fearing they will come in and see the rusty oil on the door, she frantically searches for some towels to clean up the mess. She finds nothing in the kitchen. She goes back to the bed, rips off a pillow case, and wipes up the mess, hiding the cloth below the sink. She sits back in the only chair in the room. She may possibly be meeting her death now; she thinks with every footstep that comes closer. Will it just be a new awakening as she has sometimes thought? The steps grow nearer, and Tony comes through the door.

Kira is so startled that she jumps.

"It's all right. I brought you the clothes you wanted. They probably won't fit, but it is the best I can do." He puts down the bag, reaches in his pocket, and tosses out a pack of cigarettes on the bed. "Here are the smokes." Kira looks over to see he has tucked a book of matches into the cellophane wrapper of the Virginia Slims.

"Thank you," Kira says weakly, struggling to get the words out.

"I have some food for you in the car." He leaves to get the food while Kira slips on the jeans. They are baggy but warm and comfortable. She finds some socks in the bag and slips them on as well. So much better on her feet against the cold concrete floor. Tony comes back in with a bag of groceries. He also has a bucket of Kentucky Fried Chicken. It smells good, and Kira hasn't eaten all day. He puts the items down in the kitchenette.

He closes the door behind him and bolts it. Kira is worried about the lock and how she will get it open again. The smell of the food gets to her, and she goes into the kitchen to eat the chicken. She brings it in and sits in the chair, devouring a leg. She thinks of the scene in *Gone with the Wind* where Scarlett vows to never go hungry again. That is the driving spirit inside of Kira. Once it is there, it never goes away.

Kira can hear their footsteps outside the room. It sounds like they are in a room below her. She hears the clanging of metal and ripping of papers. She hears them shouting at one another periodically and counts the minutes until they go away. It reminds her of sounds of trashmen collecting trash at 4:00 a.m., crashing and rumbling as they go. She tries to hear what they are saying, but the sounds are muffled and too distant for her to distinguish. Then she realizes, she must be in Justin's warehouse, where they keep the guns and weapons. With all the bedlam going on there, it must be a big shipment. She has got to get free and stop them—before they stop her permanently.

West Palm Beach Police Station

A NDERSON BURST THROUGH the office doors search warrant in hand. "We have got it. Let's move out." Jimmy and Dave strap on their shoulder harnesses and take extra ammo. They know Justin is armed, and they expect the worst. They get extra backup as well, four squad cars in total moving out toward the Primavera Estates. Jimmy feels his heart rate racing in anticipation of what they will find.

The guard at the gates at the Primavera Estates sees the army of squad cars. Anderson, driving the first car to the gates, pulls out his badge and the search warrant to show the guard.

"Police and the FBI here on official law enforcement business." The guard takes one look at the search warrant and waves them all in. Six police officers and the two FBI go to the door. Two more police officers are standing guard in the front of the house. Justin comes to the door, no shirt and some khaki shorts on.

"What can I do for you officers?" Anderson hands him the search warrant.

"We are here to search your house for evidence on the missing Kira Michaels."

Justin steps back, allowing the officers in. His eyes grow wide when he sees Jimmy and Dave, recognizing them from the club and the Marina. He is stunned to see them walk through his door.

It all comes together for Justin in that moment that he sees the FBI. Kira was working with them the whole time. He thinks back on how he could have missed the clues. She showed no signs at all. Two of the officers take Justin into the dining room and sit him in a chair. They hold him there and question him about Kira. Jimmy and Dave join Anderson and Parelli as they conduct the search. They search the office area, which they originally did not search. They go through the sofa, all the bookcases, the desktop, and next the drawers. Pulling open every drawer and putting the contents on the desk, Jimmy is pillaging though receipts and business cards, giving careful attention to each item. Finally, in the bottom drawer hidden carefully away, he finds Kira's driver's license, a smoking gun. He walks over to Dave, who is also searching, and flashes the license in his face. Dave's eyes grow wide and his expression very serious. They both know now Justin has done something with Kira. They place the evidence in a plastic bag and move on to the master bedroom. Searching the closet, the bed, and the nightstands, nothing. Parelli points out to them that they had found the lipstick in the trash receptacle. Looking in the trash, Jimmy sees all the broken pieces of Kira's cosmetics. He sifts through them again; he finds nothing. He walks over to the toilet and opens the lid. He sees something floating. He reaches in the toilet bowl and retrieves a cell phone screen. He pulls it out and calls over Parelli and Dave, also in the room. They all walk over and, looking over the object, confirm what it is. In closer inspection, Dave sees more particles at the bottom of the toilet. Rolling up his sleeve, he reaches in the toilet bowl. He pulls out parts of a cell phone. He takes them and dries them off, and all evidence go in the plastic bag.

"I want this bathroom sealed until we can get someone in to flush out all the parts to the phone," Jimmy says to Parelli, who nods in agreement. He places police tape across the bathroom door as they leave.

"We have enough to arrest him and take him in for questioning. Do you want to cuff him? Or should I?" Parelli asks Jimmy.

Jimmy says, "You do the honors." They walk into the dining room, and Anderson reads him his rights. They turn him to face the wall, and Parelli puts the cuffs on. They lead him out to the waiting police car.

WAREHOUSE

KIRA CAN'T SLEEP for the noise. She paces the floor instead, keeping her energy up in case Matt or Tony come through the door. She grabs the pack of cigarettes, puts one in her mouth, and lights it. She hasn't smoked in years, but the stress is breaking down her resolve. She hears the rumble of the rolling door rolling up; next comes the sound of a big truck starting. Her instincts kicking in tell her they are loading a shipment of guns. Still pacing the floor, she catches a glimpse of her reflection in a mirror hung near the bed; she looks drawn and pasty. The trauma has taken a toll on her face. She needs some clean air and sunshine; she needs some healthy food and a good laugh. There is none of that in here.

She hears the truck door slam and the truck start up again. The rumble shakes the warehouse; it sounds like a jet plane taking off. The rumbling gets quieter and fainter as it drives away. Kira is hoping with every ounce of conviction still left in her that Matt and Tony are gone. But then, the footsteps outside the door tell her someone is still there. She watches as the doorknob jiggles, and then it turns. Matt comes through the door; Kira shivers at the sight of him.

"So how do you like your new room, princess?"

"I prefer the Four Seasons, but they were all filled up."

"I bet you prefer pretty rich boys too. But there aren't many of them around either, are there? Have you ever even tried it with a real man? I'll bet you would like it."

"I prefer to stick to the rich, pretty ones, thank you anyway."

"Really? Because you look like you could really use some hot cock right now, baby."

Tony comes through the door.

"Let's get out of here. We have lots more work tonight."

"Don't want to get out of here. I was just warming up."

"Shut the hell up and let's go. Mess with this girl another time. We have to make it to the harbor."

Matt hesitates, looking lustfully at Kira.

"Move your ass out, I said! We only have twenty minutes tops to get to the harbor!"

Matt smiles a fast, lewd smile at Kira.

"Hold on, sugar, because I will be back."

Kira gives him the look of pure disdain as he walks out of the door. Matt locks and bolts the door on his way out. Kira is sickened by Matt's advances; she has to get more aggressive about breaking out of here. Matt's advances are getting more belligerent, and her life is hanging in the balance. She knows he will be back again with more fervor. It is happening quickly; she feels it in her bones.

She grabs the letter opener and the wire and goes to work on the lock. She turns it hard with all the strength she has got left. She turns the lock to the right and to the left; it clicks open. Next, she works on the bolt. It seems to be stuck again, so she twists harder. She twists the letter opener so hard, the tip breaks off. Kira breaks out in a cold sweat; she starts to panic. What if she can't turn the lock and get out of here? She has got to make this work. She digs the wire deeper into the door. She is able this time to retrieve the small tip of the letter opener. She must try one last time and give it all she has got. First the letter opener to twist the lock and then the wire. She hears a click, and with one last desperate turn, the door opens wide. There is only jet-black darkness in the room. Blindly, Kira runs her hands down the wall, searching for a switch. Finally, she reaches it, and the lights go on. Quickly she heads for the computer and plugs it back in. It is an eternity waiting for the computer to load up, but there is a break, a streak of luck, and it is on. Kira gets directly onto the internet and gets an email out to Jimmy:

> I have been locked into Justin's warehouse near the ocean. There is a shipment going out tonight. Something is going down. Stay tuned to the fire department. Then follow them to the fire.

Kira sends the message and then takes the wastepaper basket out to the center of the empty concrete room next to the office. She starts wadding up papers from the desk and throwing it into the basket until it is overflowing with trash. She lights a match and pitches it into the basket. Quickly the flames grow high. Kira takes more and more trash, throwing more fuel on the fire. The room is filled with smoke as the fire rages. Kira is choking from the fumes. She runs into her little cubicle and douses a rag with water and holds it to her face to keep the smoke out; she is coughing and choking all the while. She thinks, *What if the fire sprinklers do not work? What the hell could I have been thinking?* With the heat rising in the room, Kira starts to feel faint. She is choking and barely able to breath; she is sweating profusely. The fire has spread to a cabinet that is engulfed in flames. The heat is so strong on her face, she can feel her skin blistering. Kira holds the wet rag to her face and gets down on the floor. There may be some air to breath in a space next to the ground. Kira finds a small crack at the bottom of the roll-up door and tries to breathe air through it.

Finally, the fire alarm goes off! The fire sprinklers are activated but not strong enough to squelch the massive blaze. Still Kira is suffering and gasping for air.

She hears the fire trucks' sirens in the distance. Will she make it? The heat is searing her flesh; the sweat on her body is probably the only thing keeping the fire off her. Where are they? The sirens are getting louder now. She can hear the firemen breaking down the rolling door; a beam of light trickles in as an ax breaks through the door. Small light as it is, for Kira, the clouds have cleared, and it is like a beam of light from heaven.

With one big final sweep, the door is opened, and the firemen spray the flames that now have taken over and are burning at the rafters in the ceiling. Kira crawls toward the opening. She is catching some of the sprays from the fire hoses. Nothing has ever felt so good.

She continues to crawl toward the opening. One of the firemen sees Kira and rushes to rescue her. Picking her up in his arms, he carries her out of the burning building. Her face is blistered and black from the smoke. First, he lays her down on the grass in the warehouse courtyard. He wipes her face with the rag she is holding.

"You are going to be all right. I am going to take care of you." Kira cannot speak because the smoke has taken her voice. The fireman quickly gets her some oxygen. The mask goes over her face. They bring a stretcher; the fireman lifts her and places her on it.

The fireman who rescued Kira looks into her eyes.

"I think we got you in the nick of time. Hang in tough. I think you are going to make it." Kira nods appreciatively as tears roll down her charred face. The ambulance arrives. The firemen and the paramedics work in unison to get Kira into the ambulance. The paramedic takes over, wiping Kira's face with antiseptic, and looking very closely at Kira, he says, "Can you see me?" Kira nods yes. He takes that as a good sign then says, "We are going to get you transported. Stay with me." Meanwhile they inspect Kira's arms and face for burns. They radio in, "Female fire victim suffering smoke inhalation and minor second-degree burns." Kira is feeling relieved to hear that her burns are second-degree. They are searing her flesh; she had imagined they were worse. The cold, foggy air feels so good on her skin. The paramedics take gauze and wet it with solution and wrap her face in it. It cools the burning, but it will not stop the fire inside of her. They close the door, and Kira is being whisked away in the ambulance. *Sweet freedom* is all that is going through her mind now.

POLICE STATION

J USTIN IS TAKEN into an interrogation room. Anderson is doing the questioning. Jimmy and Dave watch through a surveillance window. They can also hear the conversation though the microphones in the room.

"How well do you know Kira Michaels?" asks Anderson.

"Not extremely well, I had just met her. Maybe it was two weeks."

"What was the nature of your relationship?"

"Romantic, sexual."

"Would you say tumultuous?"

"At times, maybe." Justin seems cool, unaffected, and aloof.

"Why did she leave? Was there a fight?"

"No fight, she said she was only going to see a friend. I expected her back."

"But the officers found signs of a fight. Her things were all broken and thrown in the trash."

"She dropped her purse. Some things broke. What is the big deal?"

"Kira is missing, that is the big deal. You were the one seen with her last." Anderson is getting tense, heating up.

"What about her cell phone being found smashed and in your toilet? Why did you smash her cell phone if there wasn't a fight?"

"I don't know anything about the cell phone. For all I know, she did that herself. Maybe she was trying to get away from someone. Did you ever think of that?"

"No, what I thought is that you smashed her cell phone and tried to flush it down the toilet. I also think you have done something with Kira, which is of course why you are here with me. You are not leaving here until you tell us where she is."

Dave walks in the room, thinking that he will have a crack at Justin.

"Listen, dude, just tell us where she is. Do you have her hidden? Locked away?"

"That doesn't make any sense. Why would I do that?"

"You had a fight. You are afraid she knows too much, perhaps."

"She works with you guys, right?"

"Is that what you think? Is that why you killed her?"

"WHAT? *No*, I did *not* kill her."

"Then tell us where she is. If we can verify she is alive, we just may let you out of here."

Jimmy paces as he listens outside the room. He knows if he goes in, he will punch this guy's lights out. He knows he is lying through his teeth. Jimmy gets a notification of a new email. He checks his phone; his expression turns to elation and relief as he reads Kira's email. She is alive; that is the best news he has had since she went missing.

Justin rushes to open the interrogation-room door. He motions to Dave and Anderson to come out. They leave Justin locked in the interrogation room. He shows Dave the message.

"I got an email from Kira. She has been held hostage in Justin's warehouse. There was a fire, and she was rescued by the fire department. We have got to move fast, though. She says something is going down. We need to get to her. Can we establish a line of communication with the fire department? I want to know everything."

"I think we can. Let's ask at dispatch." They all rush over to dispatch.

Justin asks, "Do you have an alarm of a fire at a warehouse?"

The dispatch operator says, "Yes, there is a three-alarm fire at a warehouse on Admiralty Way near the marina." She writes down the address and hands it to the officers. Jimmy and Dave rush into action, going to their office and strapping on their guns. Anderson follows them over.

"What should I do with Hamilton? I think he should be charged with kidnapping and false imprisonment."

Jimmy answers, "No, it is more important right now to catch him in the act with the gun shipment. I want you to release him. When we bring him in again, we will charge him with both crimes."

"But what if the message is a hoax? Anyone with access to a computer could have sent it. They might have sent it to get us to release Hamilton."

"You are right. Hold him until we confirm we have found Kira," says Dave. "But he should still be charged with false imprisonment."

"The FBI needs to get an illegal gun shipment on him and stop the stream of weapons to the terrorist. It's about the big picture right now." Jimmy tells Anderson this as they head out to their car. Jimmy and Dave speed away toward the marina.

WAREHOUSE BURNING

T HE FIREMEN ARE still working on getting the fire completely out. There are still some smoldering embers. Jimmy and Dave arrive. Jimmy flashes his badge at the fire chief, who is still on the scene.

"FBI, did you find anyone inside?"

"Yes, we found a girl inside. She was rescued, given oxygen and first aid. We transported her to County Hospital."

"What was her condition?"

"She is being treated for smoke inhalation and second-degree burns. She was coherent when the ambulance took her away."

"How did the fire start?" asks Dave.

"Looks like it was deliberately set, although no exhilarant was used. But it was clearly deliberate. It looks as if the fire was started in a trash can. It doesn't make sense, though. No one else was here. Who would have set it inside? We are still investigating it."

"Did you find fire arms?"

"What? There are firearms? No, we did not find any."

"That means they were all taken out prior."

"Is that what was being stored here?"

"Yes, let me know right away if you find any." Jimmy says this and hands him his card.

"Absolutely," says the fire chief.

"We have to get over to County." As Jimmy and Dave drive to the hospital, Jimmy has a pit in his stomach. Kira could have been killed again. How could she have gotten wrapped up so tight? This could have been her last mistake. With her near-death experience, he is not going to try and shove it down her throat just yet.

COUNTY HOSPITAL

K IRA HAS BEEN cleaned up, and her blistered face and hands have been treated at the hospital. The smoke in her lungs still feels heavy. It hurts to breathe deeply; when she does, she chokes. Still, setting the fire was worth her freedom. She never wants to come that close to death again, although chances are she will.

The FBI agents arrive at the front desk of the hospital. They show their badges to the attendant and are told Kira is in room 640. They go to the elevator; arriving on her floor, Jimmy gets aches in his stomach. What if her injuries are so horrific, she is left disfigured? He is anxious, not knowing what to expect. He is bracing for the worst.

As he walks into her room, she is sitting up in bed, her face still in bandages. She has an IV and an oxygen mask on. Kira looks over at Jimmy and Dave and slightly, painfully smiles. With a hoarse voice, barely being able to speak, she says, "Surprised to find me alive?" After speaking, Kira starts coughing deeply, her chest heaving.

"Not really, only the good die young." Jimmy couldn't help himself.

Kira cracks a smile at this remark, which hurts her blistered face.

"How bad is it?" Kira asks. Jimmy peels back some of her facial gauze to have a look. There is some blistering and redness, but it is better than he had expected.

"Looks like a weekend-in-Malibu-type sunburn, that is all."

"Did you set the fire?" Jimmy asks.

"Of course, I did. I had to get out. I saw the alarms and the fire sprinklers. I knew the firemen would respond, and I would be rescued. Only, I thought the fire sprinklers would come on a lot sooner than they did."

"So Hamilton locked you up?" Dave inquires.

"He accused me of being a spy. They did a background check and found out that I am educated, with degrees in criminal justice, among other things. They thought I was working with the FBI and both of you."

"If only they knew the real truth on you. You landed in some dangerous territory. Can't stop pushing it, can you?"

"Stop it, Jimmy. You know all of my reasons. Let's not go into that now. We don't have time for explanations. They are shipping a huge load of weapons to Pakistan as we speak. I have to get out of here and stop Hamilton."

"You need to stay here and recover. You are no longer on the payroll, Kira. Dave and I can handle this."

"You can't do this without me. I know where they are. I can find the ship. I know their every move. You need me."

"Don't be ridiculous. You can hardly talk. You stay here and have a full recovery. We will go out and get Justin Hamilton." Dave looks at Kira and is concerned. "Can we get you anything?"

"I need some clean clothes and a cell phone. He took all my cash and my ID."

"I can get you clothes, and we have your ID at the police station. I will get it back to you. I can go down to the gift shop and get some of the bare necessities." Jimmy leaves to go down to the gift shop and get a few things for Kira.

Dave stays in the room with Kira.

"You know, he is going to find out where you are. I need to get some police on duty to guard you in case they try and come here. Dave steps out of the room to make the call to the police station."

Kira looks out the window and thinks about how quickly things change. Just two weeks ago, she was blissful and in love with Justin. Now she sits in a hospital, recovering from a near-death experience and hating him. The FBI whom she had been trying to get rid of are by her side to help her. Is she really that confused? How could her life have gotten so chaotic that she could be so blindsided? Her eyes have been opened, and she can clearly see what she needs to do. Admitting her weakness and her downfall has given her new strength and clarity.

Jimmy returns with a bag of clean clothes and toiletries for Kira. He hands the bag to her. He reaches into his pocket and gives her forty dollars.

"Here is some cash in case you need something else."

"Thank you, I really appreciate all that you have done." Jimmy smiles and looks into Kira's eyes. He leans over and kisses her on the forehead. Kira feels almost healed by his touch.

Jimmy and Dave turn to leave. Jimmy looks back at Kira and says, "I am really happy you made it out alive." Kira thinks for a split second that the bridge between them has mended.

The two men leave the room, leaving Kira alone.

Kira is resolved to apprehend Justin Hamilton. She came here to do that, and nothing is going to stop her now. The love that was blinding her has melted away like a single snowflake in the desert. What is left now is just a burning desire to take him down. She will do that with pleasure.

Kira pulls the IV out of her arm, gets out of bed, and gets to the sink in the room, and looking in the mirror, she starts to peel the bandages from her face. She gasps as she sees how red and burned it is, raw and still inflamed. She gets into the shower to wash the ashes out of her hair. The water stings her face when it touches her burns. But it is nothing like the burning that is going on inside. She gets out and dries herself off. She puts on the simple cotton dress Jimmy bought for her. She opens her door and peers out into the hallway. It appears that no one is watching. She hopes to get out without being seen. Hair still wet, she steps into the hallway and makes her way out of the hospital. The cool air outside on the sidewalk feels good against her hot face. She will never take freedom for granted again.

She sees a cab waiting at the sidewalk. She gets into the cab and tells the driver to take her to the Breakers. As he drives, she catches her reflection in his rear-view mirror. She thinks her injuries are not too bad. Once she gets some makeup on, no one will notice.

THE BREAKERS

KIRA IS FEELING very different than when she entered the hotel for the first time. The first time was with wonder and amazement; now, she is battered, burned, and wiser. She feels like she has aged twenty years since then. So much has happened to change her from the inside out. The warrior inside Kira has been awakened. As she enters the Breakers now, it is with new eyes—the eyes of a tiger.

Trevor is startled to see Kira at the desk. He looks up and gasps.

"Kira, my god, I can't believe it. The police were here, the FBI. What has happened to you?"

"So much has happened. I can't begin to tell you. I can't take the time right now. I lost the key to my room. Can I have a new one?"

"Sure." Trevor pulls a plastic key from the desk, punching some numbers in the computer, slides the key, and instantly hands it to Kira.

"I need your help; my purse has been taken. It had everything in it, my ID, cell phone, and all my cash."

"We can help you with all of that through the concierge desk." Trevor looks at Kira intensely, seeing the stress on her face. "You look terrible. Why don't you go up and get some rest? I will take care of getting those things with the concierge."

"Thank you." Kira goes up to her beautiful suite and takes a deep breath. Trevor was right on two things—she really needs some sleep, and she does look terrible. She steps out onto the balcony and breathes in the soft sea breeze; the fatigue overcomes her. She walks back into the room, lies down on the bed, and immediately goes to sleep.

COUNTY HOSPITAL

T HE OFFICER SENT to guard Kira takes the elevator up to room 640. He knocks on the door then enters the room. He finds the bed empty; he checks the bathroom. He goes to the nurse's station to ask about Kira. They check the charts and say she has not been checked out. The hospital staff go on a search for Kira. The fear is that she may have been recaptured by Justin. The officer calls Jimmy, who is at the police station; he tells Jimmy Kira is missing.

West Palm Beach Police Station

D AVE PICKS UP the phone in the office and briefly speaks to the hospital staff. Alarmed, he turns to Jimmy.

"Oh shit, Kira is missing from the hospital."

"What? Are you surprised? I'm not. It is not Justin that got her. We are still holding him. She walked out on her own, she never listens to reason."

"Fuck that, let her do what she has to do. I can't stop Kira. I have tried before, and it doesn't do me any good," Jimmy adds.

"Let's get her ID to her and let her go, balls to the wall."

Dave pulls the ID out of the evidence bag and hands it to Jimmy, who puts it into his wallet.

Anderson walks into their office.

"What have you decided we are going to do with Hamilton?"

"We need to release him," Jimmy says.

"He holds Kira hostage, locks her up, and we are going to give him a pat on the back and tell him goodbye."

"Right, the weapons to terrorist is a much bigger issue. We have got to catch him in the act. Don't worry, he will be back."

"All right." Dave and Jimmy follow Anderson to the interrogation room. Anderson goes in and lets him know he is being released. "We found Kira. You can go now."

Justin steps out of the interrogation room, looking shocked. He flinches when he sees Jimmy and Dave standing outside the room. He stares at them in an awkward frozen gaze for a second. Anderson takes him by the arm and leads him away to the checkout desk. He is given back his cell phone. He leaves the police station, completely disturbed.

Once outside he calls for James to pick him up. While waiting, he calls Tony.

"Where the fuck are you?" Justin says when Tony answers.

"What do you mean? We are loading the boat. We are at the harbor."

"You got the guns?"

"Hell yes, we have the guns. We loaded them into the truck. We are on our way to the harbor."

"I just left the police station. I got taken there for questioning about the disappearance of Kira. They released me and told me that they found Kira."

"What the fuck? We were just at the warehouse. Kira was locked inside. We left her there."

"She somehow got out alive."

"We should have killed her like Matt said. She is nothing but trouble. Those FBI guys that are following Kira were at the police station too. Everyone is looking for that bitch."

"We got all the guns out, don't worry."

"James is on his way to get me. I can be there in twenty minutes."

"Good." They end the phone call, and Justin paces outside the police station, waiting for James.

THE BREAKERS

K IRA IS AWAKENED by a knock on the door. She opens the door and it is Trevor, she lets him in.

"I must have been so exhausted, I fell asleep the minute I lay down."

"You looked tired. Trevor hands her a bag. She spills it out on the bed, she has cash, cell phone and her ID now.

"How did you get my ID?"

"One of the FBI guys dropped it at the desk. He said to give it to you, he said you might be needing it."

"The FBI guy? So, they know, I left the hospital."

"What? You were in the hospital?"

"You were right about Justin being a bad guy."

"What? Did he beat you up? I knew something was wrong."

"You were right, something was wrong. He locked me in a warehouse, he held me hostage. The warehouse caught on fire and I was rescued by the Firemen."

"You are lucky to be alive. I just knew something was going to happen. I told you not to go there."

"I should have listened. You have been such a good friend to me. I need one more favor."

"Anything you want, just say it and consider it done,"

"I am going to need my car; can you have it brought around for me? Can you have it down front for me in about forty-five minutes?"

"Sure." Trevor leaves to call for Kira's car.

Kira gets in the shower. Getting out, she looks at her face, wondering how long before the blisters heal. She presses the towel against it, and the redness temporarily goes out and then comes back. She blows her hair dry and applies makeup. Kira dresses in an all-black outfit of leggings, sweater, and boots for camouflage. Opening the safe, she takes out her gun. She checks the chamber for bullets; it is loaded. She tucks the gun into her pants in the back and throws a vest on to cover it. Before she leaves, she grabs another clip of bullets. Finally, she is loaded and ready for action. Feeling stronger and in control now, she thinks she is back. As she walks past the front desk, Trevor is stunned to see how pulled together she looks. She passes by him and goes to the rental car waiting at the curb. She gets in and is on her way to the marina. It has been a rough week, and it is about to get rougher. Kira thinks right now is the moment she has trained for all of her life. Her life has been a chaotic mess since she left the FBI. Kira thinks tonight will be a turning point, a defining moment. She must get back on track with her life, feeling like she has been stumbling in the dark and someone just lit a match.

Driving through the streets of Palm Beach reminds her of how rich life can be, how quickly that can be taken from you. She has come so seriously close to death so many times. Can she face it and get through it again? Damn straight, she can.

THE MARINA AT MIDNIGHT

KIRA PULLS INTO the marina gate and parks away from Justin's boat. She gets out her night vision binoculars. She creeps close to the boat. Her black clothes shield her from sight. She peers at the sailboat—no one in sight. She points them further away to look across the harbor. It is a clear night. Many boats are moored in the marina. They bob up and down in the current as she looks. Kira spots something suspicious across the harbor. Adjusting her night vision to get a closer look, she gets a clear shot of Matt. He is carrying boxes onto a cargo boat. Getting a closer look, she sees Tony as well. Several Middle Eastern types are loading with them; must be some of Ullah Kahn's men. She takes the opportunity to take some close-up pictures of them loading up the boat with the weapons. Justin cannot be too far behind, so she should move in a little closer. She gets back into the car to drive closer over to the cargo boat, no headlights on, moving very slowly.

She arrives on the other side of the harbor, parking the car away from view of the guys loading the boat. She pulls out the night vision again, hoping to get some better shots of what they are loading. The boxes are marked Explosives. She gets some close-up shots of this. She moves in even closer. Some very magnified shots give her a name on the boxes, Hamilton Enterprises. That is the money shot. Just then she feels someone stick a metal object to her back. This sends lightning bolts of terror though her. A familiar voice says, "Stop it right there, Kira, and hand me over the camera." She holds out the camera in the air. He grabs it from behind. She turns to see the face of Justin, anger on his face and sweat dripping down to his chest. "I told you, you have met your match. Too bad you are going to have to die. Start walking to the boat."

Kira moves slowly toward the boat. This was not supposed to happen. She really didn't see things going down like this. Justin continues to hold the gun on her as she walks.

"You are making killing you too easy on me, proving you are a spy and then coming right here so I can conveniently dump your body at sea. Just think, surviving a burning building, only to meet death by being eaten by sharks."

Kira continues to walk to the cargo ship in silence, her insides shaking, out of control. Kira feels as if her knees will give away. Now standing at the dock just behind the cargo boat, Justin yells out to the guys on the boat, "Look who I found crawling around in the parking lot. If it isn't our good friend Kira. Apparently, she wants a boat ride." Matt steps out to the end of the boat. "You just made my night. This is going to be fun."

Just then huge floodlights come on. Jimmy and Dave appear, guns drawn, followed by a massive team of law enforcement, all holding weapons pointed at Justin.

"Drop the gun, Justin. This party is over," yells out Jimmy. Justin turns his gun on Jimmy and fires a shot. Several shots are fired back. Justin takes off across the parking lot, diving behind cars. Kira pulls her gun and takes off after Justin. Jimmy follows in hot pursuit. Dave jumps in to try and corner Justin so he doesn't get away. The rest of the law enforcement swarm the boat. The crew on the boat are well outnumbered in men and firepower by the police. They cuff Matt and Tony and start taking down the rest of the crew while helicopters and police vans move in to haul all the men and the evidence away.

Suddenly Justin drops from view. He could be underneath a car or hiding behind one. Kira, Jimmy, and Dave search in silence, pointing their guns at anything that moves. It looks like they may have lost him when, unexpectedly, he bolts up from behind a car and takes a shot at Jimmy. Jimmy jumps down behind a car. Dave, who is covering Jimmy, takes the bullet to his stomach. Dave curls over in agony. Kira runs to Dave and gets shot at three times by Justin, who is running away. Kira is narrowly missed. Dave is spitting up blood in the parking lot. Kira cradles his head.

"Hold on, buddy," she says. Jimmy crawls over to the Kira and Dave, who are huddled behind a car.

Jimmy spurts out, "Goddamn it, man, why did it have to be you?"

Dave says, "That is the risk we take. Go and get the motherfucker."

Jimmy radios in, "Officer down." Dave passes out from loss of blood. You can already hear the sirens in the background when Kira and Jimmy take off to get Justin. They have fire in their bellies this time; nothing can stop them.

They can see Justin in the distance, running like a track star at the Olympics. Occasionally he stops to hide behind a car. He is clearly making his way to the sailboat in an attempt to get away. Jimmy and Kira are gaining on him, almost to the sailboat now. Jimmy gets a clear shot at Justin and fires his gun. Justin turns and returns the gunfire. This time Jimmy gets hit in the ankle. Jimmy falls and grabs his ankle. Kira runs up to cover him and takes several shots at Justin. She manages to hit him in the arm. He momentarily grabs the arm but keeps on running.

Kira bends down to check Jimmy's ankle.

"It is just a graze. You will be all right."

"What the hell are you doing? I thought you hate my fucking guts."

"I still do, but you saved my life a couple times, so what the hell? I owe you one."

"I'll take that," Jimmy says as he gets up and starts limping his way toward Justin. He is doing good running as fast as he can with an injury. Kira is just ahead of him when they are standing at Justin's boat. They see him working like a dog in heat to shove off. Jimmy fires all the shots he has left in his gun at Justin. Jimmy runs out of ammo and tosses the gun as Justin starts to move away from the dock. Jimmy takes a running jump and grabs on to the side of the boat, trying to pull himself into the boat. Justin takes an oar and starts pounding Jimmy's hands until he falls under the boat. Kira fears Jimmy will get chopped into the boat's motor; she dives in, going underwater to save him. She grabs him by the collar and is able to pull him to the surface. They both come up gasping and choking for air.

Justin is getting away in the sailboat, which is under motor power now. Jimmy says, "He is fucking getting away." Kira reaches into her pocket and pulls a grenade. She had found it on the ground in the parking lot, apparently dropped from the shipment. Jimmy looks at her in amazement. A smile comes across his face. She pulls the pin with her teeth and throws the grenade, which lands squarely on Justin's sailboat.

The boat explodes violently and spectacularly, sending a huge fireball launching into the sky, lighting the night sky as if it were the sun! They both tread water and are in awe of the sight. They are staring in silence for some time. The fireball dies down. Then quickly two more explosions go off on the boat, and it is cut into smithereens. They watch it sink quickly down.

Jimmy looks over at Kira and says, "I guess we are even now."

Kira says, "I will let *you* know when we are even." They swim back to the dock together. They pull themselves up to the dock and sit, watching. The entire harbor is filled with law enforcement, the bright colored lights flashing everywhere. There is an army of black-and-whites, several SWAT cars and vans used to transport prisoners. All of Ullah Kahn's guys are cuffed and put on a van. Kira sees Matt and Tony cuffed and being placed into separate squad cars. Fire trucks and ambulances are also on the scene. A rescue helicopter lands close to Dave. The paramedics jump from the helicopter with a gurney to take Dave away. The paramedics reach Dave and lift him onto the gurney. One paramedic says to Dave, "Don't worry, we got you in time. Just hang in with me, man." They lift him into the helicopter, and he is whisked away. A coast guard ship moves into where Justin's boat was. They start collecting parts of the sailboat.

Kira and Jimmy walk back to the parking lot toward all the police activity. Jimmy turns to Kira.

"My night has just begun. I will be at the station all night, writing reports."

"Can't say I envy you," Kira says.

Jimmy looks her in the eyes and says, "You want back in, don't you?"

Kira answers, "I am sort of lost."

Jimmy laughs and says, "*Sort of* is an understatement."

As he looks at her for a few beats, she starts laughing as well. Jimmy finally speaks up and says, "I'll put in a good word for you." He starts walking away, leaving Kira to go to her car. He turns back around to say, "What you did tonight was truly heroic." He salutes her; Kira is beaming. She gets in her car with her wet clothes on and drives back to the Breakers—a newer, better, wiser version of herself.

Lennie– Life is either an
exciting adventure –or nothing
at all

ABOUT THE AUTHOR

KIM SIMONS IS a native Californian. She has acted in movies and appeared in network productions. She is a member of the Screen Actors Guild. Her experiences in being an actor and an adventurous woman in Los Angeles inspired the character of Kira Michaels in Dance of Deception. In her quest to inspire more meaningful roles for women, she has written six screenplays featuring strong female characters. Dance of Deception is her first novel.

Go for the adventure!

Kim Simons